Robert G. Barrett was raised in Sydney's Bondi where he worked mainly as a butcher. After thirty years he moved to Terrigal on the Central Coast of New South Wales. Robert has appeared in a number of films and TV commercials but prefers to concentrate on a career as a writer. He is the author of sixteen books, including *So What Do You Reckon?* — a collection of his columns for *People* magazine, *Mud Crab Boogie, Goodoo Goodoo*, and *The Wind and the Monkey*, his previous Les Norton adventure published by HarperCollins.

Visit Bob's official web site
and the home of Team Norton at:
http://www.robertgbarrett.com.au

Leaving Bondi

ROBERT G. BARRETT

HarperCollins*Publishers*

HarperCollins_Publishers_

First published in Australia in 2000
Reprinted in 2000
by HarperCollins_Publishers_ Pty Limited
ABN 36 009 913 517
A member of the HarperCollins_Publishers_ (Australia) Pty Limited Group
http://www.harpercollins.com.au

Copyright © Psycho Possum Productions Pty Ltd 2000

HarperCollins_Publishers_
25 Ryde Road, Pymble, Sydney, NSW 2073, Australia
31 View Road, Glenfield, Auckland 10, New Zealand
77–85 Fulham Palace Road, London, W6 8JB, United Kingdom
Hazelton Lanes, 55 Avenue Road, Suite 2900, Toronto, Ontario M5R 3L2
and 1995 Markham Road, Scarborough, Ontario M1B 5M8, Canada
10 East 53rd Street, New York NY 10022, USA

National Library of Australia Cataloguing-in-Publication data:

Barrett, Robert G.
    Leaving Bondi.
    ISBN 0 7322 6871 0.
    1. Norton, Les (Fictitious character) – Fiction I. Title.
A823.3

Cover illustration by Nice Stuff
Cover design by Darian Causby, HarperCollins Design Studio
Typeset by HarperCollins in 12/20 Minion
Printed and bound in Australia by Griffin Press on 80gsm Bulky Book Ivory

7 6 5 4 3 2
03 02 01 00

DEDICATION

This book is dedicated to Major General Peter Cosgrove and all the Australian Forces who served in East Timor. I got a lot of letters from the troops. I know they did a great job up there and they're still doing a great job. And we should all be proud of them.

A percentage of the royalties from this book is being donated to:

The Wombat Rescue and Research Project
Lot 4, Will-O-Wynn Valley
Murrays Run NSW 2325

Despite George Brennan's running gag about Les Norton getting arrested for breaking into a fifty-dollar bill, then being acquitted because it was his first offence, Les wasn't all that mean with his money. A bit tight? Maybe. Careful? Definitely. Distrustful? After watching some of the people around him whilst living in Bondi and working at Kings Cross: one hundred per cent. But mean? No. Definitely not. If it was Norton's turn to shout or he had to spend his money on something necessary, he would. And some of the money he'd come across in his jaunts here and there, Les had certainly spread around. Which, somehow, often came back to him.

However, Les wasn't into the share market or real estate. He owned his own home and was more than happy with that. Even backing some of Price's horses at short odds had lost its allure, whether they were good things or not. As far as Les was concerned, there were only three places to keep any spare cash you had lying around: In the bank. Buried somewhere, where you could get to it easily if you wanted to. Or strapped tightly to your body where pickpockets or such couldn't get to it easily if they wanted to.

So for an extremely cautious person like Norton to invest fifty thousand dollars in a movie, a movie that was virtually just another

1

Australian meat-pie western, would take close to an act of God. Or whoever talked Les into it would have to be the greatest salesperson on the planet. But Les had his reasons for investing such a vast amount of his hard-earned into a dodgy Z-grade flick. It all came about through Les hanging around Ray Tracy's Japanese restaurant next to Bondi Beach Public School.

The way things were going in Bondi, the Gull's Toriyoshi Yakitori wasn't a bad place to hang for a feed and a cool one. The old Icebergs was still a pile of bulldozed rubble money-hungry developers and Waverley Council were constantly arguing over. The Diggers had been sold to make home units, so most of the punters had moved down to The Rathouse in the North Corner, which was good value, except you had to put up with poker machines and cigarette smoke and Les wasn't a member. Les was a member of Hakoah, but mainly for the choice food. The Bondi was all right in the daytime, but you wouldn't go there at night unless you liked drinking elbow to elbow with backpackers full of drink and western suburbs home-boys full of attitude. Redwoods had been turned into an internet cafe and most of the other bars around Bondi were either too smoky or too trendy and charged an arm and a leg for a drink. The old Rex wasn't that bad and the VB on tap was good, only there were too many blokes there either Les or Billy had cuffed on different occasions and Les spent half the night looking over his shoulder. Norton could get all the dramas he needed working at the Kelly Club. And as Les only drank two or three nights a week because of his job, he liked to be able to relax when he did. So a bit of a sneak away from the crowds and the smoke was needed. And in this respect, the Gull's Toriyoshi suited him admirably.

Ray was a good friend of Warren's and Les got on well with him as did just about everybody else. The Gull always reminded Les of Peter Fonda in *Easy Rider*. The same thoughtful, winsome face, the same loose brown hair and steel-framed glasses and the same plausible nature, tinged with polite curiosity. Since Les had poisoned the big Russian swimmer there, Ray had done the Toriyoshi up. The cooking was now done out the back, there was more seating and, being a local waxhead, Ray had filled the walls with old Bondi surfing memorabilia. You could sit out the front if you wanted, where there was a well-stocked bottle shop two doors away, the Japanese staff were friendly and Ray's food was always tasty and well presented and, compared to some of the other feedbags around Bondi, extremely reasonable. Being an actor and a scriptwriter, Ray also had a good-looking French girlfriend who was always good for a perv, a blonde actress called Monique. And if she wasn't around, there always seemed to be plenty of other girls hanging about. Because of his involvement in the film game, Ray's Toriyoshi attracted much of the Bondi and Sydney entertainment industry from TV, film, radio and theatre; some of whom were all right and some of whom were absolute pains in the arse. Les preferred to sit out the front with Ray's old waxhead mates when they were around.

They were good blokes in their thirties who rode mini-mals, liked a drink and a laugh and always had an anecdote about Bondi to relate. Most of them had nicknames like Weasel, Snoopy, Hey Joe, Short-Round, Butch van Bad Skull, Munoz, The Arm, Tounger, or whatever, and all had this strange way of talking now and again in allegorical metaphors tinged with biting sarcasm. Les was sitting out the front one night having a cold one with Weasel and Hey Joe, and evidently Weasel had been seen out on the weekend with a really ugly girl.

'Nnnyyhh,' said Hey Joe, 'I'm glad the chick you were out with the other night didn't have a head on her like a kicked-in shitcan anyway, the Wease.'

'Nnnyyhh,' replied Weasel. 'I'm glad you wouldn't crawl over broken glass with your Morts out to stick it up her behind my back anyway, the Joe.'

Nnnyyhh, thought Les. I'm glad you haven't, got me fucked if I know what you're talking about anyway, the boys.

Naturally, being a writer and hanging out with the film industry in beautiful downtown Bondi, the Gull had come up with a film script. It was called *Leaving Bondi*. Thinking Les might be interested and looking for investors, he showed Les the script and the synopsis one night when it was quiet. The story was about an Australian Vietnam veteran who elopes back to Australia with a Japanese girl and was set in Bondi before they got rid of the old sewerage works — the murk — and started pumping all the shit out to sea beneath the ocean floor. Her father is a boss in the Yakuza and comes looking for his daughter. The Vietnam vet shoots the father and his gangsters, then ends up in a massive shoot-out with the police and the State Protection Unit before getting away with his girl through the sewers of Bondi, finally escaping through the main sewerage outlet under the golf links around Ben Buckler Point. There was waffle and moving dialogue and in the end you're left hanging, not knowing whether they got away or drowned in several million litres of shit.

The film was going to be shot around Bondi, Bondi Beach Public School, the Toriyoshi and Ray's father's house in Clyde Street, Bondi. Ray reckoned by cutting costs and using unknown actors he could shoot the film for less than a million dollars. The Gull had called his film company Murke Productions. Les flicked through the script and thought the the film company was aptly named and it was good the movie was about sewers and such, because it was the most shithouse thing he'd ever read. And figured anybody that would invest money in a clunker like *Leaving Bondi* would have shit for brains. Oddly enough, Ray had raised nearly all the money and was just $50,000 short of production. Les handed the Gull back his script, said he'd take a rain check and got another beer.

One night Les was sitting out the front of the Toriyoshi with Warren, Ray Tracy and Ray's French girlfriend Monique. Ron from 99FM was there with a Sydney disc jockey who raved on too much for Norton's liking, and a local film director Les wasn't too keen on either. Along with some lesbian film producer. Evidently they were the main investors in the Gull's movie. Even Warren had sunk some money into it.

The director was Max King, a humourless, narrow-eyed person about forty with a hunched, bony build and a narrow, bony head topped with short greying hair. He rarely smiled and always reminded Les of a snake the way his head sunk between his shoulders and his slitty eyes seemed to dart everywhere as if he was looking for a mouse or a small bird to eat. He'd made a number of films. His biggest claim to fame being an art film shot in Bali, which won a gong at some obscure film festival in Europe before fading without trace. He'd also been high up in the South Australian Film Corporation where he'd produced several meat-pie dramas and telemovies. King had lived in Bondi for over ten years, but before he moved to Sydney, Eddie said King had been in the army reserve in Melbourne where he'd also done community service for petty larceny. Because of his Balinese film connection, King always liked to wear batik shirts; tonight's fashion statement was black, brown and yellow.

The disc jockey was Nathan David. An average-sized, self-opinionated bigot in his thirties with tinted hair and a squashy little nose rumoured to have undergone plastic surgery. David originally arrived in Sydney from Adelaide via Melbourne. He was single, loved developers, hated environmentalists and was currently right up there in the ratings giving Sydney's talkback kings a run for their money. So far David hadn't been caught up in the cash-for-comment-keeping-the-greed-alive-scandal rocking Sydney radio. And often enjoyed referring to his opposition and anyone else who didn't share his views as vile, rotten swine. Norton, however, after what he'd heard and read in the papers, wouldn't have pissed on any of them, particularly David. And often said so. But if he ever bumped into David at the Toriyoshi, Les kept his opinions to himself. If only for Ray's sake.

The woman was Simone Mitchum. She had dark hair and dark looks, which blended in with her all-black outfit, broken up by a purple scarf and purple earrings. Simone lived in Dover Heights and also came from Adelaide, where she'd worked on a couple of King's movies with the South Australian Film Corporation. She wasn't introduced to Norton as a lesbian. But just her mannerisms, and the way she glared at Les for having the hide to perv on the same woman

6

at the table she was, told him so. Despite her abrasive manner, she seemed to be fairly intelligent, and Les was curious why she, or anybody else, would invest in a Z-grade wobbegong like *Leaving Bondi*. Warren, a mullhead working in an advertising agency, Les could understand. But the others? Maybe they knew something he didn't?

The night Les was drinking there, David had just been berating everybody about his rise in the latest radio survey; mainly because he'd escaped the cash for comment inquiry. Now he was berating Les about putting some money into Ray's movie. David was dissecting Les from behind a pair of dark sunglasses he was wearing so no one could recognise him while he was wearing a bright red T-shirt with his radio station's logo across the front so no one could miss him.

'Well, come along, Les,' chirped David, in his familiar radio-announcer's voice. 'Ante up, my boy. This could be a great investment for you.'

'Sure. Come on board, man,' said Ron. 'It's a cool thing.'

'Yeah, why don't you? You miserable big prick,' said Warren. 'You've got plenty snookered away.' He gave the Gull a wink. 'You've been leaching a fortune off me in rent for years. I wouldn't be surprised if you had all my rent money buried somewhere in the backyard in a shoe box,' he added, as a titter of mirth ran round the table.

Les looked at Warren impassively for a moment. 'Yeah, that'd be right, Warren. Trying to kick you out but you won't go'd be more like it. You greasy little bludger.'

The Gull, plausible as ever, seemed slightly taken aback by Les and Warren's rapport. 'Well, hey. Like you know, Les,' he gestured politely. 'Nathan's got a point there, man. This movie could be big.'

Max King didn't bother looking up from the table. 'I like the script,' he said assertively. His words hanging in the air, as if they were impaled on an invisible wall, to emphasise his approval of the script was all that was needed.

The Gull nodded to Les. 'Hey, he's right. It's a great script, man.'

'A great script?' said Les. 'Turn it up, Ray. A heroin addict could forge a better script than that. I read it. Remember?'

The Gull looked at Les for a moment. 'Not all of it.'

'Ohh why waste your time,' said Warren. 'Les'd rather put his hand in a meat grinder than put it in his pocket.'

Another titter of laughter rang out round the table as everybody got a chuckle out of Warren's remark except Norton.

Simone gave Monique another very heavy once up and down. 'Why don't we talk about something else,' she said.

'Yes. Why don't we,' agreed Max King, his slitty eyes flicking sideways at Les, as if a non-film person like Norton shouldn't even have been sitting with them in the first place.

Les fixed his eyes on the Gull for a moment. 'All right, Ray,' he said evenly. 'I'll back your movie. How much did you say you needed the other night? Fifty grand? Okay. You got it.'

For a moment it looked as if a nerve gas bomb had just gone off as every face at the table froze and all eyes rivetted on Norton.

'What was that, Les?' blinked the Gull.

'I said, I'll put fifty grand into your movie.'

'Are you fair dinkum?' said Warren.

'I'm always fair dinkum, Warren.' Les finished his beer and rose from the table. 'Now if you people will excuse me, I have to go.

There's a travel documentary about Kakadu on the ABC I wish to tape.' He nodded to the Gull. 'I'll have your fifty down here at the end of the week, Ray. Goodnight all.' Les turned and walked home, stopping briefly at Bates milk bar in Hall Street for a packet of CC's.

When Les got home, he knocked the top off a cold Eumundi Lager, took a swallow, then slipped a tape in the video recorder. Once that was going, he went out into the backyard, sipped some more beer and stared down at where he had all his loot buried next to the garden shed. The Krugerrands had fallen in by accident so he wouldn't miss any, and the arse appeared to be falling out of the gold market so he'd be better off getting rid of them. Fifty grand was a lot of money to waste on a meat-pie western. But it was nice to see the looks on all their faces when he dropped his bombshell earlier, and it would be even nicer to see the looks on their faces when Les Norton, major investor, started hanging round the film set, a big cigar in one hand and a set of worry beads in the other. Also, this would consolidate his position at the Toriyoshi; the Gull would think the sun shone out of Norton's arse now. And although Les couldn't conceal a certain dislike for some of the poseurs and hangers-on in the movie business parading around Bondi — Ray Tracy excluded — they definitely attracted all the choice crumpet. A lot of whom were friends of Monique's and liked to sip white wine and eat the fat-free food at the Toriyoshi. For virtually a handful of coins Les could be the next Sam Goldwyn. He could put a casting couch in the spare bedroom. And even though the government had put the squeeze on the old 10BA rort in the film game, there was still an attractive tax break for investing in a meat-pie western, so he wouldn't lose that much in the wash-up. On the other hand, there was always the chance *Leaving Bondi* could get up. People might actually pay to go and see the lemon. Stranger things had happened. Norton finished his bottle of beer and got the pinch bar out of the shed.

The next day Les saw Price, told him what he was up to and to keep it between the two of them. Price was only too delighted to oblige, as well as cop a nice pile of shiny, bargain-basement Krugerrands to add to his collection. In five minutes Les had his money, and all nicely washed through a bookie so it looked like Les had won it at the races. Five minutes later Les rang his accountant. Norton's last accountant had moved to the Gold Coast so Les had a new one. Geraldine Hardacre. A tall, coppery brunette who did triathlons with her husband Ivor, an insurance investigator. Gerry was one of Billy Dunne's in-laws on his wife's side, so she knew where Les and the rest of them at the Kelly Club were coming from. She also knew a lot of people herself and wasn't adverse to cutting corners and going straight to the heart of the matter if need be. Geraldine quickly got a prospectus on the movie and by the end of the week the Gull had his money and Les had a fifty-thousand-dollar share investment in a film by Murke Productions Pty Ltd titled *Leaving Bondi*.

This had all happened before Les went to Port Stephens with Eddie. Since then, they'd both got back safe and sound, Price had slipped Les another ten thousand for the effort, and life went on. Now it was another Sunday night at the Kelly Club in late autumn. The club was empty and Les was sitting in Price's office, wearing a char-grey shirt tucked into a pair of black trousers, about to enjoy an after-work drink. Sitting on his left, Eddie and Billy were wearing leather bomber jackets and dark trousers and deep in discussion about how much chlorine goes in a swimming pool. Price was at his desk, wearing a light green suit with a jade tie, and going over some betting slips with George Brennan. Overweight George was wrapped into a dark blue suit with a blue tie; the suit slightly crumpled as usual. Norton being temporarily left to his own devices was settled back, sipping on a cold Fourex and surmising that all up, things weren't too bad. They could have been better. But all up, they weren't too bad.

Digger and her cousin had certainly made headlines with 'their' discovery of the submarine, and with the money rolling in, they were able to leave for America so Brendon could have his eye operation. Digger even sold her story to a woman's magazine. ANNE ZACCARIAH, MY SECRET AGONY, SHARKS ATE MY FATHER WHILE MY COUSIN WENT BLIND. Because she didn't like travelling to Sydney, Les had been driving to Newcastle when he got the chance. Which sadly wasn't working out. The porking was still sensational. But Digger wasn't the happiest drunk in the world and her cooking would kill a brown dog. Besides that, Les got the distinct feeling Digger was having it away. Not out of any disrespect or lack of affection for Les, but Les had definitely turned her into a mad raving case and having that bottled up inside her all those years, she was making up for lost time. Why buy a book — even if it was a good one — when you can join a library. Digger never let on, but Les could tell. And it wasn't just the phone calls from old friends when he was at her house; phone calls always taken in the other room. Of course what Digger did when Les wasn't around was pretty much her business. Not his. But Les wasn't all that keen on sharing Digger's sweet little whatever with strangers. And now you could bet Digger was cutting a swathe through the medical fraternity in Fort Worth, Texas, while Brendon was recovering in hospital. So Les knew it was only a matter of time before it would be the end of the affair. Oh well, thought Les. You win some, you lose some. I guess I was just born to go through life another broken-hearted clown, laughing on the outside, crying on the inside. That's show biz. And talking about show biz, tomorrow was the first day of filming for *Leaving Bondi*. He took another sip of beer and felt a tap on his left shoulder. It was Billy Dunne.

'You're very quiet there, old mate,' he said.

'Eh? No, I was just thinking about something, Billy,' replied Les. 'You and Eddie were talking anyway.'

Eddie stretched his arms above his head and yawned. 'I know what I'm thinking,' he said. 'I'm thinking of going straight to bed when I get home. I worked on the house all day today, pouring concrete. And I'm rooted.'

'Hey, talking about work,' said George Brennan, locking the safe. 'That lazy, loafing nephew of mine Kevin's got a part in a movie tomorrow. They're shooting it at Bondi Beach public school while the school holidays are on. He's a cop.'

'Kevin?' said Price. 'How could he do a day's work? They'd have to take an X-ray first to see if he had one in him.'

'He'd make a good cop,' said Billy.

'Yeah,' chuckled Les. 'It runs in the family.'

'Hey, how come you haven't got a part in the movie, Tom Cruise?' said George. 'It's being shot in your backyard. And you're an actor and a model. Did your agent forget to ring you?'

Les brushed his fingernails lightly against his shirt then glanced at them indifferently. 'It's funny you should say that George. Because I just happen to have a share investment in that very same movie.'

'You what?' said George.

'I bought some shares in the movie,' replied Les. 'It's called *Leaving Bondi.*'

'Shit! You kept that quiet,' said Billy.

'Well,' drawled Les. 'I didn't want to start running around big-noting, Billy. Just because I've become a major player in the Australian film game.'

'Major player in the film game.' Billy shook his head. 'Fuck off, will you, Les.'

'How much did you stick into it?' asked Eddie.

'Enough.'

George turned to Price. 'Can you believe this cunt? Sticking his money into a movie.'

Price gestured with one hand. 'I don't know, George. Taking a punt on an Aussie movie's not a bad idea.' He turned to Les. 'This could turn out to be a very wise investment, old son.'

Les nodded. 'That's right. It could turn out to be another *Crocodile Dundee.*'

'*Crocodile Dundee,*' scoffed George. 'I know one thing. You won't be crying crocodile tears if you do your money. They'll hear you howling the other side of Cape Barren lighthouse.'

'Hey, I'll be down Bondi tomorrow,' said Eddie. 'I got to see a bloke about something. You reckon it'd be worth me hanging round the movie set for a perv?'

'I don't know,' shrugged Les. 'But I'm going to have a look. I might see you down there.'

'Okay. We'll have a coffee,' said Eddie.

Price changed the subject to something that had happened at the club earlier in the night. Then they talked about something else. It was the end of the week and everyone was feeling tired and looking forward to a few days off. They drank and talked for another thirty minutes or so then left. Driving home in the back of Price's new Mercedes, Les was thinking. Yes. Things ain't that bad. I've just earned a few Oxford Scholars tonight. My job definitely isn't the Burma Railway. And I'm getting a lift home in an air-conditioned Merc. Yes. Things could be a lot worse. Eddie dropped him off at his door, Les said he'd see them all later and went inside.

Once more, Les had the house to himself. This time Warren was down the south coast at Ulladulla, in a weekender with a blonde actress he'd met at the Toriyoshi. A blonde Les fancied. But unfortunately Warren tap danced too fast for him. Les got out of his work clothes and into his tracksuit pants and a T-shirt, made an Ovaltine then walked out into the backyard and looked up at the stars shining down on a crisp autumn night. He sipped his Ovaltine and shook his head, finding it hard to believe how time went so fast. It only seemed like a few days ago they were trying to get the money together to make *Leaving Bondi*. Now they were actually filming it. Les yawned and had a slight chuckle to himself. He'd got a postcard from Neville Nizegy early in the week. From San Diego of all places. It didn't say who it was from. But Les knew. I wonder what Nizegy would think if he knew some of his money was going into an Aussie movie? He'd probably be rapt. Naturally, Nizegy didn't leave a forwarding address, so Les couldn't tell him. Les finished his Ovaltine. Yawned again then went to bed. In ten minutes the big Queenslander was snoring soundly.

By the time Les rose from his sleep-in, got cleaned up then climbed into his blue tracksuit and trainers to walk down and get the paper, it was ten o'clock. After throwing his dirty clothes in the washing machine, before taking his own sweet time over poached eggs and coffee, it was after eleven. Outside it wasn't too bad a day; mild, with a few clouds around and a light nor'wester rustling through the few trees in Cox Avenue. An excellent day for filming smiled Les, as he flicked through the sports pages. Filming, I say filming my movie that is, boy.

By the time Les cleaned up in the kitchen and hung his washing out on the Hills Hoist like any other good Bondi housewife, it was getting on for twelve. Les had a glass of filtered water for the road, locked the house up and headed for the film set.

Walking fairly briskly, Les went straight down O'Brien Street then took a left into Gould, slowing down as he crossed Curlewis to wave to a couple of girls he knew going past on ten-speeds. He crossed

Beach Road, finally stopping in Gould Street at a metal gate set into the rusty cyclone-wire fence running along the back of Bondi Beach Public School. Behind the metal gate, a set of concrete steps angled down to the old schoolyard, the tar criss-crossed with white markings to form a basketball court. A row of scrubby trees ran below the cyclone-wire fence towards Warners Avenue and on the right a couple of tall pines and other trees stood in front of a grey paling fence that separated the schoolyard from the flats in Beach Road. On the left side of the schoolyard was a children's play station flanked by two basketball hoops and across the playground, opposite Les, was a two-storey block of classrooms, then the rest of the school sprawled across to Campbell Parade. Joining the other interested bystanders in Gould Street, Norton leant against the metal gate and peered into the playground where the circus was well and truly in town.

All over the schoolyard were actors and extras dressed in State Protection Group or army uniforms. Walking amongst them, in a grey dust coat with a holstered magnum on his hip, was the armourer, keeping an eye on the M–16s, Heckler and Koch sub-machine guns and Glock pistols the actors and extras were having a great time playing with. Two make-up girls were bustling about, wiping the actors' faces or whatever while two wardrobe girls were busy double-checking their uniforms and another girl was walking around taking polaroids. Through the sprawl, other film crew were wandering around the playground, sucking on styrofoam cups of coffee as they squawked into two-way radios. Some of the extras, including George's nephew, were leaning up against the school block.

Others were seated around a hot water urn next to one of the basketball hoops. While all this rattle was going on, another scene of organised confusion was being enacted next to the children's play station.

A camera was set up on a cherry picker and beneath it electricians, carpenters, grips and various other film crew were bustling about laying down tracks or securing things with grey gaffer tape. At the epicentre of all this and looking every inch the uber-director was Max King, wearing a red batik shirt and Ray Ban sunglasses. King was staring morosely at the ground, his hand under his chin, in earnest conversation with the cameraman and the first assistant director, who was in earnest conversation with the soundman and the second assistant director, who was in earnest conversation with the assistant to the assistant assistant's whatever. Hovering in the background was the man with the clapper-board. He was in earnest conversation with a girl carrying a stop-watch and a clipboard who was checking the continuity. More film crew were coming and going and the dress was everything from ferocious black to Mambo Surfie and King's batik shirt. All topped with weird haircuts in every colour of the rainbow and facial piercing. It was as if the inmates had taken over the asylum and the inmates were waiting for Max King to rise majestically above the mob, give the nod to the first assistant director who would give the nod to the second assistant director who would then utter the magic words.

'All right. Quiet everybody. First positions please.'

Les leant against the gate to watch all the sizzling action and beautiful girls in the movie business. There was neither. Every girl on the set would have got kicked off a ghost train and the whole scene was about as exciting as watching an endless American gridiron huddle. Les watched everyone on the set play hurry up and wait for a while longer, then decided to walk down to Campbell Parade via Warners Avenue and have a look in the front gate just in case something might be happening there.

Through a line of trees behind the school fence in Warners Avenue, Les could see all the film company trucks lined up along the drive at the main entrance; wardrobe, make-up, generators, etc. The crew and cast had their cars parked nearby and in front of the drive was a grassy area about seventy metres square. Benches and tables were set up on the grass and behind the benches and tables was a dark blue catering van, its back nestled up near some scrubby trees running behind the school fence in Campbell Parade. Les strolled casually round the corner just as a 380 pulled up at a bus stop in front of the fence. As he slowed down for the people getting off the bus, Les noticed his left shoelace had come undone. He walked to the other side of the bus stop then turned round and rested his foot on the seat. Through the trees on his left, a flash of colour caught Norton's eye.

It was a thin, pale man with a shock of pink and yellow hair, wearing a black T-shirt, greasy black jeans and an apron round his waist. The man had come from a set of steps at the back of the catering van and Les surmised he was the cook. He was carrying a small tupperware container in one hand and a fork in the other, and had his back to Les as he picked something up from the grass near the steps. It was a couple of small, dried-up white dog turds. Les watched from behind the trees as the cook carefully put the two turds in the plastic container then clipped the lid on and disappeared back inside the catering van. Les closed his eyes and shook his head for a moment wondering what was going on. Les was still wondering what was going on when he felt a light punch under his floating rib. It was Eddie, wearing a black Balance tracksuit and matching trainers.

'Righto, Shifty. What are you up to?'

'Eddie,' replied Les. 'How are you mate?'

'Good. What's happening on the film set?'

'Not a great deal,' said Les. 'Hey Eddie, you're not going to believe what I just saw.'

Les finished tying his shoelace and told Eddie what he'd seen, pointing to the catering van on the other side of the trees. Eddie seemed to think for a moment, a smile tugging at the corners of his eyes.

'You reckon the cook was picking up dog shit? And putting it in a tupperware container?'

'Yeah,' nodded Les. 'You could almost smell it. I wonder what he was up to?'

'Buggered if I know,' said Eddie, thoughtfully. 'But I know how we might be able to find out. Follow me over to my car, I'll show you something. It's just round the corner.'

Les followed Eddie across to his maroon Calais which was angle parked on the opposite side of Warners Avenue. Eddie opened the boot and took two aluminium binocular cases out of an overnight bag. He opened the cases and handed Les a pair of black binoculars. They were wider and heavier than normal, with green tinted lenses and there was a switch built into the lens on the right with a tiny light in front of it. Stamped across the top was CANON IMAGE STABILIZER 15X 451S.

'What are these?' asked Les.

'Image stabilizing binoculars,' replied Eddie. 'I just bought them. You focus on what you want to look at. Then press that button and it cuts out any movement.'

'Yeah?'

'That catering van's facing this way. Come on over the road and we'll have a look from behind those trees. We might be able to see what he's up to.'

Les had another look at the binoculars. 'Righto.'

They crossed Warners Avenue, found a clear view of the catering truck through the trees, then rested their arms on the metal fence and raised the binoculars to their eyes. Les gave a double blink. The catering van was a hundred metres away, but the binoculars were so powerful, you would have thought you were inside it. There were gas bottles behind another door on the right and a white laminex counter at the front with a blue awning over it. Pink Hair was chopping up broccoli behind the counter. Les pressed the image stabilizer switch and could scarcely believe his eyes. Everything stood perfectly still; there was absolutely no shaking at all. It was like watching TV, only better.

Les could easily make out the cook's facial features now. Under the pink hair, he had a lean, grainy face with a pointy nose and a long pointy chin, where a silver stud glinted through a blonde goatee beard. There was a dark-haired girl in another black T-shirt and jeans, wiping over the tables on the grass, leaving the cook alone in the kitchen. The cook finished what he was doing, had a quick look around then reached under the counter and took out the tupperware container. He removed the two white dog turds then very deftly sliced them into six neat portions and placed them on a plate. Through the binoculars, Les could see everything clear as crystal. Next, the cook got a bottle of chocolate sauce from beneath the counter and poured some over the portions of dog shit. While the sauce was sinking in, the cook reached into a cabinet above the counter, got a packet of shredded coconut and sprinkled it liberally over the pieces of sliced dog shit. Satisfied, he put the plate to one side as Les put the binoculars down and turned to Eddie.

'Did you just see that?'

Eddie had his binoculars down too. 'Did I ever. What a cunt.'

They raised the binoculars again and Les pushed the stabilizer switch. A fat, orange blowfly drifted languidly into the catering truck and landed on the counter. The cook kept his eyes on it then picked up a plastic fly swat and carefully flattened the blowfly where it landed. The blowfly had scarcely stopped kicking when the cook descended on it with a small pair of scissors and quickly trimmed off its wings and legs. He flicked them off the counter then got another small tupperware container, opened it and dropped the blowfly inside with several other trimmed up blowflies. The cook looked at them for a moment before tipping the lot into a pot of bean casserole simmering on the stove behind him. He gave the casserole a stir then put the two tupperware containers into a dishwasher as his assistant came in through the door on the right.

Les brought the binoculars down again, shook his head and looked at Eddie in disgust. 'Ohh yuk!' he said. 'That's enough to turn you off your fuckin day.'

'It is making it a bit willing,' agreed Eddie.

'Making it a bit willing?' said Les. 'It's enough to make you sick.'

'And on your movie too.'

'Yeah. My grouse bloody movie. What's his caper?'

'I don't know. But are you going to cop it?' asked Eddie.

'No fuckin way Jose.'

'Then there definitely has to be a square up.'

'Oh! A square up for sure, mate.'

'You got any ideas?' enquired Eddie.

'Yeah,' nodded Les. 'How about I go over there and pour that casserole down his pink and blond throat. Then force-feed him those dog shit lamingtons for dessert.'

Eddie wiggled his eyebrows. 'I got a better idea.'

'You have?'

'Yeah. The old exploding-cake-full-of-shit trick.'

'The exploding-cake-full-of-shit trick, Ninety-Nine? What's that all about?'

'Come on. Let's put these back in the car, and I'll tell you.' They walked back across the road to Eddie's Calais. Eddie returned the binoculars to his overnight bag and closed the boot. 'I'll put a thundercracker in a cake full of shit. Then rig it so when Pink Hair opens the box it goes off and he gets a face full of shit. Along with his chuck wagon.'

'Sounds good to me,' said Les. 'How's it work?'

'I'll explain it to you in the morning. All I want you to do is find out his name, so we can write it on the cake box. Then you deliver it to him. You reckon you can do that?'

'I don't see why not, Edward.'

'I got a couple of blokes coming to see me tomorrow morning. I'll bring it over your place about ten-thirty. Is that okay?'

'Good as gold.' Norton turned towards the catering van. 'In fact I can't wait.'

'Okay.' Eddie looked at Les for a moment. 'You still feel like a cup of coffee?'

Les shook his head. 'Not particularly.'

'No. Me either. You want a lift home?'

'No. I might walk. I want to pick a couple of things up at the shop.'

'Okay. Well, I'll see you in the morning.'

'Righto. See you then, Eddie.'

Eddie drove off towards North Bondi. Les had another look at the catering van then walked back to Gould Street. So much for my first day on the wonderful film set. Bloody hell! What's the world coming to?

When he got back to Chez Norton, Les put the groceries away then changed into his old training gear, wrapped a sweatband round his head and went for a lap of Rose Bay Golf Links and back, finishing in the backyard with what felt like a half-a-million sit-ups. Les was in a funny mood while he was exercising. One half of him was dirty on what he'd just seen on the film set. The other half was laughing at the square up coming the next day. After a shower, Les threw a steak under the griller, nuked some vegetables then settled back for a quiet afternoon at home. He wrote a letter to his parents, washed the car, and by the time he'd tidied up and farted around the house the day was over. Les could have watched the news. But instead he thought he might call into the Toriyoshi, say hello to the Gull and congratulate him on the first day of filming. Les changed into a pair of jeans and a grey Toriyoshi T-shirt Ray had given him, put his gaberdine bomber jacket on and strolled down to Campbell Parade. The Gull was on the phone, wearing a red Hawaiian shirt and jeans, when Les arrived at the restaurant. Les gave him a wave through the window, then bought two bottles of Stella Artois, placed them on a table out the front and gave Ray a nod to let him know there was a cool one waiting for him when he was ready. The Gull was out in a couple of minutes.

'That was Monique,' he said, joining Les at the table. 'She can't find her key.'

'She's a blonde,' winked Les. 'Give her a break.'

Ray couldn't help himself. He was absolutely beaming when he picked up his beer. 'Well, what do you reckon, Les?' he said. '*Leaving Bondi*. It's a happening thing, baby.'

'It sure is, Ray. I came down today and had a look. Congratulations, mate.' Les clinked his bottle against Ray's.

Ray clinked his back. 'Thanks Les. And thanks again for investing your money in it.'

Les made a magnanimous gesture. 'Hey. What else could I do?'

Ray shook his head. 'I swear to God, Les. A lot of my blood, sweat and tears went into that movie, man. And me nearly going over the gap a couple of times.'

'Down and out in Gullsville.'

Ray nodded. 'Yep. Fat city. No soles in my shoes. And no strings on my banjo. But not now, Les. The Gull's back in town.'

'Drinkin' TNT. And smokin' dynamite. Good luck to you.' Les clinked the Gull's bottle again. 'Hey how come you're not doing the catering on the movie, Ray? That would have been a nice little earn for you.'

Ray shook his head. 'I couldn't be bothered making that many pork balls, Les. I'm flat out here.'

'Fair enough. So who's doing the catering?'

'Kreative Katering,' replied Ray. 'Spelt with a K.'

Les snapped his fingers. 'I think I know the bloke who runs that. I used to work with him at Pyrmont. Skinny nosed bloke with a skinny chin. Wears a beard. Do you know him?'

'Sort of,' replied Ray.

'What's his name?'

'I'm not sure. But I can find out for you. I got a call sheet under the counter, I'll get it.'

'That's all right, Ray. You don't have to.'

'Won't take me two minutes,' said Ray, rising from the table. 'Besides, you're a major investor.'

'Thanks, mate,' smiled Les. The Gull walked inside the restaurant, Les had another swallow of beer and looked up at the night sky. Does it always have to be this easy Boss? Honestly. Where's the challenge? Where is the challenge?

Ray came back out with what looked like a small filmscript printed on blue paper. He placed it on the table and flicked through the first few pages. 'Here it is. Kreative Katering. Albert Knox, Proprietor.'

'That's him,' said Les. 'Knoxie. I must call in and say hello.'

Suddenly some people began to arrive, so Les finished the rest of his beer. 'I'd better make a move, Ray. You're starting to get busy.'

'Hey. Stick around, Les. Have another beer.'

'No. I only called down to say hello. And to offer my congratulations.' Les offered his hand. 'Good on you, Ray. You've killed 'em.'

Ray shook Norton's hand. 'Thanks, Les. And thanks for coming down. It's always great to see you, man.'

'You too, Ray. I might see you tomorrow.'

'See you then, Les.'

Norton got up and left, leaving Ray to look after his customers.

Back home, Les got another beer from the fridge and settled back in front of the TV. Albert Knox. That shouldn't be too hard to write on top of a cake box. Les slipped on a video Warren had brought home from the advertising agency. *Analyze This* with Robert de Niro and Billy Crystal. Les was still laughing when he went to bed. What's a sandwich that ain't fattening? A haf a sandwich. Beautiful. Just beautiful. In ten minutes Norton was snoring like a baby. Tomorrow was definitely going to be another day.

Les was out of bed by seven; feeling good and looking forward to the day. Outside it was pleasant enough again; mild, a bit of an offshore breeze and sunny. Les got cleaned up, had some coffee and a mango smoothie then decided to get his exercise out of the way early. He got back into his training gear again and did the Rose Bay Golf Links, sit ups in the backyard ghastliness, same as the day before. By the time Les got that over, scoffed some poached eggs and read the paper, it was ten-thirty and the doorbell was ringing. It was Eddie, wearing the same tracksuit as the day before, carrying a white cake box in his hands, sealed with Sellotape.

'G'day, Eddie,' Les greeted him. 'Come on in.'

Eddie followed Les down the hallway into the kitchen. 'Did you find out the bloke's name?'

'Yes. Albert Knox.'

'Good old Knoxie, eh. Well done, Les.' Eddie placed the cake box on the kitchen table.

'So that's it.'

'Yep. That's it,' replied Eddie, looking proud of his work. 'One exploding shit cake to go.'

Les gave the cake box a perusal. 'So how does it work?'

Eddie shrugged. 'It's mainly a lot of fucking around with electrical tape. And I can tell you one thing, Les. I'm not over rapt in the smell of my own shit.'

'Don't worry, Eddie. I've been on the wrong side of your farts at work.'

'But it's just a thundercracker from Chinatown with a shortened fuse. A matchbox, matches and a mousetrap. The hard part's slowing down the spring on the mousetrap.' Eddie looked at his watch. 'I'll show you how you do it one day back at my place. But believe me, Les. These work a treat.'

'I'll take your word for it, mate.'

Eddie cursed. 'Bad luck I won't fuckin be there to see it go off.'

'You won't?'

'No, bugger it. I've got to go over the north side and I don't know when I'll be back. But when you give it to the cook, hang around and take some photos. I want to see them.' Eddie gave Les a wink. 'And don't piss yourself when you see what happens.'

Les smiled back at Eddie. 'I'll try. But I can't promise you anything.'

Eddie stayed while Les printed the cook's name on the cake box in blue texta colour. He told Les the thing was safe and couldn't go off unless you opened the lid. But keep it upright, don't drop it or knock it around too much. Les promised to obey Eddie's instructions to the letter.

Eddie drove off, leaving Les in the kitchen staring at the cake box. What a weird bloke, thought Les, looking at the cook's name written across the top. I wonder why he did that? Either he's dirty on the world, or there's just some people on the set he wants to get at. Maybe Max King. I wouldn't blame him there. I'll find out somehow over the next few days. In the meantime, Albert's Karma at Kreative Katering is going to katch up with him. Les looked at his watch. Now, what would be the best time to deliver it? I reckon … about one o'clock. That gives me time to go to the bank, pay a few bills then get to the set when they're all having lunch. That way, everybody will see the cook get splattered and I can mingle in with the crowd. I'll use the telephoto lens first for some action photos then get a few close-ups. The cook won't have a clue who it is, either. Les chuckled to himself. And next day, me and Eddie'll send him a postcard. *We called in to see you. But you were shitfaced so we left. Love, Thelma and Louise.* Les changed into a pair of jeans, a green T-shirt and his Bugs Bunny cap, got his credit cards and whatever else he needed and drove up to Bondi Junction.

Everything went surprisingly easy. He had no trouble getting a parking spot and the queues weren't long. He was back home in time for a cup of coffee and a biscuit before going to the film set. That done, Les picked up the cake box, slung his camera over his shoulder and set off for Campbell Parade.

The big Queenslander was whistling cheerfully as he strolled past the Toriyoshi and through the school gates. The two wardrobe girls were standing near the gate in their multi-coloured clothes and dyed hair. They'd just finished a joint and picked up on Norton's vibe.

'Hey. Someone's in a good mood,' said one, with cherry red hair teased up around her head like a big red broccoli.

'On a day like this,' smiled Les, 'you'd have to be in a good mood.'

Her friend with jet black hair full of dark blue streaks and coloured beads, noticed the cake box. 'Is it somebody's birthday?' she asked.

'Yes. Albert the cook's,' replied Les. 'I baked this for him myself.'

'Oh,' said the dark-haired girl. 'He should like that.'

'Oh yeah,' smiled Norton. 'He'll get a bang out of this, I guarantee it.' Les left them and walked towards the chairs and tables on the grass. He was a little disappointed to find there weren't many people around. One or two film crew, a couple of voyeurs, the ubiquitous Japanese tourist armed with a video camera and the cook's dark-haired assistant, back wiping the tables. Still whistling cheerfully, Les gave the Japanese tourist a smile and a cheeky bow of his head as he went past, straight up to the girl wiping the tables.

'Excuse me, is Albert around?' he asked politely.

'Yeah,' replied the girl, pointing to the blue van. 'He's in the kitchen.'

'What time are you serving lunch today?'

'One-thirty. They're behind with the shoot. So they're having a late wrap.'

'Okay. Thank you.'

Les walked over to the van, tapped on the counter and placed the cake box on it.

'Parcel for Albert Knox,' he called out.

'What?' A lean pink head appeared from behind a wall oven.

'Parcel for Albert Knox. You don't have to sign anything. See you mate.'

Norton quickly turned and walked off, looking for somewhere to hide while he waited for the cook to open the cake box. The cook, however, was in one of those moods where he didn't have time to be stuffed around. He saw the cake box with his name on top and tore it straight open. Les had just got to the edge of the grass when he heard a muffled explosion and a loud curse. Shit, that was bloody quick. Les laughed and turned around to aim his camera. Next instant, there was a deafening blast and the catering van disintegrated in a spiralling ball of orange flames and a billowing cloud of thick black smoke. Instinctively Les threw his arms across his face as the steps at the rear of the catering van sailed over the school fence before smashing into the back of the bus stop and pieces of metal, wood and fibreglass rained down all over the front of the school, showering the parked trucks and cars with burning debris. The cook, minus one arm and half his face burnt away, was blown through the side entrance at the right of the van, along with the fridge and parts of the stove. Looking like a wobbly mess of charred meat in the remains of his smouldering clothes, Knox was dead before he hit the ground. His ears ringing like a burglar alarm Les tried to gather his senses as people started running from everywhere. Some carrying fire extinguishers, others had blankets, most were just startled people from the film crew or bystanders wondering what had happened. By rights, Les should have stopped and offered assistance. But something told Norton the best place for him was out of there. Holding his camera, Les pushed through the people coming in the school gate and walked home as fast as he could.

Back at Chez Norton, Les poured himself a bourbon and ice and with his ears still ringing from the explosion, flopped down in the lounge room dumbfounded. He took a slug of bourbon and tried to get his thoughts together. Jesus bloody Christ! What the fuck did Eddie put in that cake box? Les had another sip of bourbon and shook his head. No, he told himself. No way. There were definitely two explosions. I know I heard the first one. It was just a bit of a bang. Then that other fuckin thing went off. Bloody hell! Les sipped some more bourbon, feeling it burn down his chest and into his stomach. Maybe the thundercracker set something else off? Like those Elgas tanks. No. Les shook his head again. I've heard tanks go. It's a different sound. That was gelignite or some kind of explosive.

Les reflected into his glass and was forced to realise the only possible explanation: somebody had let a bomb off in the catering van at the same time he'd bowled up with his firecracker. But why? The cook might have been a low bastard doing what he did. But it wasn't worth killing him for. Was it? Christ! What a lousy, fuckin coincidence. I don't believe it. Then a thought hit Les and it didn't warm his body like the bourbon. It chilled him to the bone. What if somebody saw me leave that parcel there? Saw me leave the parcel? About six bloody people saw me. Those two weird-looking sheilas for a start. The cook's assistant. That Jap with the camera. And anybody else that was there. See me? Fuckin hell! They couldn't miss me. Les stared anxiously at the phone. I think I'd better ring Eddie.

Eddie's mobile wasn't answering. Neither was his answering service at home. That figures, thought Les. Lyndy's taken the kids away for the school holidays so Eddie's up to something. Fuck it. Les put the phone down and started to pace. The more he paced, the more worried he got. Shit! I'm a good chance of getting a tug over this, he told himself. A bloody good chance. He paced some more. Yep. You can back it in. I'm going to get my collar felt. I know it. And what am I going to tell them? Oh, it was only a cracker in a cake box, officer. Yeah. Righto. Les paced some more. No. This is not good. Not good at all. I'd better make another phone call.

'Hello?'

'Yeah. Hello Price. It's Les.'

'Les. How are you, mate? What can I do for you?'

'Price, I think I'm in a bit of serious bother with the cops. I might need a big favour off you later on tonight.'

Les didn't have to spell it out. 'I understand, Les. What time?' asked Price.

'I'm not sure. But I'd reckon early tonight.'

'No worries, Les. I'll make the necessary arrangements. Ring me here. I'll be home all night.'

'Thanks, Price. I appreciate it.'

'You do sound worried, Les.'

'I am.'

'Don't be. Just settle back. And ring me when the time comes.'

'Thanks, Price. I'll get back to you.'

Les hung up and finished his drink. He didn't make another one. Instead he switched on the kitchen radio just in time for the dramatic news.

'One person was killed and several others injured in a bomb blast at Bondi early this afternoon. The device, believed to be remote controlled, was set to go off in a catering van on the set of a movie, *Leaving Bondi*, being filmed at Bondi Beach Public School. Fortunately, the school was closed for the holidays so casualties were kept to a minimum. However, a caterer was fatally injured in the blast and several members of the film crew have been hospitalised. Police have not released any names. But they wish to question a tall, solid man, wearing a T-shirt and baseball cap, seen leaving Bondi Beach Public School shortly after the bomb was detonated.'

'Fuckin hell!'

Les switched off the radio. He'd heard all he needed. A tall, solid man in a baseball cap. That's me. And it'll only be a matter of time before they put a name to the face. Yep. I'm off tap. Les stopped pacing. Okay. No need to panic. But you can bet they'll search the place when they get here. And there's things to be done.

Les got the jemmy from the shed and levered up the pile of wood above where his loot was buried. He removed the slab of wood over the hole then got a shovel and filled the hole with earth. After patting the earth down solid, he dumped the pile of wood on top of it and straightened the tarpaulin. It was going to be a bit of a pain in the arse getting to his swag again, but at least now there was less chance of the police finding it. Next item on the agenda was the boarder's pot. Luckily, Warren had just harvested his plants from the backyard, but he had about half a kilo of juicy heads squashed into a shoe box under his bed. Les took the shoe box out to the kitchen, stood on a chair, moved the manhole cover in the ceiling and hid it in the roof. A thorough search would soon find it, but at least it was better than just sitting under the bed. Warren's lousy fuckin pot, thought Les, after he put the manhole cover back. As if I haven't got better things to worry about than that. Like fuck-all chance of me getting bail for starters. Les gathered his money, wallet, credit cards, passport and anything else he could think of and put them in the pocket of his bomber jacket. He didn't bother ringing his family or Billy Dunne. It was no use alarming everybody for the time being. He'd contacted Price. That was enough. Price would handle it from there. Les could have taken it on the toe and got out of town. But that would only make it look worse and they'd find him sooner or later. No. He had to wear it. It was just plain bad luck. Les had another drink, then made some more coffee and waited. The knock on the door came in the early evening.

Les opened the front door to find two detectives standing there in sports coats, and a uniform cop in overalls with a Jack Russell terrier on a lead. Both detectives were about the same stocky build; one had dark hair going bald, the other had brown hair cut close to his scalp. The uniform cop was tall with a brown moustache. The dark-haired cop had the warrant.

'Les Norton. Cox Avenue, Bondi?' said the dark-haired detective.

'That's me,' nodded Les.

'I'm Detective Caccano. This is Detective Tait and Sergeant Plackett. We have a warrant to search your premises for explosives.'

Les stood back from the door. 'Go for your life.' He turned to the cop with the dog. 'You won't find nothing, mate, so try not to wreck the place will you? There's a tool shed out the backyard too. It's unlocked.'

'Righto, mate,' said the uniform cop indifferently. 'Come on, Oscar. Good boy.'

Les watched as Sergeant Plackett and his sniffer dog started searching round his bedroom, then motioned to the two other cops. 'The lounge is through there. You want to sit down?'

'We'll follow you,' said Detective Caccano.

They went into the lounge room and sat down. Les on the lounge, the two cops facing him on the loungechairs.

'You live here on your own?' asked Detective Caccano.

Les shook his head. 'No. I got a flatmate. A bloke called Warren Edwards. He works for MM and B Advertising.'

'Where's he?' asked Detective Tait.

'Down the south coast with a girl. At Ulladulla. I don't know when he'll be back. About Thursday, I think.'

'You work at the Kelly Club, don't you?' said Detective Tait.

'That's right,' answered Les.

'With a bloke called Billy Dunne.'

'Yeah. We work on the door.'

'Price Galese has gone very respectable these days,' said Detective Caccano.

Les looked at the two detectives expressionlessly. 'I was under the impression he always was.'

The two detectives looked expressionlessly back at Les as Sergeant Plackett and his dog gave the house a swift but thorough going-over. The dog sniffed all over the lounge and kitchen, then they went out into the backyard. Les offered the two detectives some coffee. They declined. There was a modicum of chit-chat then Sergeant Plackett came back into the lounge and shook his head.

'Nothing out there,' he said to the two detectives. He turned to Les. 'How do I get up in the roof?'

'There's a manhole cover in the kitchen. Above the sideboard next to the fridge. The stepladder's in the shed.'

'I won't need it.'

Les watched the cop go into the kitchen then heard him push the dog up through the manhole cover. The dog barked a couple of times as Les heard it running about in the roof. Well, there goes Warren's pot. Now they'll get me for supply. As well as murder, arson, and whatever fuckin else they're going to charge me with. Fuck it, cursed Les.

Les heard the manhole cover being replaced, then Sergeant Plackett and his dog came back into the lounge room empty handed.

Sergeant Plackett shook his head. 'Nothing in there, either,' he said. 'The place appears to be clean.'

'I had a feeling it would be,' said Detective Tait.

'What do you want me to do?'

'Go back to the yard. We'll give you a call if we need you again.'

Les had nearly fallen through the back of the lounge. He knew he had to say something. Anything. Or his facial expressions would give him away.

'If you don't mind me asking,' Les said to Sergeant Plackett, 'that's a funny-looking police dog. I thought they were all German Shepherds. Or Rottweilers.'

'Oscar?' replied Sergeant Plackett. 'Oscar's okay. Oscar used to be with Customs. But he accidentally snorted a big pile of pure heroin one night and nearly died from an overdose. He's been useless with drugs ever since. Couldn't tell dope from donuts. But he's the best in the business when it comes to explosives. Aren't you Oscar?' The dog panted and smiled up at his handler. 'He's a good boy.' Sergeant Plackett turned to the two detectives. 'Okay. I'll see you later.'

'Righto. Thanks for your help, Geoff,' said Detective Tait.

Les heard Sergeant Plackett and his dog leave and studied Caccano and Tait pretty much the same way they were studying him. From his dealings with police in the past, their attitude and body language told him these two knew what they were doing. They hadn't carried on with any great drama so far and they'd obviously done their homework on him. They were probably mystified why Les would want to set a bomb off on a film set. But by the company Les kept, where he worked and his past form, it wouldn't have surprised them.

Up to this point, they'd been very low key. Now Les was waiting for the penny to drop. Though Les had to admit, luck had certainly been on his side so far. Detective Caccano spoke first.

'Well, I imagine you know what this is all about, Les?' he said quietly.

Les made a small gesture with his hands. 'Not ... really. Maybe you'd better fill me in.'

'An explosive device was set off on a film set in Bondi early this afternoon,' continued Detective Caccano. 'In which one person was killed and a number of other people were injured.'

Les nodded. 'Yeah. I heard it on the news earlier.'

'You've been identified by at least five people leaving a parcel in the catering canteen at the precise time of the blast,' said Detective Tait.

'You've been positively identified by the film's director,' Detective Caccano flipped open his notebook. 'A Mr Max King.'

'And there's film of you leaving the parcel on the school's outdoor security camera,' said Detective Caccano. 'Which is what Mr King was able to make a positive identification from.'

There was a brief silence, then Detective Tait spoke. 'So what have you got to say to all this, Les?'

Les studied the two detectives for a moment. 'What have I got to say?' he replied. 'I don't quite know what to say at the moment. But I imagine you'd like me to accompany you to the station. Where I could be of further assistance with your inquiries?'

Detective Caccano half smiled. 'We certainly would.'

Les nodded to his bomber jacket on the lounge. 'I'll just get my jacket.'

Les stood up and so did the two detectives. Detective Caccano reached behind his sports coat.

'If you don't mind, Les,' he said easily. 'Your hands.'

'Yeah,' said Detective Tait. 'It's not that we don't trust you, Les. It's just that we don't trust you.'

Les felt the handcuffs snap round his wrists and knew exactly where he stood with Detectives Caccano and Tait. Two minutes later he was in the back seat of a Holden heading for Waverley Police Station.

Christ! This is getting to be a habit, Les fumed to himself, as the units in Old South Head Road went past. How could anything fuck up so bad? The bloody security camera. I didn't even think of that. But why would Les have thought of that or anything else? It wasn't as if he and Eddie had planned to murder anyone. All they had in mind was more or less a harmless prank. Les would have told the neighbourhood what they were up to. It was a hoot. Now this. Les shook his head and put himself in the two detectives' shoes for a moment. Les was their man all right. They were short on motive, but they had a red hot suspect. And Les knew for sure the best evidence was yet to come.

Waverley Police Station in Bronte Road looked exactly the same as the last time Les was in there. And the time before that. Except there was a platoon of journalists, photographers and TV cameras milling round out the front. Les just had time to pull his jacket up over his head as cameras started flashing and TV cameras began whirling. The police drove down the back of the station and with the media still howling like jackals in the background Les was bundled out of the Holden and through a door into the station. The only view Les got was his feet beneath his bomber jacket, going up the familiar concrete stairs before he was led into the detectives' room.

'Christ! That was a lot of fun,' said Les, straightening his jacket around him after he walked through the door.

'Yes. Our friends in the media,' said Detective Tait. 'They're all right, aren't they.'

Les had a look around him. He was in the same room as he'd been in last time he was at Waverley Police Station. The same dusty window looking out over the surrounding flats, the same grey metal filing cabinets against the walls. A skinny pot plant in the corner opposite the vinyl chairs and desk. Even the wanted posters on the walls hadn't seemed to change. The only difference was the blue grey carpet looked new, there was a computer on the desk with a TV and a VCR beneath and a video camera mounted on a black metal tripod sat near the computer. Detective Tait motioned Les to one of the seats. Les sat down as the two detectives loosened their ties.

'All right. We won't fuck around, Les,' said Detective Caccano, picking up a video and slipping it into the VCR. 'This is a copy from the school security camera. Have a look and see what you think.'

Les sat back as the video began rolling. It was grainy and jerky with a time lapse. But there was no mistaking Les coming into view and placing the cake box on the counter of the catering van. You could even pick up the maniacal grin on Norton's face as he walked back out of range. Next, there was a great flash of flame and smoke as the van erupted and the chairs and tables closest to the van flew into the others. Then the cook's body tumbled down the stairs through the smoke. Detective Caccano wound it back a couple of times more. Freeze framed it on Norton's grinning face, then switched it off.

'Well, what do you think, Les?' asked Detective Tait. 'I'd say that's you. I'd even hazard a guess and say you're still wearing the same T-shirt.'

'Yes,' agreed Norton slowly. 'There is a certain resemblance.'

Detective Caccano flipped open his notebook. 'We've also got a statement from a Ms Robyn Cornish, one of the make-up girls on the movie. She said to you, quote, "Is it somebody's birthday?" And you replied, quote, "Yes, Albert the cook's. I baked this for him myself. He'll get a bang out of this. I guarantee it." This is also verified by a statement from the other make-up girl,' the detective consulted his notebook, 'a Ms Jacintha Gillings.'

'Albert the cook certainly got a bang out of your cake, Les, didn't he?' said Detective Tait. 'I'd say half of Bondi did.'

Detective Caccano looked evenly at Norton. 'Do you wish to make a statement, Les?'

Les stared at the handcuffs round his wrists. This was the evidence he knew the two detectives had. And he was stuffed, six ways to Saturday. Or as Billy Dunne liked to say, he had two chances: none and slim. And Slim left town last week. But Les did have two chances. He could tell the truth; not that it would do him much good. And he could make a phone call.

Les sucked in some air. 'Okay. You're right. That is me.'

'Thanks, Les,' said Detective Tait. 'At least you're not playing us for complete mugs.'

'And I want to make a statement. You ain't gonna believe it. But I'll make it anyway. And it's the truth.'

'Okay, Les,' said Detective Caccano. 'Now as this is a very serious charge, I'm going to record it on video.' The detective swivelled the video camera on the tripod, spoke briefly into the recorder, then gave Les the go-ahead.

Without implicating Eddie, Les told them everything that happened. He said he made the device in the cake box, and he was alone when he saw the cook tampering with the food. He left the scene because he panicked and intended contacting the police the following day, but the two detectives called round before he had the chance. Detective Caccano switched off the video recorder, looked at his partner, then turned to Les. Whether they saw the funny side of the situation Les wasn't sure. It certainly didn't appear that way.

'You say you made the explosive device in the cake box?' said Detective Tait.

'That's right. At home. In the shed out the back,' replied Les.

'And you bought the cracker from a friend in Chinatown?' said Detective Caccano.

'That's right.'

'What was his name?'

'His name? Ahh, I'm not sure. He's just a bloke I know.'

'And the image stabilizing binoculars?' asked Detective Tait. 'Where are they now?'

'I loaned them to a bloke. To take to the races.'

'I see,' nodded Detective Tait. 'And the cake you used to put the firecracker in? Where did you buy that?'

'I baked it at home. Out of a packet,' replied Les.

'And you went to all this trouble,' said Detective Caccano, 'because you saw the cook putting flies in the stew. And dog shit in the lamingtons.'

'That's exactly right,' said Les. 'Hey, like I told you, I invested some money in that movie, and I didn't like what I saw going on.'

'I suppose the money you invested in the movie,' said Detective Tait, 'you won that at the races, too.'

'As a matter of fact I did.'

Detective Caccano looked at his partner. Then back at Norton. 'Okay, Les. That's one of the greatest loads of bullshit I've ever heard. It's such a load of bullshit it could almost be fair dinkum. But ...' Detective Caccano shook his head. 'So I am now officially charging you Les. With murder. Five counts of malicious wounding. Malicious damage. Endangering public safety.' He looked directly at Norton. 'That'll do for starters.'

'Okay,' conceded Les, nodding his head slowly. He'd played his ace. Now it was up to his right bower. 'But bullshit or not, I've been straight up with you blokes, haven't I? I haven't carried on like a cunt. And I haven't treated you like mugs.'

'True,' agreed Detective Tait.

'So how about a phone call?'

Detective Tait pushed the phone across the table. 'Be my guest.'

Les picked up the receiver and dialed awkwardly with the handcuffs still round his wrists. 'Hello Price. It's Les. Yeah. I'm in

Waverley Police Station. Okay. I'll put Detective Caccano on the line.'
Les handed the receiver to Detective Caccano. 'Just have a talk to Price for a sec, will you?'

Detective Caccano picked up the phone. He didn't speak. He just nodded his head a couple of times. 'All right, Mr Galese,' he said, then hung up.

'What was that all about?' asked Detective Tait.

'I'm not sure,' replied his partner. 'But we'll know soon enough.'

A minute later the phone rang. Detective Caccano picked it up and seemed to stiffen. All Les could hear was a muffled, 'Yes sir. Yes sir. No sir.' Then Caccano handed the phone to Detective Tait. There was another muffled, 'Yes sir. Yes sir. No sir,' before Detective Tait hung up.

Both detectives sat and stared quietly at Les. 'You sure know some people, don't you, Les,' said Detective Caccano.

Les shook his head. 'Not really. But Price does.'

Detective Tait gave a mirthless smile. 'Yeah. Good old Price.'

Les gestured as best he could with the handcuffs on. 'Like I said, he's a very respectable man. Always has been.'

Detective Caccano looked at Norton then undid the handcuffs. 'All right, Les. We'll give you half a break. I'm still charging you. But we'll give you conditional bail. Six days. That means you're back here next Monday at nine-thirty to appear before a magistrate for a hearing.'

'Thanks.'

Detective Caccano tapped the table, then pointed at Les. 'You surrender your passport. You report here every day between nine and three. You don't leave the state. And if we so much as see you walk in an exit door, we'll be all over you like flies on shit.'

'I got the picture,' nodded Les, rubbing his wrists.

'And when you front on Monday,' said Detective Tait, 'we'll oppose bail. The prosecutor will oppose bail. So as well as your lawyer, bring a toothbrush.'

'Fair enough.'

The two detectives then processed Les. He was fingerprinted, they took a photo, and they took his passport. And in no uncertain terms, they warned Les to obey to his bail conditions to the letter. Everything was painstakingly typed up in quadruplicate then they went over everything again with him so there was no mistake. Finally Les was given his bail papers and a report card to bring with him when he came to the station.

'Okay, Les,' said Detective Caccano. 'You're free to go.'

'For the time being,' added Detective Tait. 'And I'll be fair dinkum with you, Les. We're filthy on having to watch you walk out of here. We saw what was left of the cook. There could have been another dozen like him.'

'Fair enough, fellahs,' said Les. He stood up and looked at the two detectives. 'Look, I know how you feel. No one likes being compromised. But this is just one big fuck-up. And that's the truth. I just want a chance to see if I can sort the shitfight out.'

'It's a shitfight all right,' agreed Detective Caccano, emptily. 'See you later Les.'

'Yeah, see you on Monday. And thanks again, anyway.' Les turned and walked out of the detectives' room.

Fuckin hell, thought Les as he came down the steps to the front desk. How heavy was that? Bloody Price. I wonder what strings he pulled to get me out of there? Yeah. Only for six days. But the way it was going, I'm bone lucky to get that. Then another thought struck Les. Now I've got to get through all those miserable pricks out the front. The last thing I want is my head plastered all over the front of the papers and the late night news. Over at the front desk Les recognised a familiar face. It was the old fat sergeant who farted in the front seat of the wagon when Bob McKenna's daughter got pinched for shoplifting. He wasn't a bad bloke if Les remembered right. The sergeant was standing next to two other uniform cops who were listening to some woman in a black dress having a beef about an AVO.

'Hey boss,' Les said to the sergeant. 'How can I get out the front without those bludgers swarming all over me?'

The old sergeant recognised Les and remembered what Les had done the day they drove him back to the station. He showed a bit of sympathy. 'Here,' he said, 'take this newspaper and read it walking out backwards.'

'Read it walking out backwards?'

'Yeah. They'll think you're walking in. Christ! They're only journalists. They're not rocket scientists.'

Les hesitated for a moment then took the *Wentworth Courier*. 'You're right. Thanks, sarge.'

This might just work, thought Les. They still don't know for sure what I look like. Les opened the paper in front of him, and went out through the door backwards. The media scrum was still pushing and shoving each other all over the footpath like wild dogs round a dead sheep. Les went round them cooler than Michael Jackson moonwalking; straight into the front seat of a passing taxi. The taxi driver had thick black hair, a moustache and a cap pulled down around his ears.

'Where to mite?'

'Bondi. Cox Avenue. You know it?'

'Sure I do,' said the driver, setting the meter. 'No worries mite.'

Les settled back as the driver headed for Old South Head Road.

'Hey, what you think about the bomb in Bondi todiy mite?' said the driver.

'What do I think about it?' Hello. Here we go, thought Les. 'I don't think much about it at all. It's ... no good,' he answered.

'You know who done it. Don't you, mite?'

Les shook his head. 'No. Who done it?'

'The blackfellahs.'

'The what?'

'The bloody abos, mite.'

'The abos?'

'Yeah mite. Didn't you see the bloke on the tivee the other night. Sayin' burn all the place down for the Olympic games. This the start mite.'

Les looked at the driver. 'You could have something there. I never thought of that.'

'Hey. I know I'm right, mister. Make it hard for me to get the quid now. Should send them all back where they come from, bastards.'

'Come from? They come from here,' said Les.

The cab driver shook his head. 'No. They come from New Guinea.'

'Fair dinkum?' said Les. 'I've lived here all my life and I never knew that.'

·'It's the truth, mite. Should send them all back. And Pauline Hanson with them.'

Les stared at the cab driver. 'She's not an abo.'

'No. She's a pom. And they's just as bad. Whinge, whinge, whinge. Allatime.'

'You know,' said Les. 'You might just have something there … mite.'

'Hey. I know what I'm talkin' bout, mite. Don't you worry.'

The taxi pulled up outside Chez Norton. Les paid the driver and went inside. Fair dinkum. Somebody tell me I'm dreaming, thought Les, as he shut the door behind him.

There were three messages on the answering machine. All from Eddie. Les listened to the last one and the phone rang again. It was Eddie.

'Les. I've been trying to ring you. I just heard all this weird shit on the news. What the fuck's goin' on?'

'What's going on, Eddie,' answered Les. 'Some cunt put a bomb on the film set. And it went off just as I delivered that cake box.'

'Fuckin hell! I don't believe it,' said Eddie. 'So what happened to you?'

'What happened to me? I got pinched. The cops think I did it. I just managed to get bail.'

'You're on bail? Ohh this is fuckin unbelievable.'

'You can believe it all right, Eddie,' said Les.

Les told Eddie what happened. The police coming round to his house. Not believing what he told them and Price managing to squeeze bail for him.

'And you didn't mention me, Les. You wore the lot.' Eddie was impressed. 'Jesus, you're staunch, mate.'

'Yeah. Well, it's not much good the two of us getting nicked,' said Les. 'You're better off helping me out in the street.'

'Hey. Don't worry, Les. I'll be doing everything I can.'

'Thanks.'

'Look. It's not much good talking over the phone. How about I call round your place tomorrow morning? Early. About eight o'clock. That okay?'

'Yeah. Good as gold.'

'And don't worry. We'll sort this fuckin thing out somehow.'

'I hope so, Eddie. Because I'm in deep fuckin shit.'

Les hung up then thought he'd better ring Price.

'Les. How are you mate?' said Price. 'Eddie rang me earlier. And I heard the news. What a gigantic balls up.'

'Unfortunately the cops don't seem to think so, Price. They've charged me with everything but the Wanda Beach murders. I'd still be up there if it wasn't for you. Thanks for that.'

'That's okay, Les. It's the least I could do.'

Les told Price what happened in the police station and how the cops weren't too happy about letting him go.

'So they've got me on a pretty heavy pinch, Price. After seeing the evidence, I don't suppose you can blame them.'

'Look, don't worry, Les,' said Price. 'We'll do our best to get you bail on Monday. If not we'll appeal or some bloody thing. But we'll work it out. My blokes are the best in the business.'

'Thanks.'

'In the meantime, just hang in. And we'll all get our heads together through the week and see what we can come up with.'

'Okay Price. I'll be in touch.'

'Do that, Les. See you mate.'

'Yeah. See you, Price. Thanks again.'

They'll do their best to get me bail. Great, thought Les. That cop wasn't joking when he said bring a toothbrush on Monday. Les shook his head in frustration. Why me? Why fuckin me? He went to the bathroom, cleaned the fingerprint dye off his hands and tidied himself up, then got a beer from the fridge and sat in the lounge drinking it, but not enjoying it. About half way through his beer, Les decided sitting around doing nothing wasn't going to help. He had six lousy days to come up with something. So he'd better get his finger out and start asking questions. And there was a very plausible person not too far away who might know something. And if he didn't, a bit of friendly persuasion might jog his memory.

Les was just about to walk out the door when the phone rang. It was Warren, sounding very excited.

'Les. It's Warren. Are you there? Pick up.'

Les reached across for the receiver. 'Hello Warren. How's things?'

'How's things?' replied Warren. 'Christ! I saw the news earlier. I've been trying to ring all night. What the fuck's going on? What happened to the movie?'

'What's happened to the movie?' answered Les. 'It got blown up.'

'Did you do it?' said Warren bluntly.

'No. I didn't fuckin do it, Warren. It's a frame-up.'

'Bloody hell!'

50

'Warren, I'll give it to you straight,' said Les. 'I've been charged with murder.'

'Murder?'

'Yeah, I'm out on bail till Monday. Then I go for a hearing and they'll refuse bail when I front.'

'Bloody hell!'

'So it looks like you're going to have the house to yourself for a while.'

'Fuck. This is unbelievable. I'd better come home now,' said Warren.

'No. Stay where you are,' replied Les. 'There's no need to spoil your holiday.'

'It's spoiled already,' answered Warren.

'Yeahh. But there's nothing you can do up here. Just be back by Monday to take me to court.'

'Are you sure?'

'Yeah. Positive.'

'All right. I'll come home Saturday, Sunday morning at the latest. You've got my mobile number. If you need me or whatever, call me.'

'Yeah. I'll do that, Warren.'

'Shit! This is unbelievable.'

'Yeah. Ain't it. I'll see you on the weekend, Woz.'

'All right. See you then, Les.'

Les hung up and looked at the phone. Good old Woz. I could think of worse blokes to be looking after the place while I'm away. But I don't need him around at the moment. If me and Eddie should have to drag someone back here for a few answers, I think Warren might get a little squeamish at the smell of burning flesh and blood all over the walls. Les finished his beer. Now, where was I? Out the door if I remember right.

The Toriyoshi was closed when Les got there. So was the bottle shop. The front of the school was roped off with yellow police tape and there was a wagon parked in the driveway. The film crew had long packed up and gone; all that remained was the blackened shell of the catering van sitting near the fence. Mmmhh, mused Norton. Looks like the Gull's flown off. I reckon there's a chance he might be having a drink. And I know where Ray likes a cool one when he's not in his chicken shack. C.C.'s.

C.C.'s was a bar in Curlewis Street just near the TAB. It used to be a wine bar, but a young ex-bookmaker had just taken over and acquired a beer and spirits licence. It was family roomy, with a coloured sign out the front featuring a blinking cocktail glass, and inside was green carpet and green walls dotted with posters for Boags Stout, Caffreys Irish Ale and Jim Beam. Several fans spun under a latticework ceiling, and through an archway at the rear, bands performed on a small stage. There were plenty of stools and tables along the wall on the left as you walked in, the bar was on the right and the windows near the front door opened onto the street to let the smoke out. Les liked C.C.'s and used to pop in for a drink now and again. if C.C.'s had got its spirit licence before Les settled in at the Toriyoshi, he would have drunk there more often. The band had stopped playing and about thirty casually dressed punters were sitting or standing around having a drink when Les walked in the front door. The Gull was perched on a stool at the bar, dressed in a blue Hawaiian shirt, staring into a bourbon and coke like he wished it was a deep, dark pool of water and he could have jumped in with a Mack gearbox wired to his neck.

Les walked over and stood on Ray's right. 'Nnnyyhhh. So what's happening the Gull? I'm glad you're face isn't looking like a six-month-old passionfruit, anyway.'

Ray looked up and gave Norton a heavy double-blink from behind his steel framed glasses. 'Les? What are you? I mean ...'

'You mean, what am I doing here, Ray?' replied Les. 'I got bail. That's what I'm doing here, Ray.'

'You did? I mean. I heard on the news ... Hey, what do I know about the news? That's good, Les.'

'Yes. It is. But you don't look too good, Ray me old. What's the matter?'

'What's the matter?' The Gull took a sip of bourbon then shook his head and went back to staring into his glass. 'The police don't know if somebody's going to plant another bomb on the set so they've stopped the shoot. Nearly everyone on the set's getting trauma counselling after seeing what was left of the cook. The rest got hit by flying debris. Max has pulled the pin. Simone's pulled the pin. The whole gig's over, man. Finished.'

'Finished?' said Les.

'Yeah. It couldn't sink any further if they buried it at sea. And I'm sunk with it.'

'Back to Gullsville, Ray.'

Ray nodded. 'Yeah. Not a pot to piss in. Or a window to throw it out.'

'Or a feather to fly with,' suggested Les.

'Right on, baby.'

Ray had another mouthful of bourbon. Les caught the eye of a blonde barmaid in a white top and ordered a bourbon and unleaded for himself.

'Well so much for *Leaving Bondi*, Ray,' said Les, raising his glass. 'It didn't even get on the 380.'

Ray shook his head. 'I don't even want to know about it, man. It's turned out a complete bummer.'

'What about my lazy fifty, Ray? I imagine that left Bondi all right. Never to return.'

'It might be covered by insurance, Les.'

'Yeah.' Les had a sip of bourbon. 'Look, Ray, no matter what you're thinking, I didn't set the bomb off.'

'Hey Les, that didn't even enter my head man,' the Gull assured Norton.

'But the cops think I did. And I'm in deep shit. So I need some information, Ray.'

'Sure Les. How can I help?'

'I need the Tom Thumb on that cook. Albert Knox. What do you know about him?'

'What do I know about him?' Ray blinked helplessly behind his glasses. 'Shit Les. I don't know that much about him at all.'

After being grilled at Waverley Police Station for hours in a pair of handcuffs, Norton wasn't wearing his happy hat. 'Well you must know some fuckin thing, Ray,' he said. 'Christ! You knew his name when I asked about him before. You're both in the fuckin food game.'

'Okay. Okay. I'm with you, man.' Ray thought for a second. 'All right. He got the catering job on the movie off his own bat. I didn't do anything for him there. He … he lives … I mean, he lived in Darlinghurst. He shared a flat there with some guys.'

'Darlinghurst?'

'Yeah. I heard he was into some weird gay scene.'

'Weird gay scene?' said Les.

Ray nodded. 'Yeah. He's bi. I know that. Was. Whatever.'

'So Albert was AC/DC was he?'

'Yeah. Bowled underarm. Look, the bloke you should talk to is Brett Rittosa.'

'Brett Rittosa? Who's he?'

'Brett and Albert used to be partners in a restaurant at Glebe. The word is, Albert ripped Brett off for a lot of money.'

'Did he now? That's interesting. So where do I find this Brett Rittosa rooster?'

'In rooster territory, Les,' smiled Ray. 'He runs a takeaway breakfast kitchen in Bondi Junction. Near the entrance to the railway station at the back of the mall. It's called Brett's Brekky.'

'Brett's Brekky. I might have seen it.'

'Yeah. He does sausage sandwiches. BLTs. Coffee, whatever. For people on their way to work. It's only a small business. He doesn't make a lot of money.'

Les had a swallow of bourbon and looked at the Gull over his glass. 'What time's he open?'

'Six o'clock in the morning. He closes about eleven.'

Les had a think for a moment as the band came back on. 'All right. Thanks Ray,' he said, finishing his drink. 'That's a start. I'll go and see him first thing in the morning.'

'Okay. And Brett's not a bad bloke either. He's done it tough.'

'Ain't we all,' Les looked directly at the Gull for a moment. 'Hey Ray. All jokes aside, who do you think did it? You got any ideas?'

Ray shook his head despondently. 'Les, I haven't got a clue, man. I still can't believe it's happened, to be honest. The karma on that set was beautiful. Just perfect. Now this.' Ray shook his head again. 'All I can say is, that Knox cat must've been toting some heavy vibes, man.'

'Right,' nodded Les. 'That definitely makes sense, Ray. Oh, have you heard from Max King and the rest of them?'

'No. Max had split from the set when I went round. The others haven't called me yet. I can't even find my business partner.'

'Okay. Well, I'll see you, Ray.'

'Yeah. See you, Les.' Ray stared back into his bourbon as Les stepped round the other drinkers in C.C.'s and out the door.

Back home, Les had a shower then changed into a clean white T-shirt and a pair of shorts. He got a beer from the fridge and took it into the lounge room to sit and have a quiet think. Unexpectedly, he felt dog tired. Instead of his mind racing at a thousand miles an hour, it was almost blank. All Les could think was, one minute you're up there laughing your head off and life's a bowl of cherries, next thing it's the absolute bloody pits. He ran his eyes around the house at all the creature comforts he enjoyed — along with Warren — and how you take things for granted. Now in six short days he could lose the lot. Along with his freedom for probably the rest of his life. And this time he hadn't done anything. Les looked at the bar and all the bottles of choice booze sitting there. An idea would be to get pissed out of his brain and blot everything out. Then climb up in the roof, get Warren's pot and stone himself into the netherworld with the stereo blasting. Instead, Les finished his beer and went to bed. He intended being up nice and early in the morning and hitting the ground running. He slipped a Steely Dan CD into the stereo in his bedroom, lay back and closed his eyes. By the time 'Aja' had cut out, Norton was in a deep, dark sleep.

Les was out of bed around six. Outside it was cold and the previous day's breeze had turned to a biting sou'westerly. He made some tea and sipped it over a toasted sandwich while he listened to the news. The bombing was the lead story and Norton's name was mentioned; Les finished his sandwich and couldn't wait to read about it in the papers. He got into a pair of jeans, black desert boots and a black leather jacket and drove up to Bondi Junction. The traffic was light and he had no trouble finding a parking spot in Oxford Street around from Newland. He locked the car and walked across to the mall.

Brett's Brekky was a white kiosk with a shutter front and matching awning, in the middle of the walkway near the Grafton Street entrance to the railway station. Les stood back amongst the people hurrying for the trains and checked out the owner and his female assistant. He was lean, with a grainy face and brown hair receding in the front, and had that look of tired humour in his eyes people get after working all their life to get nowhere before finally accepting what life has thrown up.

He was wearing white jeans and a white T-shirt with a blue bib and brace and a butcher's apron tied in the front. His dark-haired helper was wearing the same. The owner was cooking food on a small stove next to a coffee urn while the girl was buttering toast; there was one customer. A metal step led up to the back door. Les walked over and knocked lightly on the side of the kiosk.

'Are you Brett Rittosa?' he asked.

'Yeah, that's me,' replied the proprietor, glancing up from a frypan full of sausages. 'I suppose you're from the taxation department?'

'No,' answered Les. 'Quite the opposite. In fact I'd like to give you some money.'

'What?' Brett looked up again. 'Yeah that'd be right.'

'Do these look all right?' Les flashed a roll of hundred-dollar bills.

Brett looked at them and his thin mouth filled with saliva. 'They sure do, mate.'

'How about making me a flat white with two sugars. And I'll see you on one of those seats in the mall.'

'I'll be there in two minutes.'

Les walked up to the mall, found a wire seat, then sat down and made himself comfortable. Brett was along shortly with a carton of coffee and a can of Coke. He handed Les his coffee and sat down next to him. Les offered his hand.

'I'm Les.'

Brett nodded and shook Norton's hand. 'Les Norton. I've seen you around.'

'I live in Bondi. And I work up the Cross.'

'The Kelly Club. Price Galese.'

'That's me.'

Brett took a mouthful of Coke and smiled. 'So Les. I imagine this is about the unfortunate demise of Albert Knox.'

'You're right on the ball, Brett,' Les smiled back, then tucked a hundred-dollar bill into the top of Brett's apron. 'And you can have that for starters.'

'Thanks. That'll come in handy, I can tell you.'

Les removed the top of his carton and took a sip. The coffee was surprisingly good. 'All right Brett, I'll get straight to the point. You were partners in a restaurant with Albert Knox. Tell me all about him. Anything.'

Brett looked directly at Les. 'He was a cunt. How's that for starters?'

'Fair enough,' said Les.

'He ripped people off. Dope dealers. Women. Old ladies. Me. Anybody.' Brett shook his head. 'Somehow he managed to keep getting away with it. Up until now.'

'What did he do with all the money?'

'Shoved most of it up his nose.'

'Into the sentimental bloke, eh. That figures. Was he dealing?'

Brett nodded over his can of Coca-Cola. 'Yeah. Not in a big way. Mainly to feed his habit.'

'Did he have many friends?'

'Friends? I'll put it this way, Les, I wouldn't like to be selling sausage sandwiches at his funeral.' Brett swallowed some more Coke. 'He used to hang with some strange people though. Sort of heavy. In a weird kind of way.'

'What? Dope dealers?'

'Probably. But weird.'

'Gays?' said Les. 'I heard Albert sat on both sides of the fence.'

Brett laughed. 'Albert'd be in anything. No. These people were into Wicca.'

'Wicca? What the fuck's that?'

'Witchcraft. Spells, rituals, all that sort of shit.'

'Albert of the occult,' said Les, taking another mouthful of coffee. 'The plot certainly thickens.'

'He had a place in the Blue Mountains. He used to go there and write poetry and stuff. I went up there a couple of times. But he'd never let me stay overnight. Or have a good look round the house. I thought that was a bit odd, seeing I was his business partner.'

'Whereabouts in the Blue Mountains, Brett? Do you know the address?'

Brett shook his head. 'I can't remember. But it was in Medlow Bath and it had a red gate. And a blue letter box. And there was a big red gum out the front, too.'

'When you say had a place in the Blue Mountains, has he still got it?'

'Oh yeah,' replied Brett. 'He'd never let that go. He has people stay there while he's in Sydney. You know, boarders, some of his weird friends, whatever.'

'Uh huh.'

Brett finished his Coca-Cola about the same time Les drained his coffee.

'Well, Les, there's not much more I can tell you,' said Brett. 'And I'd better get back to the kiosk. Michalina only knows about five words of English.'

'Okay,' said Les, getting to his feet. 'You've been a big help though. Here.' Les stuck another two hundred dollars in Brett's apron.

'Shit! Thanks for that, Les.' Brett offered his hand again. 'If there's anything else I can do. You know where to find me.'

'Okay. Thanks Brett.'

'Call in anyway. I'll shout you a coffee.'

'I might do that, Brett. It's bloody good coffee.' Les turned to walk away. 'Hey Brett. One more thing?'

'Sure.'

'Where was Albert from? Sydney?'

Brett shook his head. 'Adelaide.'

Les watched Brett walk back to the kiosk, then dropped his empty coffee carton in a garbage bin. He bought the morning paper and headed for Bondi.

Back home, Les had a glass of water and flicked through the paper. The first three pages were headlined BOMB OUTRAGE AT SCHOOL. KILLING ON FILM SET. TEN PEOPLE INJURED. Here we go, thought Les. But it could have been worse.

The photo of him being driven into Waverley Police Station gave nothing away. He'd managed to get his jacket up over his head, so they could have had Elvis in the car for all anybody would have known. And apart from Knox's assistant, the injuries weren't too bad and some of the film crew were probably hitting the workers' compensation trail, seeing that the film shoot was finished. Plus they had him down as Les Norton, a waiter from Kings Cross. That old sergeant was right, mused Les, going over it again before flicking to the sports pages. You definitely don't have to be a brain surgeon to get a job on a newspaper. Les was reading about a disappearing prima donna rugby league player when the doorbell rang. It was Eddie.

'Shit Les. What can I say, mate?' Eddie waved his newspaper around as Les closed the front door and they walked down to the kitchen.

'We've managed to make the headlines again, Eddie,' said Les. 'It could be worse, though. At least I'm Les, the inoffensive waiter. Not Les, the thug gangster doorman.'

'Yeah. It's still a fuckin heavy pinch they've got you on mate.'

'Yeah,' agreed Les. 'It sure is. And if I said I wasn't worried, I'd be a liar. And a dill.'

Les told Eddie everything that happened. From the bomb going off. Cleaning out the house. To the police coming round and charging him. Then what Ray Tracy had told him and his meeting with Brett Rittosa earlier.

'So it looks like our mate the cook was a shifty no-good prick,' said Les. 'You almost had to queue up to hate him.'

Eddie shook his head. 'I wish we'd never gone near that silly fuckin film set.'

'You and me both, mate,' agreed Les. 'What about you, Eddie? Have you found out anything?'

'No. I didn't get back home till late last night. And I only got up a while ago. But George'll be ringing you soon. Evidently he's on to something.'

At that instant the phone rang in the lounge room.

'This'll be him now,' said Eddie.

It was Billy Dunne. 'Les, how are you mate? You okay?'

'As good as I can be under the circumstances, thanks Billy,' answered Les.

'Eddie told me what's happened. Fuckin hell! I can't believe this.'

'It's true, Billy. Eddie's here now. Have you got this morning's paper?'

'Yeah. At least you can't see your head. But everybody around the traps is going to know who it is.'

'Yeah,' admitted Les. 'Great, ain't it.'

'I've spoken to Price and we're all on the case. I've got Big Danny to fill in for you at work.'

'Thanks, Billy.'

'And I reckon you should be sweet on Monday.'

Despite his workmate's effort, Les didn't detect a great deal of confidence in Billy's voice. 'Yeah. We'll see what happens, mate.'

'Look, I'll leave you with Eddie. And I'll call round this afternoon. You be home?'

'Probably.'

'Okay. Well, I'll see you then. Take care, mate.'

'Yeah. Thanks Billy.' Les hung up and walked back into the kitchen. 'That was Billy. He's going to call over this afternoon.'

Eddie nodded. 'I rang him earlier.'

Les was going to say something when the phone rang again. 'This might be George.' It was.

'Hello Les. How are you goin', mate?'

'I'm hanging in, George,' replied Les. 'Hangin' in.'

'Good on you son.' Les and George might have constantly bagged and poked shit at each other at work, but when it came down to business, that was all forgotten. 'Price told me what's going on Les. I can't believe your bad luck.'

'I suppose you saw the papers this morning George?' said Les.

'Yeah, the pricks. At least they didn't get a decent photo of you. And I always said you'd make a good waiter.'

'Thanks George,' laughed Les.

'Okay. I'll tell you what's going on. Evidently they love a bit of scandal and rumour, the show biz mob, and while he was hanging around that movie set, Kevin picked up a bit of gossip.'

'Go on, George.'

'That cook who got blown up. His name's Albert Knox. He was a small-time coke dealer.'

'I already knew that.'

'He'd also been in a bit of strife with the law,' said George.

'Dealing dope?'

'No. You remember about a year ago, a bloke got murdered in the Blue Mountains and they found his body on a walking trail. He was a barrister, had a wife and kids. And it turned out he was a mad raving poof on the side.'

'Vaguely, George.'

'Well, they never found the murderer. But Knox had tried to blackmail the barrister. He was going to out him and a couple of his mates. The cops charged Knox with extortion, but between the bloke getting himself murdered and whatever, Knox beat it.'

'Yeah. According to a bloke I've been talking to, Knox was a bit of a shifty,' said Les. 'Something like that'd be right up his alley.'

'There was also this old bird in the Blue Mountains,' continued

George. 'Kicked the bucket and left all this money and real estate in a disputed will. Knox was half pie pally with the old girl and forged her name on a letter giving him part of the estate. He got sprung. But somehow or other he beat that, too. So besides being one step in front of the gendarmes, Knox had quite a few people offside.'

'Christ! You'd think those two coppers'd know all this,' said Les.

'They probably do,' replied George. 'But unfortunately they've got your head on the block, Les.'

'Yeah. Terrific.'

'Anyway, Kevin's calling over this afternoon. He might've found out something else. And me and Price have got our ears to the ground.'

'That's good. Well, thanks for your help, George. I'll keep in touch.'

'No worries. Look after yourself, big fellah.'

Les hung up and walked back into the kitchen. 'George's nephew found out a couple of interesting things.' Les told Eddie what George had said over the phone.

'Fuck. It looks like our mate Knox barred nothing when it came to hustling a quid,' said Eddie.

'Yeah,' agreed Les. 'He'd steal the filling off a shit sandwich and leave you with the dry bread.'

Les and Eddie sat silently staring into space for a while before Eddie spoke.

'Well, what do you think, Les?' he asked.

'What do I think?' shrugged Les. 'I'm fucked if I know, Eddie. Anybody could have murdered that prick Knox. Coke dealers he'd ripped off. People he'd tried to blackmail. That old girl's relatives in case he's still disputing the will. His ex-partner in the restaurant. Witchs, warlocks, whatever.'

'Not counting punters who didn't like his nouveau cuisine,' said Eddie.

'Yeah. I forgot about them too,' said Les. 'Christ! It's a cast of thousands.'

'So what are we going to do?'

'What are we going to do?' Les looked at Eddie for a moment. 'I know what I'm going to do. I'm going to take a trip to the the Blue Mountains.'

'The Blue Mountains? What the fuck do you want to go there for?'

'I'm going to see if I can find Knox's house. There's definitely a Blue Mountains connection to this, Eddie. And if I can get into his house. I reckon I might find a clue.'

'Clue?' said Eddie. 'Turn it up Les. Who do you think you are? Cliff Hardy?'

'Well, I may as well be sniffing around up there, Eddie, as walking around Bondi with every cunt pointing at me behind my back saying, look, there's the bloke that set the bomb off on the film set.'

'Yeah. I suppose you've got a point,' agreed Eddie.

'I know I've got nothing to lose,' said Les. 'I can punch the bundy at Waverley Police Station on the way up. Stay the night. And be back in time to bundy on again Thursday. And you can keep sniffing around down here.'

'Fair enough,' agreed Eddie. 'When are you going to leave?'

Les looked at his watch. 'By the time I root around here and pack my swag, a couple of hours. I'll get there in time for a late lunch.'

'You know where you're gonna stay?'

'Haven't the foggiest,' shrugged Les. 'First decent hotel I come to in Medlow Bath, I suppose.'

Eddie gave Les a look of grudging approval and got to his feet. 'All right. Well, I'll get cracking and see what I can dig up. And I'll see you when you get back. If you need me, give me a call. I'll be straight up.'

'Thanks mate. I will.'

Les saw Eddie to the door, waved him off then walked back out the kitchen. He made a cup of coffee and as he was sipping it thought of something the Gull had told him earlier. Les looked at his watch again. Yeah. She'd be at work now for sure. He took his coffee into the lounge room and picked up the phone.

'Geraldine Hardacre, accountant.'

'Hello Gerry. It's Les Norton.'

'Les?' replied his accountant. 'How are you?'

'Oh. Okay Gerry, I suppose.'

'That's not you in this morning's paper is it Les? Surely?'

'Yeah. That's me all right,' admitted Les.

'Good lord! What's the world coming to?'

'Well I can tell you now, Gerry, it's not what it seems.'

'I didn't think so. I know you're a pretty willing lot at the Kelly Club, but I didn't think you went around blowing up movie sets.'

'We don't. Especially after one of us has shoved fifty grand into the bloody thing.'

'Yes. That could be looking a bit shaky at this stage. I'm sorry to say.'

'Great,' said Les. 'Anyway, that's the least of my worries at the moment, Gerry. I'm wondering if you could do me a favour?'

'I'll certainly do what I can, Les.'

'Could you ring Ivor and find out if anybody's taken any … any special sort of an insurance policy out on that movie?'

'I can do that for you, Les. He's busy this morning. But if you ring me back late this afternoon he should know something. Say about four-thirty.'

'Thanks, Gerry. I'll ring you then.'

'Bye Les.'

Les hung up, sipped his coffee and looked at the phone, shaking his head. That's something else we didn't think of. An insurance scam. Add that to the list of suspects. Christ! Forget Cliff Hardy. This is more like Agatha fuckin Christie. Les took his coffee back out to the kitchen and glanced at his photo on the front page of the paper again. Then another thought struck him, giving the big red-headed Queenslander even less joy. Somewhere out there, someone who couldn't believe their luck was having a good laugh at his expense. They didn't even need any luck. All they had to do was hang in and by Monday they were home and hosed. Les threw the paper in the garbage, finished his coffee and started packing for a quick trip to the Blue Mountains. I wonder what the weather's going to be like up there, he mused. Les had a look out the front window. The sou'wester had picked up and it was starting to rain. Cold and wet. Better toss in my GAP anorak. An hour later Les had packed everything he thought he'd need from warm socks to a pair of binoculars and a torch. He locked the house, wished himself luck and drove up to Waverley Police Station.

Signing his report card was pretty much a formality. There were no journalists or TV cameras around and Les was more than likely just one of a host of villains forced to report when told. A grizzled desk sergeant processed him and as soon as he got that out of the way, Les headed for Parramatta Road and the M4, stopping briefly at Camperdown to fill up with petrol.

The rain increased and so did the traffic along Parramatta Road till eventually Les found the entrance to the M4 at Strathfield. He still wasn't too sure where he was going. According to his roadmap, get to the other side of Penrith and climb west. A set of tollgates appeared out of the gloom. Les couldn't see how much it was, so he impatiently flung whatever change he had in the basket and quickly wound the window up. The light turned green and he continued on his way to the steady beat of the windscreen wipers and the rain hitting the roof. The traffic was slow and heavy. Trucks and prime movers hissed by leaving plumes of road water in their wake and every vehicle had its headlights on. Another truck went past spraying water everywhere as the FM station quietly playing in Norton's Berlina pumped out another pop record. Les caught his eye in the rear-vision mirror and shook his head. You know what I am, he told himself. An idiot. A complete bloody idiot. I'm driving somewhere in the pissing rain, to find a house with a red fence and a blue letter box. With a fuckin gum tree out the front. Then if by some remote chance I happen to find it, what do I do? Knock on the door and say hello, do you mind if I take a stroll around, I'm looking for some evidence in a murder. Unbelievable. The traffic ground on and the radio played another pop song. Ahh fuck it, thought Les, as he crossed the Nepean River. I may as well have some ad-free music on my road to nowhere. He slipped a tape into the cassette and Dutch Tilders and The Blues Club started hoofing into 'Bad Books'. By the time this cut into 'Long Way From Brooklyn — Down to the Bone', Les had gone under Knapsack Bridge and was approaching Blaxland.

At Faulconbridge the fog got thicker and if Les wasn't driving slow enough already, the council was doing up the road. All he could make out in the way of scenery was trees, a few churches and old houses with cars for sale parked out the front. At Hazelbrook Les got stuck behind a tour bus, then when he reached Lawson the fog set in like a monstrous grey blanket over everything and he got stuck behind a petrol tanker. Les shook his head in disgust. What did George say up the club one night? If brains were ink, I wouldn't have enough to write a full stop. He's not wrong. You would have got up here faster in a horse and buggy a hundred years ago. The road and the traffic ground on. 'Paying Cost To The Boss' — B.B. King and The Rolling Stones were picking and honking out the speakers as Les went past the turn off to Katoomba. Shouldn't be too far now, he mused. B.B. King faded into Mollie O'Brien wailing 'Denver to Dallas' when Les made out a sign on the left. Medlow Bath. Hello. I'm here. Thank Christ for that. Les looked for some shops and houses. I am? There was nothing but trees and a railway line on the right. What the fuck? A railway station came into view and suddenly what looked like a palace appeared out of the gloom on the left. It was all maroon and gold with gold arches out front, set under a huge grey dome next to a bigger building resembling a white castle. A hedge and an old mossy sandstone fence ran along the front with a black and gold sign above the hedge saying, MEDLOW ASTORIA — WELCOME. Hey I've heard of this joint, thought Les. Price said he used to come up here for dirty weekends before he got married. It's supposed to be el schmicko. Why don't I prop here? I can't get any closer to Medlow Bath than this. Les swung the Berlina into the driveway and pulled up outside the main entrance.

Norton got out of the car, stretched his legs then took the red carpeted steps to the front doors and into the warmth of the foyer. Hey, this is all right, he thought, pausing to take a look around. Everywhere was beautifully restored art-deco, featuring maroon, gold and white. Arches and small columns stood under a domed ceiling hung with sparkling chandeliers, while thick scatter rugs covered a polished oak floor spread with velvet lounges and plump matching cushions. Alongside the lounges were ornate wooden tables and lamps made to resemble ancient Egyptian figurines. There was an open fireplace under a white archway on the left and in front of another white archway on the opposite side of the room two polished oak tables formed the front desk. An attractive, dark-haired woman in a crisp char-grey uniform and matching tie smiled up from the desk on the left.

'Yes sir. May I help you?'

'I'd like a room for the night, please,' replied Les. 'A single.'

'Certainly sir.' The woman consulted a register. 'I can let you have a room in the Concordia Wing at three hundred dollars a night. Or, if you wish to take advantage of our mid-week special, you can have two nights for four hundred dollars.'

Les thought for a moment. 'Yeah okay. I'll take the two nights.'

Even though he intended staying only one night, it was now mid afternoon and in the thick fog outside he'd be flat out finding a herd

71

of elephants with bells round their necks let alone a house. So he'd have to leave his searching till the morning, when hopefully the fog would lift. For the sake of an extra hundred he could take his time checking out and relax a little before he went back to Sydney. The woman took Norton's credit card number, did the details and gave him a key to room 123. Les said he'd be right with his bag, went out and parked the car near the sandstone fence then came back inside, turned right at the foyer and went looking for his room.

The Medlow was huge and plush and was probably *the* place years ago. Long carpeted corridors ran to the left and right with signs saying Del Monte Room, Savoy Lounge, Gaming Room, Caledonia Wing, etc. Les walked past the old gaming room on his right, that was now a conference room, and the breakfast room on the left where a scattering of punters were taking tea and sandwiches in front of huge windows overlooking the Megalong Valley. Further on, a double-glass door opened into an extensive, art-deco lounge room called The Kurrajong Room. Logs crackled in a big open fireplace on the left and more plush furniture, lamps and ornate tables sat on a polished wood floor spread with thick rugs. On the right was a cigar room, another glass door, then a chrome-railed bar next to a pool table tucked into the corner. Delicate chandeliers hung from the ceiling, paintings and mirrors looked down from the walls and running past a balcony on the left, massive windows with brown drapes offered stunning views of the Megalong Valley. From a set of speakers hidden somewhere in the ceiling, a reedy version of 'Pennies From Heaven' played softly in the background. Les stopped and looked around with a half-smile on his face. It was like stepping back in time. Any

72

moment he expected either Agatha Christie and Hercule Poirot to stroll in ready to take tea and cucumber sandwiches, or Fred Astaire and Ginger Rogers to come dancing down the staircase in the corner on the left singing 'You And The Song And The Moonlight'. The doorway to the Concordia Wing was near the staircase. Les picked up his bags and headed towards it.

A corridor with scalloped light fittings along the cornice led to a short set of stairs on the right where two chrome statuettes of women holding outstretched beach balls were set in a wall alongside some glass bricks. Les took the stairs to his room. For three hundred dollars a night, or whatever he was paying, Les felt his room could have been a little bigger. It was no larger than the spare room at Chez Norton. But it was cosy enough, with a comfortable double bed, a small TV, a bathroom and a table with two leopard-skin seats. A sash cord window offered a sweeping view of the Megalong Valley; only the fog and rain cut the view to a path below and the surrounding trees and ferns. Les tossed his bag on the bed and sat down facing the window. Well, here I am, he thought. Now what? The rain pattered down on the roof and the breeze coming from the valley flicked at the rainwater in the trees. I suppose I'd better drive into Katoomba, buy a map and see if I can figure out where they've hidden the rest of Medlow Bath over a cup of coffee or something. Les unpacked his travel bag, freshened up a bit then headed back the way he came.

On his way out through the Kurrajong Room, Les stopped beneath a painting near the main door, titled *Nile in Flood*. It showed the pyramids and the sphinx and Les was thinking how nice it looked, when a girl about twenty-five came bouncing down the stairs in the far corner carrying a clipboard. She was wearing a light blue pleated dress cut above the knee, long white socks and dainty white shoes. A blue crepe de chine top fitted over her dress and a brimless white sequinned hat sat tight on her head like a bathing cap. She had a pretty pixie face, blue eyes and two thin bangs of blonde hair flicked across her cheekbones from beneath her hat. Les gave the girl a double blink as she stepped daintily across the room. Did I say something about Agatha Christie? It's Vera Claythorne taking a brief holiday after the coroner's inquest. As the girl approached the main door she dropped a fountain pen from her clipboard. Les bent down and picked it up.

'Excuse me, miss,' he called out. 'You dropped something.' The girl either didn't hear Les or she ignored him. 'Okay,' said Les. 'Bleed to death.'

The girl turned around from the door. 'What was that?' she said.

Les held up the fountain pen. 'You dropped this. I said, okay, if you don't want it, I'll have it.'

'Oh, I'm ever so sorry,' apologised the girl. 'I didn't hear you.'

'That's quite all right,' replied Les, handing her the fountain pen.

'Thank you very much,' she said. 'That's very gentlemanly of you.'

Les gave a slight bow. 'My pleasure, madam. Hugo would have done the same for Vera Claythorne.'

The girl stared at Les and her cheeks coloured slightly. 'Oh my goodness,' she said, then opened the door and bounced off down the corridor like the white rabbit in *Alice in Wonderland*.

Have a nice day, Vera, Les chuckled to himself. Now, what was I doing before I was so rudely interrupted?

Les got in the car and headed through the drizzling rain and fog towards Katoomba. After the warmth of the hotel it seemed colder than it already was, making things even more miserable. Before long he reached the lights at the turn-off and took a right across the bridge over the railway line.

The road curved left past some shops on the right and a few more on the left next to a tunnel beneath the railway station, then it went right again into the main drag. From what Les could make out through the fog and rain, Katoomba was trying to be the art-deco capital of Australia. Most of the shops, especially the restaurants, had that 1930s black and chrome look about them. The main street sloped down on the left, past restaurants, banks, clothes shops, a couple of churches and whatever before levelling off at a pedestrian crossing on an intersection. Les did a U-turn and came up the other side. It was much the same. More shops and art-deco restaurants, a medical centre, butcher, newsagent, the town centre arcade, an antique furniture centre then the grounds of another old hotel at the top, the Kensington. The hotel was at the back but a set of steps off the street led up to two double-glass doors and a bar. A sign on one of the doors said, Piano Man — Thursday Night. Back at the top of the hill, Les noticed a hotel across the railway line called the Gordon. He did another U-turn and found a parking spot, outside a cluster of restaurants opposite the Kensington, then got out of the car and had a look around for a moment. With his breath turning into small clouds of steam in the cold mountain air, Les strolled down to the newsagency and got a map and the local paper. That didn't take long and when he returned Les decided to try Cafe Zappa.

Like the others it was either restored — or just left the way it was to save spending any money — art-deco. The floor was bare boards with booths on either side and a counter at the rear where they did the cooking. Les went for a bowl of pumpkin soup and a flat white; the woman said she'd bring it to him. Even though it was cold and miserable outside, Les chose a footpath table left of the front door, opposite a table full of hippy-gothics on the right.

Along with the men at the table there were three women with prams and babies and everyone had this arty, 'Okay, so I might be on the dole or getting a pension and I dress like a rag picker and I'm half broke. But I'm still really cool, you know' look about them while they sipped their coffees and smoked skinny roll your owns from a communal packet of Champion Ruby. Like most of the other punters shuffling past in the rain, carrying string bags or backpacks, the dress code at the table opposite was thick beanies, army pants, loose knitted jumpers and leg warmers. Purple Doc Martens, rainbow-coloured stockings and crushed velvet dresses was another look, along with denim dresses, greasy jeans and ugh boots. And of course nose rings, ear rings, ear studs and cheap Indian jewellery. Some bloke with a cane at a table outside the restaurant next door was wearing a floppy velvet hat, a white jacket and a long scarf. He looked like Dr Who minus the Tardis. Norton's pumpkin soup and coffee arrived. He left the locals to it and sipped and supped while he studied his map.

Medlow Bath wasn't all that big. Just a cluster of cul-de-sacs on the other side of the railway line, not far from a water catchment area, with one long road leading out to the airfield. Depending on the fog and rain, Les felt he was in with a chance. He still didn't know what he was looking for and if he did find the house with the red fence, he was just going to hope no one was home and break in. He'd brought a jemmy with him for that purpose. He still didn't have much to go on. But he didn't have much to lose. And the alternative was the remand yard at Long Bay. Les put the map aside and flicked through the paper while he finished his soup and coffee. The soup was a bit bland and could have done with some chilli and garlic. The coffee was okay. By the time he'd finished, the street was emptying and it was getting dark. Les paid his bill and left for the hotel.

Driving back to The Medlow, Les found himself developing a kind of 'who gives a stuff' attitude. He had nothing much to go on. And he was more than likely wasting his time. So why not to have as much fun as he could before the chop, and try not take it too seriously. If something turned up, great. If it didn't, well, at least he'd had a go. Les was also feeling, although he'd been off his food a bit, the pumpkin soup and the mountain air had put the edge back on his appetite. Dinner at the hotel would definitely be in order. After a few gin and tonics in the Kurrajong Room of course. I wonder should one wear one's tuxedo to dinner? He mused. And take one's ivory cigarette holder? One should certainly give it some thought. He found the same parking spot by the sandstone fence and locked the car.

There weren't many people around as Les walked to his room; a few Japanese tourists, one or two couples and the smiling staff going past. Les took his time having a shower and a shave, then changed into a blue shirt with little white roulette wheels on it Price had given him, jeans, black desert boots and his leather jacket over the top.

Then dabbed a drop or two of Eau Sauvage on his face. He also took a book with him to read while he had a few drinks. It was a book he'd bought off Billy Dunne for two dollars. Billy's wife had bought it for three dollars in an op-shop. It was called *The Portable Beat Reader* and had a photo of William Burroughs and Jack Kerouac on the cover. The main reason she bought it was because the photo of Jack Kerouac on the cover looked a lot like Billy. Billy however couldn't get into the book. Especially the poetry. Les didn't mind the book. There was a bit of Charles Bukowski, and Burroughs' views on drug addiction made interesting reading. Like Billy, however, Les too thought the poetry was VFO. Very fuckin ordinary.

Apart from a young barman in black, there was no one in the Kurrajong room. Les ordered a gin and tonic, chose a plush lounge facing the side door and took in the art-deco ambience while he sipped his gin and tonic and read his book. He was looking at a poem that consisted of, 'Scissor sceptre cutting prow' repeated four times, followed by, 'Ahh, swark, swark,' and thinking, did some wally actually get paid to write this? when who should come bouncing down the stairs, wearing the same clothes, but the girl he saw earlier. Vera Claythorne. She too was carrying a book. She couldn't have missed Norton sitting there, but she didn't catch his eye and Les didn't make a point of catching hers. She went to the bar, got a drink, then sat down on a lounge a little to Norton's left. She opened her book and started to read. Les continued to read his and sip his gin and tonic. He was reading a list of instructions some hippy had written during the Vietnam War on how to beat the draft. Three suggestions were develop a bleeding stigmata, contract tertiary syphilis, when the doctor tells you to spread your cheeks, have a firecracker stuffed in your date. At the word firecracker, Les wasn't sure whether to laugh or cry. He looked up at the same time Vera did. This time he caught her eye.

'Hello,' he said pleasantly. 'What are you reading?'

'Agatha Christie,' replied the girl. '*The Mysterious Affair At Styles.*'

'I should have guessed,' replied Les.

'Oh? What makes you say that?'

'Nothing,' said Les. 'Just a guess.'

The girl looked at Les for a moment. 'Do you mind if I join you?' she said. 'There's something I'd like to ask you.'

'Certainly not,' answered Les, shuffling along the lounge. 'Be my guest.'

The girl came over and sat down on Norton's left. She put her drink on the table in front of them, then placed the book she was reading on her lap. In the process, Les managed to sneak a glimpse of lacy white knickers under the short blue dress.

'You said something to me earlier when I dropped my pen,' said the girl. 'Hugo would have done the same for Vera Claythorne. What did you mean by that?'

'Nothing,' smiled Les. 'It was just a joke. I hope I never offended you?'

'No. Not at all,' replied the girl. 'On the contrary.'

'Really?' purred Les. 'Why's that?'

'That's Agatha Christie. They're two characters in *And Then There Were None.*'

'That's right,' said Les.

'Do you read Agatha Christie?' asked the girl.

'Of course,' said Les. 'Not as much as I'd like to. But I read what I can.' Les hated Agatha Christie. If he could have, Les would have organised a book burning and incinerated every Agatha Christie book he could find, along with the author. When he was at high school, a sadistic female English teacher made the class read three Agatha Christie novels. To Les, it was about as interesting as studying for a degree in law. But being young it got brainwashed into his head and to this day he still remembered most of the corny names and places.

'I study Agatha Christie,' said the girl, patting her book. 'I absolutely adore her.'

'I don't blame you,' enthused Les. 'Agatha Christie's one of the great women writers of our time.'

'Thank you,' smiled the girl. 'I also write poetry.'

'Really?' Les nodded to his book. 'I love poetry.'

'And I'm also working on a novel at the moment.'

Les looked surprised. 'Well I'll be,' he said. 'This is just the most amazing coincidence.'

'Why? What makes you say that?'

'I happen to be a publisher.'

'A publisher,' gushed the girl. 'No.'

'Yes.' Les offered his hand. 'Allow me to introduce myself. Forrest McNamara. Roulette Publishing, Sydney.'

'Oh dear me,' flustered the girl, placing her dainty hand in Norton's huge, calloused mitt. 'This is incredible.'

'Yes. Like I said,' smiled Les. 'It's certainly a delightful coincidence. So what's *your* name? If I might ask?'

'Blythe. Blythe Selby.'

Les shook his head. 'That's poetry in itself.' He took another mouthful of gin and tonic and let Blythe get her breath back. You would have thought she'd just met Elvis.

'And what brings you to the Blue Mountains and the Medlow Astoria, Blythe?' asked Les.

'I was invited to read my poetry at The Blue Mountains Songs Of The Wind Festival,' answered Blythe.

Les slanted his head slightly to one side. 'How simply marvellous.'

Blythe gave Les the low-down on how her father ran a furniture company in Bathurst. It was a family business. She did the books and Daddy was picking up the tab at the Medlow. She'd just had a reading and had to go back home in the morning, but she was returning to the Blue Mountains on the weekend.

'I got a really good response,' said Blythe. 'And on Sunday they're doing a play at the Varuna Writers' Centre. Agatha Christie's *Black Coffee*. I'm playing Lucia Amery.'

'Congratulations, Blythe,' beamed Les. 'You're an actress as well as a writer.'

'I'd rather write,' said Blythe modestly.

Les finished his drink and offered to buy Blythe one. Blythe accepted and had a Brandy Alexander. Les had another gin. A double. They sat sipping politely away and Norton found himself starting to feel pretty good along with Blythe's dress starting to look even shorter.

'Are you here for the festival too, Mr McNamara?' asked Blythe.

Les held up a hand. 'Please. Forrest will do. No, Blythe, I'm up here to interview a writer. I'm trying to get him to join Roulette.' Les smiled over his drink. 'It's called head hunting.'

'Goodness,' said Blythe. 'Who is he?'

Les shook his head solemnly. 'I'm sorry Blythe. But I can't tell you at the moment.'

'I understand,' said Blythe. 'You're still secretly negotiating.'

'Exactly.'

Blythe took a healthy hit on her brandy. 'So which poets and writers do you publish Forrest?' she asked politely.

'Publish?' Les tried to look thoughtful for a moment. 'Adolph Glunshnutter, the German author. Marvin Schwartz, the Jewish author.'

'Marvin Schwartz?' said Blythe. 'I think I've heard of him. What did he write?'

'*Abraham's Ashes.*'

'Oh.'

'Amongst our Australian authors we've got Murray Scrartenvitch, Raymond Tracy, Georgina Brennan, Wilhelmina Dunleavy. To name a few.'

'I can't say I've come across them in Bathurst,' said Blythe.

'You haven't?' Les stroked his chin. 'I must make a note to contact our country rep when I get back to the office and see that he gets some out there.'

'It sounds like you run a pretty tight ship at Roulette Publishing,' said Blythe.

'Oh yeah, we're out there, Blythe,' said Les. 'We've got our finger on the publishing pulse. We're watching the watchers.'

Blythe looked at Les for a moment. 'Would you like to hear some of *my* poetry, Forrest?'

Les nearly swallowed all his drink. 'Why I'd ... only be too delighted, Blythe.'

'It's in my room. I'll get it.'

Les watched as Blythe skipped up the stairs like the white rabbit again, giving him another glimpse of her knickers when she reached the first landing. Christ! This is going to be nice, he thought. Stuck with some bimbo trapped in an Agatha Christie time warp while she reads me her poetry. I think I'd better get another couple of drinks. Still, I wouldn't mind shoving my face into Miss Selby's present participle, if she'd grab me on the personal pronoun. Agatha bloody Christie. God! If only old Miss Crowther could see me now. Les got two fresh drinks and sat back down on the lounge, before Blythe returned with a book binder and made herself comfortable next to him She opened the folder and started up.

'This one's called "The Singularity Of Narcissism",' said Blythe.

'Fired with desire

I peered into the river of

x-rayed souls

trawling for mythical endurance.

My view obscured

by thoughts

too perceptive to be dreamed.'

Les caught his reflection in a mirror near the bar. He'd seen that expression before. In the meatworks when a steer cops it in the back of the head with a stun-gun. He took another slug of gin as Blythe served up her next offering.

'This one's called "Uncompromisation and Patience".

'She wanted solitude

so she clothed herself in delusion

knowing the demons of antiquity

would soon be knocking on the door of redemption.'

Before long Les was looking for the cyanide pill. Blythe's poems would stink in a deep-freeze. They made absolutely no sense, and any that did weren't worth listening to. Eventually, after what seemed like days, she came up for air.

'Well,' she asked shyly. 'What do you think so far, Forrest?'

Les looked at her impassively. 'Wonderful, Blythe,' he said quietly. 'Just wonderful. Did it take you long to write them?'

'Oh, yes. Years.'

'I thought they might have. They're so full of hidden passion. Or dare I say, more, an assertive passion. You've obviously written these poems from your heart, Blythe.' Only because your arse was probably blocked up at the time.

'Yes. Yes I did.' Blythe touched Les on the thigh. 'You obviously know literature Forrest. Would you like to hear some more?'

'I certainly would,' said Les. 'But I've got an idea. How about while you're reading your ... works, I compare them to some of the poets in here.' Les held up *The Portable Beat Reader*. 'I'd like to balance your writing against these people. I feel it would make an interesting comparison.'

'All right,' smiled Blythe. 'That sounds like a great idea. This one's called. "Irreligious Shadows Killed The Rainmaker".'

While Blythe waffled away, Les immersed himself in his book, looking up every now and again to smile and nod his head in approval. Norton's book was still heavy going, but compared to putting up with Blythe, it was like reading *Peanuts*. After a while, Blythe ran out of steam and her voice developed a slight croak. Les applauded softly.

'That was absolutely marvellous, Blythe,' he said serenely. 'The comparisons between you and some of the writers in here, especially Diane DiPrima, are absolutely fascinating.'

'Diane DiPrima,' gushed Blythe. 'Surely you're not saying my poetry's in the same class as hers?'

'In the same class?' Les reached over and touched Blythe on the leg. 'It's almost as if Diane could learn from you.'

'Oh dear. I . . . I don't know what to say.'

Les rivetted his eyes on Blythe. 'Blythe,' he said quietly. 'There's something I have to ask you here.'

'Certainly, Forrest. What is it?'

'Would you be interested in Roulette publishing some of your works?'

'Publish my works?' squealed Blythe. Her knees started to shake and it was all she could do to stop from peeing herself. 'Oh yes. Yes. That's been my dream.'

'Excellent,' said Les. 'Then how about we discuss it further over dinner? Would you care to join me?'

'I'd love to.'

'All right. Let's go have a literary luncheon. Dinner ... whatever. And we can have another drink too.'

'I'll just go to the Ladies first.'

'I'll wait here for you,' smiled Les.

As Blythe skipped off to the Ladies, Les caught his reflection in the mirror again. The girls at work have got a name for blokes like you, he told himself. SAAB. A swine and a bastard. Les gave himself a look of grudging approval. Fair enough. But I prefer dropkick, myself. It's got more of an Australian ambience to it. Blythe returned from the Ladies and Les stood up.

'Are you ready to eat?' he asked.

'Yes,' replied Blythe, and picked up her poetry.

'Excellent.' Les motioned with one hand, 'After you, Blythe.'

Les opened the door for Blythe and they took the corridor past the gaming room and foyer through another door leading into a long, gently sloping corridor lined with huge, velvet chesterfields, lamp tables and indoor plants. Landscapes, hunting scenes and framed etchings hung on one wall, the other was arched windows overlooking the Megalong Valley. The corridor ended at a staircase and access ramp leading into another room full of more art-deco furnishing, mainly cream and white; with chess sets, a library and an enclosed bar at one end. A doorway on the left led along a shorter corridor to the dining room.

Les and Blythe stepped into a dining area with room for over a hundred, one half blocked off where it was divided by an arch across the middle. About twenty diners were seated round polished wooden tables with crisp, white tablecloths. Again it was all very plush; thick red carpet on the floor, cream and gold decor round the walls; chandeliers above and tiny white lamps on the tables. There was a velvet lounge setting as you walked in on the right with a grand piano in the middle and an old fortune-telling machine sat against one wall. Music from the 1920s played softly in the background and several waitresses in black uniforms and black bowties hovered round the guests. Wearing an immaculate grey suit, a maitre d with a shaved head stood behind the bookings desk on the left. On his lapel was a name tag. Angelo. Les caught his eye as he looked up from the guest list and had a fifty palmed into the maitre d's hand quicker than it took him to shampoo and condition his hair.

'Good evening, Angelo,' said Les brightly, producing his door key. 'I believe you have a table for me. Mr McNamara. Room 123. Forrest McNamara.'

The maitre d had seen this many times before. He ran a highlighter across the guest list then bowed and scraped like his head was going to fall off and roll across the dining room. 'Of course, Mr McNamara,' he said, then made a gracious, sweeping gesture with one well-manicured hand. 'This way sir.'

'Easy as one, two, three,' smiled Blythe.

'Something like that,' winked Les.

Angelo led them to a table for four facing away from the other diners. He placed a wine list in front of Norton while a waitress removed the unnecessary cutlery. 'What sort of wine would you like, Blythe?' asked Les.

'I think I'll have the same as what you were drinking before,' she answered. 'A gin and tonic.'

'Make that two gin and tonics please, Angelo.'

'Certainly Mr McNamara. Tanquerray ... ?'

'Bombay Sapphire.'

'Of course. Thank you, Mr McNamara.' The maitre d laid on some more bow and scrape and sent one of the waitresses hurrying out to the bar.

'Have you been here before, Forrest?' asked Blythe.

'Once or twice,' replied Les.

'They certainly look after you.'

'Yes. I guess it just comes with the territory. Publishing.'

'I can't wait to see my poems in print,' fluttered Blythe.

'Me either,' said Les.

Two crisp gin and tonics arrived and Les proposed a toast to Blythe's success. Blythe modestly accepted that. She had another sip of gin and looked at Les.

'Do you mind if I ask you a question, Forrest?' she said.

'Sure,' shrugged Les. 'What is it?'

'How did you get that broken nose?'

'Playing rugby union at university.'

'You went to university? Which one?'

'New South Wales.'

'I never went to uni. I went straight into Dad's business when I left school.'

Les clinked her glass. 'You never know Blythe. It might have been all for the best.'

Les went for the smoked salmon and asparagus mille feuille for starters and veal Illawarra with plums and Madeira and macadamia nut mash potatoes for mains. Blythe sensibly just had mountain stream trout with basil and Spanish onion salsa.

They nattered away about different things. Les said he'd get her phone number and address before he left. She'd send him a copy of her poetry, his company would send her a draft agreement. They'd discuss the advance later.

'I'm going to get an advance?' gasped Blythe.

'Only a small one at this stage, Blythe,' said Les. 'Just a few thousand. It's only your first book, remember.'

'Just a few thousand ...'

Blythe was a completely shot bird. Between the drinks and getting a contract she hardly knew which way was up. However, despite taking advantage of Blythe's gullibility and his outright filthy lies, Les was one hundred per cent certain he wasn't going to throw Blythe up in the air. No one ever got rooted in an Agatha Christie novel. The female characters kept their legs clamped together with super glue; tighter than the women in Barbara Cartland. And you could bet Blythe would play the part to the letter. Still, there was no harm in dropping a quiet sexual innuendo should the occasion arise or making a cultivated lewd comment.

The food arrived and neither could complain. It was tasty, well-presented and served with an absolute abundance of bow and scrape. They had two more gin and tonics and finished with coffee. They didn't bother about sweets.

'Did you enjoy your meal Blythe?' asked Les.

'Yes. It was absolutely lovely. Thank you.'

'What would you like to do now?'

Blythe smiled and gave her shoulders a dainty shrug. 'I don't really care. I have to be up fairly early in the morning, though.'

'Me too,' inclined Les. 'So how about we go back to the Kurrajong Room and have a couple more drinks before we call it a night. There's something I was thinking of doing.'

'Okay.'

Les put the bill on his room, gave the waitress a fifty, the maitre d gave him some more bow and scrape then they walked back to the Kurrajong Room.

There were a few people clustered around the fire and two couples playing pool in the corner. Les and Blythe sat at the same lounge as before and Les went to the bar, returning with two more gin and tonics. Blythe took Les's book, flopped around on the lounge and started reading one of Bob Dylan's songs as a poem. 'A Hard Rain's A-Gonna Fall.' Whether it was all the gin he'd soaked up, Norton wasn't sure, but he had to admit Bob Dylan's songs made great poems. Blythe hit him with two clunking choruses of Philip Lamantia's poetry then closed the book. Les was more than glad because he was starting to develop corns on his ears.

'And to think you compared my work to what's in here, Forrest,' sighed Blythe. 'I can hardly believe it.'

'Yeah. It's hard to believe all right,' agreed Les. He looked at Blythe over his gin and tonic. 'Blythe, did Agatha Christie ever write a book called *Death in the Cigar Room*?'

Blythe thought for a moment. '*Death in the Clouds. Death on the Nile. Death Comes as the End*. There was *The Body in the Library*.'

'Blythe,' suggested Les, 'why don't you get your drink and that and follow me over to the cigar room?'

'All right, Forrest,' smiled Blythe, rising a little unsteadily to her feet.

A row of full length windows curved round the cigar room to the doorway. Inside was a high ceiling and more plush furniture. A tapestried lounge setting filled one corner and a maroon velvet lounge sat against the opposite wall. Paintings of smokers looked down from above the velvet lounge and next to the front windows was a polished teak cabinet. Sitting on top was a cigar menu, an ashtray and several books of matches. Les had noticed a menu at the bar and it made him curious. He picked up the one on the cabinet and showed Blythe. There were several cigars on the menu: Cuban, Dominican or Canary Islands. They ranged from Tobacos Vargas Capitolios at $9.50 to Galeon Robusto at $15.50 or Romeo y Julieta Dedros de Luxe No. 3. at $18.50.

'How would you like to puff on a nice Cuban cigar, Blythe?' said Les. 'Like Mr Justice Wargrave might do, writing a letter to Constance Culmington.'

'Oh yes,' enthused Blythe. 'That sounds exciting.'

'Wait here, my dear.' Les gave a slight bow and walked round to the bar as Blythe sat down on a tapestry lounge chair in the corner.

In a couple of minutes Les was back with two fresh drinks and two Romeo y Julietas, snipped at the end and ready to fire up.

'There you go, Blythe,' he said, handing her a cigar and an ashtray.

'What do I do Forrest?' she asked. 'I don't smoke.'

'Neither do I,' said Les. 'But just put your lips round the end and suck. And don't inhale.'

Les struck a match and held it to the end of Blythe's cigar; after about half a dozen puffs she was away. Les got his going and sat down opposite her as swirls of sweet blue smoke drifted above them. Although Les was a non-smoker, the cigar didn't taste too bad. Pretty much like what it said on the menu. Dark, sweet, with a hint of cocoa beans and coffee and a core of earthiness. Les began feeling quite contented as he puffed away and sipped his gin and tonic. Blythe looked like she was feeling quite contented also. She was all over the lounge chair, her top loosening noticeably, giving Les a nice glimpse of snow white breast behind the crepe de chine. And her skirt had crept up considerably, giving Les an eagle's eye view of Blythe's sweet little map of Tasmania beneath her lace knickers.

'So what do you think, Blythe?' asked Les. 'Something different.'

Blythe tapped some ash into the ashtray. 'Yes. They're nice. Sort of sweet. And rich.'

Les blew a smoke ring across the room. 'What was it Ernest Hemingway said? A woman is a woman, but a good cigar is a smoke.'

'I'm not sure,' said Blythe. 'But I don't think it was Monica Lewinsky,' she giggled.

'No,' replied Les slowly.

'What do you think, Forrest?'

'I don't know, Blythe,' replied Les. 'I haven't finished my cigar yet.'

Blythe managed to blow a smoke ring and Les blew one into it. He held up his cigar and smiled. 'Romeo y Julieta. That's us, Blythe. Hasta la vista and buenas noches.'

'Oh Forrest, I didn't know you spoke Spanish.'

'I don't,' replied Les. 'I speak in tongues. And if my tongue could talk right now, you know what it would say, Blythe?'

'What would it say, Forrest?' purred Blythe.

Les nodded to Blythe's crumpet poking out under her pleated dress. 'That looks good enough to eat.'

'Ooohh Mr McNamara,' fluttered Blythe. She spread her legs a little more. 'Well, like Candye Kane says, all you can eat, and you can eat it all night long.'

Les almost ground the end off his $18.50 Romeo y Julieta. 'Why don't we go back to your room when we finish these, Miss Selby, and discuss your draft agreement some more? Mine's a little untidy at the moment.'

'That sounds like a good idea,' smiled Blythe. 'Let's do that, Mr McNamara.'

They finished their gin and tonics while 'Putting On The Ritz' played out of the speakers in the ceiling next door. Then they stubbed their cigars and Les followed Blythe across the lounge and up the stairs back to her room.

Blythe's room was almost identical to Norton's. Only she had a fake tiger skin lounge and a bigger window with a better view. The bed lamps were still on when she opened the door.

'I'll just go to the loo,' she said, dropping her keys by the bed. 'Help yourself to the mini-bar if you want to.'

'I might have a beer,' said Les. 'Would you like something?'

'A small Scotch and water. No ice thanks.'

'Okey doke.'

Les knocked the top off a bottle of Hahn Premium then opened a bottle of Mount Franklin and made Blythe a Scotch. He placed her drink on the coffee table in front of the lounge, sat down and had a mouthful of beer. Blythe came out of the bathroom, sat down next to him and picked up her glass. Les clinked his bottle against it.

'Well. Here's to success, Blythe,' he winked. 'May all your poems be little ones.'

'Thank you, Forrest.' Blythe took a sip of Scotch and smiled at Les. 'I just can't believe my luck. I gave a reading at the writer's festival and now I'm getting a publishing contract. All in two days. It's almost too good to be true.'

Les sipped his beer and shrugged. 'I think it was meant to be, Blythe. Fate.'

'Yes, Forrest,' breathed Blythe. 'Fate.' They sipped their drinks and Blythe moved her knee against Norton's. 'Do you believe in fate, Forrest?'

For a second a picture of the catering van exploding just as he left the cake box there flashed across Norton's mind. 'Do I ever, Blythe,' he said slowly.

'Would you say I had a fatal attraction Forrest?'

Les put his drink down and placed his hand gently inside Blythe's thigh. 'You've got a fatal something Blythe. I can tell you that.'

Blythe tilted her head up slightly. Les bent forward and kissed her. There was a slight hint of cigar smoke, but her lips were still sweet and soft and her tiny tongue as delicate as the white lace in her knickers. Whether it was the cigar, the mountain air, or just something about Blythe herself, Les wasn't sure. But in seconds he had a rock hard boner ready to blast off. He kissed Blythe a while longer then stood up, took her hand and led her across to the bed.

'Daddy missed out on dessert downstairs, momma,' he smiled. 'And daddy needs something for his sweet tooth.'

'Ooohh Hugo. Do you think Emily Brent would approve?'

'Vera. Poor old Emily never knew what she was missing.'

Blythe kicked off her shoes and lay back on the bed as Les slipped her knickers off and spread her legs. Then without any further ado, he pushed his face into Blythe's beautiful little ted and went for it.

It was absolutely sensational. Les couldn't remember ever coming across one like it. Blonde and soft and trimmed. It was like a little rosebud. Pink and soft. If you put it out in the morning sun the dew would have settled on it. Blythe had also rubbed some sweet smelling oil around herself, making things even more enjoyable. Les chewed and licked and sucked like it was a slice of watermelon at a country picnic. Best of all, Blythe was going almost spare at the end of the bed. She kicked and bucked and wriggled her hips, screamed and moaned and sighed. It was music to Norton's ears. Before he knew it, Mr Wobbly was frothing at the mouth and Les was ready to blow his bolt all over the inside of his jeans.

'Ohhhhh Vicar,' Blythe was in some kind of Agatha Christie dreamland. All she could do was moan.

Les didn't say a word. He just kept eating Blythe's gorgeous pussy, getting hornier by the second. It was that good, he could have eaten it all night then backed up for seconds in the morning. Suddenly Blythe gave a little scream, grabbed Les by the hair, pushed her hips up and emptied out in his face. Les gave it one more lick then came up for air; eyes sparkling, a grin from ear to ear. He fell down alongside Blythe, pulled a hanky from his pocket and wiped his face while he picked a few hairs out of his teeth. Blythe's eyes eventually stopped spinning around, she got most of her breath back and faced Les with her hands against his chest.

'I'm sorry, Forrest,' she panted. 'But I can't have sex with you.'

'Don't worry, Blythe. I was counting on that.' Les unzipped his fly and pulled out Mr Wobbly, gave it a couple of strokes then put his hand on the back of Blythe's head. 'So get your literary laughing gear around this, sister. And tell the vicar why you weren't at church on Sunday.'

Blythe didn't need much persuasion and Les didn't need any prompting. Blythe hardly had her lips around Norton's knob before he started blowing. Blythe gave it about half a dozen decent sucks and Les almost levitated from the bed as he emptied out. Poor Blythe. It looked like she'd walked in front of a flying lemon meringue pie. It was in her mouth, down her throat, in her hair, across her eyebrows, running down her chin. After he stopped howling, Les gave himself one last stroke and some went on the curtains and the top of the TV.

'My goodness, Forrest,' exclaimed Blythe. 'You certainly were excited, weren't you.'

'Excited,' spluttered Les. 'Blythe I haven't been this excited since Australia won the America's Cup.'

Blythe slipped her knickers back on and went to the bathroom. By the time she came back, Les had his fly done up and was lying on the bed with his hands behind his head.

'What time are you having breakfast in the morning?' asked Blythe. 'I have to get up early myself.'

Les took this as a hint. Blythe had got her contract. She'd given her publisher a decent blow job. Now he could pack up the casting couch and hit the road.

'I might have a bit of a sleep in,' replied Les. 'I'm not sure. So why don't you give me your phone number and all that, in case I miss you.'

'Fantastic.'

Blythe wrote down her phone number and address. Plus where she worked. Les gave her Warren's phone number at the advertising agency and told her to ring him there. Ask for Warren Edwards, his assistant, just in case he was in a meeting or interstate.

'Well goodnight, Forrest,' said Blythe, opening the door. 'It's been marvellous. I'm so excited.'

'Yes,' said Les. 'Me too. I've got a good feeling about this.'

Blythe batted her eyelids for a second. 'I just hope you don't think I'm awful.'

'Awful?' said Les. He placed his hands on Blythe's shoulders. 'Blythe. You're not in the slightest bit awful. You're wonderful. And you're a gifted writer. Believe me.'

Blythe handed Les *The Portable Beat Reader*. 'Goodnight Forrest.'

'Goodnight, Blythe.' The door closed and Norton was left standing on his own.

Boy, can I find them, thought Les, as he slowly trudged back along the corridor. Blythe bloody Selby. Anyway, I'm sure Mr Edwards will look after her when she rings. Shit! I wouldn't have minded slipping her one though. What about Blythe's grouse little lamington? I wonder did they eat lamingtons in any of Agatha Christie's books? Les picked another tiny blonde hair out of his teeth. Not the way I just did, that's for sure.

The bar was closed and the Kurrajong Room was empty when Les came down the stairs. 'Song Of India' was playing from the speakers in the ceiling. Les went straight to his room, stripped off down to his jox and T-shirt then cleaned his teeth and got under the sheets, leaving one bed lamp on. He yawned a couple of times and stared up at the ceiling for a while, his mind a complete blank. It felt good. Suddenly Les found himself dog tired. Between driving up there in the rain, the booze, the rich meal and the blow job, he was knackered. Oh well, Les thought, as he switched off the light. It hasn't been a bad trip so far. See what happens tomorrow. In less than a minute, the big Queenslander was dead to the world.

Norton's bed was that comfortable and the room was so warm, he probably would have slept in till noon, except that whoever had the room before him had set the radio alarm for eight o'clock. Les was abruptly woken to the news, relayed from a Sydney radio station. Nathan David's station. The news finished with the local weather report and Les was still half asleep wondering what day it was when Nathan David's voice came blustering over the airwaves giving a slant on the news. Instead of sticking to music, it was a law and order rave about the leniency of the courts and Norton got a guernsey.

'Now, as I've been saying,' trilled David, 'I do have an interest in this particular film. But I am one hundred per cent up front with my financial dealings. And always have been. Not like some of the vile swine in this town whom we won't mention at this time. But that has nothing to do with it. I saw the security camera video of this Norton character, allegedly placing the bomb on the film set. Allegedly? It's there in black and white. He even smirks at the camera. Then the bomb goes off and a poor, innocent cook is killed. So how does Les Norton get bail? What? Are the police running some kind of open door policy at Waverley Police Station? Heavens above. Now this Norton character is out there walking the streets, probably to plant another bomb somewhere. I think I'd best leave it at that. But you do have to ask yourself, what in God's name is going on with our judicial system?'

Norton couldn't believe his ears. Thanks David, you prick. I always said I wouldn't piss on you. Why don't you just hang me and be done with it? Christ! Les scowled at the radio as he switched it off. It wouldn't surprise me if you had something to do with it, you little cunt. You and your mate King. And that miserable fuckin dyke. Shit! That reminds me, I was supposed to ring Gerry. It's too early now. I'll do it after breakfast. Les sat on the edge of the bed and stared out the window. The fog had lifted but it was still raining steadily and the thick clouds covering the Megalong Valley looked like huge waves as the wind pushed them over the mountains. Les opened the window, shivered, then slammed it shut again. It was still bloody cold. He took off his T-shirt, got cleaned up then put on his blue tracksuit and walked down to get something to eat.

There were about twenty guests in the breakfast room, but no sign of Blythe. I suppose she'd be halfway to Bathurst by now, thought Les. Still rumblin' from the grumblin' and howlin' from the growlin'. I wonder what she'll tell them at the furniture shop? The register was on the left as you entered and the bain-marie started there. Les told the pleasant woman in charge his room number, then found a table with a view and filled up with fruit, scrambled eggs, bacon and whatever, washed down with coffee and orange juice. A number of thoughts went through Norton's mind while he ate and hearing his name plastered all over the airwaves was one of them. Apart from a good breakfast, the day hadn't got off to much of a start. He had one last coffee and signed the tab.

Back in his cosy, warm room, Les could think of better things to do than be driving round in the rain trying to find some house in the middle of nowhere. He tossed the jemmy and a torch in his backpack, then perused his Blue Mountains street directory, deciding to check out the main cluster of streets first. He put his GAP anorak on, locked up and walked out to the car.

Cars and trucks hissed by in the rain as Les drove past a car yard and some old disused buildings belonging to the hotel, then took a right over the railway line. A hairpin bend brought him alongside the train station and an old red building that was once the Medlow Bath Post Office and had since been turned into a book shop and tea room. The road curved round again to the left, stopping at a dead end in the bush and another road went down to the right. Les followed it down amongst more trees and bush, stopping at a longer street intersected with cul-de-sacs. According to his map, there were two small ones on the left and the rest angled off on the right before the long road to the airfield. Les swung the Berlina right.

Medlow Bath was quite hilly, with more houses than Les thought, most of them built back from the road amongst the surrounding trees, making it even more difficult to find what he was looking for. All the cross streets ended in thick bush and the cul-de-sacs ran down towards a lush green valley dense with trees. A lot of the houses looked new and well built in either polished wood or rumbled bricks and nearly every home had a neat front yard full of flowers or ferns. Clusters of trees were turning from emerald green into beautiful shades of red and orange as they lost their autumn leaves. Others had shed huge strips of bark, which hung in the branches or lay across the road. Even in the mist and rain, Medlow Bath had a noticeable country elegance. There was the odd shack here and there with a rusting car body out the front, plus several overgrown blocks of land. A few had For Sale signs and in one driveway Les made out a truck with Blue Mountains Bushfire Brigade painted on the side. He wound the window down a little and the sounds of magpies and currawongs calling to each other drifted in along with the smell of wood fires burning in some of the homes.

Les drove up and down, slowly crisscrossing each street and cul-de-sac as he checked everything out; there were plenty of yards with red gums or blue gums, but no red gates or blue letter boxes. He found one wooden building on a corner with a Japanese Shinto arch under the trees and a coloured lotus on the front gate. The Blue Mountains Insight Meditation Centre. Les shook his head. I don't think that's what I'm looking for. Les drove around some more then took the long road towards the airfield. After a few kilometres the houses began to run out and Les was starting to run out of patience. He did a U-turn near a council dump and drove back to where he started. Les drummed his fingers on the steering wheel and peered out the windscreen as the wipers click-clacked back and forth. It felt like he'd been driving round in the rain half the morning. Les looked at his watch. He had. This is fucked, he told himself, shaking his head in annoyance. I knew it was going to be a waste of time. There were two more cul-de-sacs to go, then the ones on the other side of the railway line and that was it. Les shook his head again, hung a left towards the end cul-de-sac and turned right.

It was much the same as the others; a short street full of houses and trees, ending in a turning area at the bottom, and no red gate. Les came back and drove down the last cul-de-sac. A sign on the corner said Red Gum Road. It was almost identical to the other cul-de-sac, except it included a big house built from sandstone blocks on the right with palm trees out front, and further down on the left, a white Holden utility and a grey Ford F 100 parked haphazardly across a driveway belonged to several builders working inside a partially constructed brick cottage. Slowly and a little tiredly, Les reached the end of the cul-de-sac, when — bingo! There it was on the right-hand side. A blue mail box sitting on a low sandstone fence next to a red iron gate. A tall blue gum, covered in peeling bark, leaned over the sandstone fence, all standing in front of a small blue timber house with a red trim and a green-galvanised-iron roof. A vacant block of land sat opposite; Les pulled up in front of the vacant block and wound the window down for a better view.

The front of the house had a small verandah on the left with a seat next to the front door, and on the right, a bedroom faced the street with two gables built over the window. Two windows ran down the right-hand side of the house along the driveway and on the left side was one window. The surrounding yard was fairly neat before it stopped at the bush. The sandstone fence half circled round the front of the house with the gate and the letter box on the right. Painted on the blue letter box was a yellow sun, moon and stars. Parked in the driveway was a black Ford station wagon with a wire grille at the back and sitting out the front was an old brown trailer covered in leaves. A faded sticker was peeling off the back near the tail light. Les could just make out what it said: Witches Do It In Spells.

Les wound the window up then did a U-turn and drove back up the street, parking near the corner so he faced down the cul-de-sac. That has to be Knox's house, he told himself. Rittosa had the tree out the front mixed up with the name of the street. The sticker on the trailer is the clincher. Les smiled tightly. That's the good news. The bad news is, someone's home. And the worst fuckin news is, that station wagon's parked too far down the driveway, so you can't tell if it's gone from up here. Which means I have to wait here to see them go. And if I go away and come back I'll have to drive past the house again. Les looked at his watch. Oh well. May as well make myself comfortable.

Les waited almost an hour. One or two cars went past in the rain and Les could feel the drivers looking at him. He snatched another glance at his watch. That car's not going anywhere. I could be sitting here all bloody day. Les drummed his fingers impatiently on the steering wheel. I may as well ring Gerry. There's a phone booth opposite that book shop. Les started the car and drove back to the old post office.

The phone was out of order and there was a note on the book shopdoor. Back In An Hour. Les shook his head. Warren's right, I've got to get myself a mobile bloody phone. Bit late to be thinking of it now, though. He got back in the car and drove to the hotel.

After parking the car, smiling and nodding to the staff as he walked up to his room, then dialling Sydney, Les had timed it perfectly to find Gerry's phone engaged. He waited and rang another three times. Maybe he had the wrong number? Les checked with Telstra. No. He had the right number. The line was busy. Les stared at the floor, shook his head then walked out to the car and drove back to Red Gum Road. This time he took *The Portable Beat Reader* with him.

The builders were still hammering away and the station wagon hadn't moved. Les did another U-turn then parked in the same spot at the end of the street and continued waiting. Another car went by and not long after that, the white utility belonging to one of the builders backed out of the driveway and drove past. Out the corner of his eye, Les saw a young, thin-faced bloke, wearing a gold earring and with his dark hair tucked under a black beanie, watching him from behind the wheel. Les kept reading his book and waited. Before long the utility returned, and Les didn't have to look up to know this time the driver was staring at him. Les began to feel one of his legs going to sleep and put the book down. Bugger it. I'll try and ring Gerry again. He started the car and drove back to the hotel. Another ten minutes on the phone and her number was still engaged. Fuckin hell, cursed Les. This is getting ridiculous. He pulled his hood up against the rain, walked out to his car again and drove back to Red Gum Road.

When Les reached the end of the cul-de-sac he couldn't believe his eyes. The station wagon was gone. Yes, he beamed. There is a Santa Claus. Right. No time to fuck around. Les pulled up in front of the gum tree, grabbed his backpack and without bothering to lock the car, walked across to the front gate. He was about to open it when a movement to his left filled Norton's stomach with ice and made the hair stand up on the back of his neck. Two Rottweilers with thick black studded collars raced up to the other side of the gate and snarled at him with gleaming fangs and eyes full of menace. They didn't carry on with a lot of barking or jumping up and down. However, Les knew as he watched the ridges of black hair bristling along their spines, they'd do exactly what they were told to do. Tear anyone to pieces that came through the gate. Les might have flattened one with the jemmy, but the other would have got him and he'd be minus a calf muscle and half his thigh.

'Nice doggies,' said Les, slowly backing away from the gate. 'Nice doggies.'

Without moving, the two Rottweilers watched him get inside the car and drive off. By the time Les got to the old post office, his heart had stopped racing and he pulled over to have a think. Bloody hell! What about those two monsters. Another couple of steps and in two seconds I'd have been minute steak. I didn't even think of that. Les banged a fist into his hand. Fuck it! All that waiting around for nothing. Angrily Les rubbed at his chin and glared out the windscreen. No. He was too close now. The two dogs weren't going to stop him. Les swung the Berlina back over the bridge and headed for Katoomba.

The main street was busy with Thursday afternoon shoppers and there were cars everywhere. Les did two frustrating laps up and down looking for a parking spot before leaving the car unlocked in a driveway next to a bank. He had a quick look around then ran straight across the road into the butcher shop. There were four customers and two butchers serving; an older one going bald and a young one with fair hair and pimples. After a few minutes Les got the young one.

'Yehmadewodillyav?' the butcher asked in perfect strine.

'Gizdoogillosachugstag,' replied Les.

'Rydo.'

'Njobidubwillya,' asked Les.

'Nowurriesmade.'

The young butcher got two kilos of chuck steak from the window, chopped it up and put it in a plastic bag. Les paid him, thanked him and ran back to the car just as a black 4WD pulled up to enter the driveway. Before the woman driving had a chance to start blowing her horn, Les got behind the wheel and was on his way. He was back in Medlow Bath just as a long, freight train rumbled slowly through the station. Les drove straight back to the house and parked in the same place as before. He threw his backpack over his shoulder, opened up the plastic bag and walked across to the gate. Immediately the two Rottweilers rushed up to the other side looking meaner and more threatening than ever. Les decided to try a little animal psychiatry. He wasn't sure who owned the two dogs, but they might recognise a name.

'Albert,' he said, slowly and clearly. 'Where's Albert?' The two dogs looked at Les, cocked their ears up and tilted their heads to one side. 'Yeah. Good boys,' said Les. 'Where's Albert? Albert.' The Rottweilers watched Les suspiciously as he opened the bag of chuck steak.

Then they got a sniff and drool started pouring from their mouths like a tap had been turned on. Whoever was looking after the two dogs was probably just slinging them a can of Pal each and a few Meaty Bites. It had been a while since they'd seen choice lean beef. The two dogs gave a little whine and their tails started to wag. 'Yeah. Albert,' smiled Les. 'Good boys. Good boys.'

Les tossed a handful of meat over the fence and eased the jemmy out of his back pack. The two dogs wolfed the meat down in seconds and looked up for more. Les threw the rest over the fence and slowly opened the gate. The two Rottweilers tore into the chuck steak ready to kill each other for it and totally ignored Les. Righto boys, smiled Les as he stepped inside and closed the gate behind him. Time for a different kind of animal psychiatry. He brought the jemmy up and belted the first Rottweiler across the forehead. It gave a grunt of pain, then went cross-eyed and fell face first into the chuck steak with its back legs twitching. Before the other Rottweiler even noticed, Les back handed the jemmy down across its neck. It gave a slight yelp and went down next to its mate with its eyes closed and its tongue lolling. The first Rottweiler looked like there might be a kick left in it. Les gave it another quick belt in the head and it went still. Just to be certain, Les gave the second Rottweiler one in the head as well. That was it. Les slipped the jemmy into his backpack then took the two dogs by their collars and quickly dragged them behind the house. There was a short set of steps leading up to the back door; Les took the steps two at a time and shoved the jemmy behind the lock. Two good wrenches and he was inside the house. He took a torch from his back pack and had a look around.

Norton found himself standing in a small verandah, the windows facing the backyard. An old grey chesterfield sat against the opposite wall, scattered with black cushions, and a tatty green rug covered the floor. Several abstract art posters hung on the walls and the running shelf held assorted bric a brac and thick candles. Les couldn't see anything to get excited about. He moved the torch to a corridor leading inside and followed it.

There was a kitchen and bathroom on the right and two bedrooms on the left. The corridor ended at a lounge room then another room facing the street. The first bedroom had two deadlocks on it. Les left it for the time being and pushed the door to the second one open. It was fairly plain. A brass double bed, a wardrobe, a dressing table, dark curtains over the window and a few prints and rock posters on the wall, Les figured this room would belong to whoever shared the house. Les stepped to the end of the corridor and ran his torch over the lounge.

It was very dark; thick velvet drapes covered the windows, stopping most of the light. A dark blue lounge suite, covered in red and gold scatter cushions with gold tassels, sat on a red rug and faced an open fireplace in the corner. Against one wall was a TV, a stereo and a CD stacker. Around the remaining walls were strange-looking gothic posters and paintings plus a framed poster of *Rosemary's Baby*. There were gold stars and pentangles painted on the walls, bric a brac and candles along the running shelf and a candleholder made from a skull sat on a coffee table. Hanging over the fireplace was a double-handed sword and sitting on a small shelf above it was a copper chalice. Hanging on the wall above the chalice was a framed tapestry containing the words:

Drink from the cup of the Wine of Life,
which is the Cauldron of Cerridwen,
and the Holy Grail of Immortality.

Fill it full of cold Fourex and you've got me, thought Les. Despite his flippancy, the lounge room gave Les the creeps. He stepped through and opened the door to the front room.

There was a little more light and the first thing Les noticed was a chef's hat lying across a wooden chair. Yeah, this is Knox's room, thought Les. If I owned the house it'd be mine. The bedroom was almost twice as big as the other one. A four-poster bed sat against the windows facing the street, the wardrobe was bigger and the dressing table had a full-length mirror. There was a stack of cookbooks on a small table, more gothic posters on the walls and more fat candles in holders round the running shelf along with several incense burners. Amongst the posters was another framed tapestry with a cryptic little pocm.

I do not like thee, Dr Fell,
the reason why, I cannot tell.
There's only one thing I know well
I do not like thee, Dr Fell.

So much for Dr Fell thought Les. I wonder if he bulk bills? On the wall near the tapestry were some framed photos. Les ran the torch over them. A couple were of Knox standing outside the house. Another was Knox with the two Rottweilers. Next to that was Knox and Brett Rittosa wearing chef's uniforms in a restaurant called The Moondance Diner. The last photo was of four men, taken from the knees up, standing in front of an old boat — a half-cabin, wooden clinker. There were three portholes along the cabin and on the bow was written *Trough Queen*. It was moored at the edge of a park, next to a sign saying Victor Harbor and in the distance was a rocky island with a jetty running out to it. Three of the men were wearing T-shirts with Victor Harbor Sea Scouts on the front, the fourth man had *Trough Queen* printed on his. The man wearing a sea scout's T-shirt on the left was Albert Knox. The others were all wearing floppy white captain's hats and sunglasses and Les couldn't recognise any of them.

The only standout feature was two had big noses and another was smoking what looked like a joint. They weren't quite facing the camera full on, but all four men seemed to be cracking up at some private joke. Les shone his torch over the photo. I'd say they're the crew of that boat. One of them's the skipper. And Knox and the other two are wearing sea scout T-shirts for a joke. I wonder if they've been using the *Trough Queen* for a bit of dope smuggling? From what I know about Albert Knox, it wouldn't surprise me in the least. Find those other blokes in the photo with him and you never know what might turn up. This could be what I'm looking for. Les took the photo from the wall and put it in his back pack. He flashed his torch around the dead man's room again, had a quick look in his wardrobe and left it at that. Les didn't want to be in the house any longer than he had to. Apart from whoever was living there coming back, the house had a weird feel about it. It belonged in a Stephen King movie. Les stepped back into the lounge room then walked down to the room with the locks on the door. He got the jemmy from his back pack and shoved it in the jamb. The noise in the empty wooden house was horrendous, but three good wrenches and the door was open.

Les gave it a push and walked straight in on a well-organised hydroponic operation. Twenty healthy marijuana plants were growing in tanks placed neatly under Gro-Lights hanging from the ceiling. Each plant was over a metre high and they were all starting to head. Les gave the operation a grudging nod of approval. Very nice boys. There should be a few dollars' worth there. Les, however, wasn't in the least bit concerned about the late cook and his cohorts' indoor drug plantation. He stepped out the back door and closed it behind him. The two Rottweilers were still lying where he left them. Les took the steps two at a time again, got in his car and drove back to the hotel.

The first thing Les did was try to ring Gerry again. The number was still engaged. He changed into a clean blue T-shirt then got the photo out of his back pack and studied it. After finding the hydroponic set up in the house, Les was now convinced drugs were behind all this and Knox and other men in the photo were dope dealers. They'd just pulled off a shipment and that's why they were all laughing and clowning around. And Knox was laughing loudest because he'd ripped the others off. They found out and arranged his murder. Find the men in the photo and you could bet you'd find the killer. Or killers. But where the fuck was Victor Harbor? Les had never heard of it. He placed the photo on the bed then walked down to reception and asked for a booklet of post codes. It didn't take long to find Victor Harbor was in South Australia. But whereabouts in South Australia? Les returned the booklet and strolled back to his room. There was one way to find out. They'd have to have a Victor Harbor Motel or something. Les rang Telstra. They found him a Victor Harbor, Ezy Rest Motel. Les wrote the number down then picked up the phone.

'Hello Ezy Rest Motel. How can I help you?' came a woman's voice.

'Yes. Have you any vacancies?' asked Les.

'How many people?'

'Ahh ... two.'

'No problem. When did you want them?'

'On the weekend. Look, we're new to South Australia,' said Les. 'How far are you from say ... Adelaide?'

'Eighty-five kilometres, if you come via Mount Compass.'

'Thanks. I'll see you when we get there.'

Les hung up and looked at the photo again. Eighty-five kilometres from Adelaide. This bloody Adelaide connection kept cropping up all the time. Knox, King, David. Simone Mitchum. The men in the photo. Yeah, but that's South Australia. This is New South Wales. It's a long way away. Even if this Victor Harbor is just a short drive from Adelaide.

'Ohh shit!' Les sat up on the edge of the bed. 'Oh fuckin hell!'

Talk about short drives. What about a short drive to Sydney? And report in to the police? Les had forgotten all about it. He looked at his watch. There was no way in the world he could get there on time now. And what did those two cops say? If he was one minute late they'd arrest him. If he couldn't report in, don't bother ringing up, they'd come looking for him, with the rest of the NSW police force, and shooting him on sight would be a pleasure. What did Tait say? *We're filthy on having to watch you walk out of here.* They meant every word. They'd had pressure put on them in the middle of an arrest and they didn't like it.

'Shit! Fuck! Fuck it!' Les punched the bed, almost dislodging the mattress.

He felt a film of sweat form on his brow. Les wasn't starting to panic, but there was a cold surge in the pit of his stomach. Things had suddenly changed. For the worse. He'd breached his bail conditions and now he was a fugitive. He could be arrested on sight. And after what he was supposed to have done, you could bet the cops would be looking for him everywhere. What about when Nathan David found out? He'd have a bulletin on him every half-hour. Have you seen this man? What are the police doing about it? How did he get bail in the first place? Les fell back on the bed and looked up at the ceiling. What should he do? Ring Eddie? No. With everyone running around for him, Eddie would think he was a complete dill breaking his bail conditions. Ring Price? After all the trouble Price went to, to get him bail, he'd probably tell Eddie to shoot him. Les cursed and banged at the bed. Then he settled down. No. It was time to do his own thing. He'd been listening to people all his life and got dumped on, and if he hadn't listened to Eddie and his silly fuckin ideas, he wouldn't be in all this shit in the first place. Les stared at the photo on the bed and felt he'd found something to go on. Not much. But it was better than hanging around Bondi. Or Sydney. Les absently looked at his watch and picked up the phone again.

'Hello,' came a familiar man's voice. 'Travelabout Clovelly. Gary Blair speaking.'

'Hello Gary. It's Les Norton.'

'Les. How are you? I'd thought you'd be ... well I don't know where I thought you'd be, to be honest.'

'I'm in the Blue Mountains.'

Gary was the team's travel agent. He was a good style of a bloke and a snappy dresser and always with a twinkle in his eye. Like Gerry the accountant, Gary could cut corners and didn't ask too many questions.

'So Les. What can I do for you?' asked Gary.

'Gary, I need a ticket to Adelaide. Leave tomorrow. Come back Sunday night. A cargo plane. A room at the Y. Anything. I don't give a fuck.'

Gary chuckled over the line. 'Les, you're not going to believe this. I've just had a bloke, some company director, pull out of a trip I had organised. I'm out a bit of time and money ringing Adelaide and that. But it's yours if you want it.'

'I'll take it,' said Les. 'Even if it's in the back of a Hercules.'

'It's not in the back of a Hercules,' said Gary. 'It's a package.'

'A what?'

'A package. You fly business class. You got Golden Wing. A driver's waiting for you at the airport. You stay in a Regency Suite at the Adelaide Grande. And there's a car booked for Saturday and Sunday if you want it. A Hyundai Grandeur.'

'Shit!'

'The plane leaves at twelve fifty-five tomorrow. The driver picks you up again at the hotel, five-thirty Sunday. And you fly out at seven. How's that sound?'

'Unreal.'

'You can pick the tickets up on the way to the airport tomorrow. When you get there, say your name's Conrad Ullrich.'

'I'll tart my hair up and say I'm Kylie Minogue, Gary, I don't give a fuck. How much do I owe you?'

'Ohh for you, Les,' Gary pressed the buttons on a calculator. 'Two grand. You'll have to pay for the car down there. And your meals. But you get a free continental breakfast in the Regency Club. All right?'

'I've got my credit card right here, Gary,' said Les.

Norton couldn't believe it. Some luck at last. He might be going down, but at least he was going down in style. He gave Gary his credit card details, got a few more details himself, and that was it. All he had to do now was get back to Bondi, get his gear, pick up the tickets, hope the cops weren't waiting for him and he was on his way to Adelaide. It might turn out to be a wild goose chase, but if he did find out who those other men in the photo were, at least it was something to offer Tait and Caccano before they flung him in the nick. What did he have to lose? Especially now. Norton's eyes flicked back to the phone. He still had to ring Gerry. This time the line was open.

'Hello Gerry. It's Les Norton.'

'Hullo Les,' replied Norton's accountant. 'How are you?'

'Good Gerry. Look, I'm sorry I didn't ring you yesterday. I honestly forgot. I'm in the Blue Mountains and I've been trying to ring you all day.'

'That's all right. I've been super busy. And we've had trouble with the phones and the computers all day. But I spoke to Ivor for you.'

'You did? What did he say?'

'There is another insurance policy on that movie. Max King took it out through his company, King Productions. With one other beneficiary: Simone Mitchum.'

'What a lovely quinella,' said Les.

'The way it's structured, if anything happens to production, they each get two thousand five hundred dollars a week for up to six months. Then another hundred thousand. Plus their original investment back.'

'Nice work.'

'Yes,' agreed Gerry. 'The premium was fairly stiff. But it's quite clever how they worked it. If *Leaving Bondi* never gets off the ground, it's in their best interests. And it's doubtful now it ever will. So they're laughing.'

Les nodded and gritted his teeth. 'Laughing. Like a pair of hyenas.'

'Sorry Les. But ... that's show business.'

'Yeah. Like no business I know. Okay. Thanks for that, Gerry. I appreciate it.'

'Anytime Les. Bye.'

Norton replaced the phone and lay back on the bed. So. Max King and Simone Mitchum, eh. Maybe one of them did it? It certainly added another angle to the dangle. King especially. All those radio do-dads on the film set. King could slip a remote control device in amongst them, make sure he was safe, then detonate the bomb. And no one would know. His arse was covered and with their money from the insurance policy, he and Simone could go on to make more award-winning movies. But how could you prove it? Not easily. Still. It was something to go on if nothing eventuated in Adelaide. Les smiled bitterly. Not for me though. My lawyers — hopefully. I'll be in the nick. Anyway. What now? Les swung his feet over the bed. Get cleaned up and have a feed in the restaurant. Then have a quiet one at home and pack my bags ready to split in the morning. I suppose I'd better ring the maitre d and inform him Mr McNamara will be dining alone tonight.

Les took his time having a shave and a shower then got dressed again. Outside it had stopped raining, but the wind had picked up and it was still bleak and cold. He had a read, but half the time he kept thinking about his predicament and the room started to get that gaol feel about it again. It certainly was a nice mess he'd got himself into. Eventually he switched on the TV. The reception was awful. But a repeat episode of *Seinfeld* got Les going again. The one where George's mother catches him with a full hand going alone and starts running around screaming: 'My son's a pervert. My son's a pervert.' Still laughing, Les threw his leather jacket on and walked down to the restaurant.

Angelo wasn't on. Instead Les got a fair-haired woman in a black suit. She was extremely charming and polite. But when it came to bow and scrape, she wasn't in the event compared to Angelo. Les got a nice table facing the door and looked at the menu. What he had the night before tasted that good he ordered the same; plus a Hahn Premium, coffee and bread rolls: hold the sweets. Like the previous night, the meal was delicious. Les put it on his tab, gave a tip and left.

He paused momentarily in the Kurrajong Room, but didn't feel like sitting on his own listening to Super Hits of the Twenties and Thirties. So he went straight to his room.

There was nothing on TV; and if there had been, the reception was that bad it wouldn't have been worth watching anyway. Les opened *The Portable Beat Reader*. He'd finished all the Bukowski and Kerouac. And after half a page of Joyce Johnson Les felt it'd be more fun beating his meat. He closed the book and stared out the window again into nothing except cold and darkness. It wasn't much of a night. But Les felt anything would be better than sitting around like a battery hen. What did it say out the front of that hotel yesterday? Piano man Thursday night? Why not go and have a couple of quiet beers and check it out. If I keep my head down I should be all right. Les zipped up his leather jacket and walked out to the car.

Not a great deal was happening in Katoomba when Les got there. A few taxis were parked in front of the tunnel to the railway station, one or two people were walking by and that was about it. He parked the car on a bus stop right outside the Kensington and walked up the front steps.

There was one room as you entered, a small bar on the right then a few stairs led up to another room at the back. Chairs and tables dotted the red carpet and bench seats ran round the walls in the first room. The usual booze posters and sepia photos of pioneer days clung to the walls and a set of stairs on one side of the bar ran up to a bistro. Built above the bar was a wooden stage where a bloke on piano was hammering out Elton John's 'Benny And The Jets', aided and abetted by another bloke on a guitar. About forty punters, mostly men, were scattered around both rooms. There were a few attractive girls and three of the ugliest lesbians Norton had ever seen, wearing Levi jackets and gelled mullets. Sitting along the opposite side of the bar under the stage were four young blokes in sweatshirts and baseball caps, sucking schooners and smoking cigarettes. They were hair raiding the musicians and making plenty of noise in general, somewhere between boisterous fun and drunken attitude. Apart from them, everybody else was quietly drinking and the dress code ranged from corduroy trousers to plastic raincoats, tracksuits to black dresses. The only exception was an overweight woman with a face like a pie tin standing at the bar wearing a long grey woollen dress. She had copper-coloured hair, combed into two braids, junky green earrings and wrapped loosely round her neck was a green, tartan scarf. Sitting on the bar was a cheap bottle of sparkling domestic in an ice bucket and she was carrying on like she'd just won lotto. Les edged his way around her and got a middy of VB then found a vacant bench seat and a table. He sat back looking up at the stage and had an enjoyable sip of beer as the two musicians gave it to Neil Young's 'Heart of Gold'.

The first beer went down easy and was just what Les needed. Feeling a slight glow, he walked over and ordered another one, getting a heavy once up and down from the woman with the ice bucket. Les half smiled back at her and returned to his seat. The two musicians got stuck into Stevie Ray Vaughn's 'Pride and Joy'. Then the piano man announced they were taking a break and he was going to relieve his bladder. One of the young blokes at the bar held up a half empty schooner glass and yelled up to him.

'Here. Fill this up while you're at it.'

All his mates thought it was as funny as all get up and fell about laughing like drains. Les thought it wasn't a bad call and finished his second beer. He got up for a third and got another once up and down from the woman with the ice bucket. Again Les half smiled back and returned to his seat. Over the top of his middy Les could feel her watching him. Finally, she picked up her ice bucket and walked over.

'Mind if I join you?' she said in a throaty voice that vibrated through her double chins.

Les looked at her like she had a tarantula crawling over her face. 'Yeah, why not?' he answered.

Tartan scarf plonked her ice bucket on the table in front of Les and crammed her ample backside into a chair. 'I'm Lareina,' she said.

'How are you Lareina,' replied Les. 'I'm Marvin.'

'Nice to meet you, Marvin.'

'Yeah. Likewise.'

'Are you from round here Marvin?'

Les shook his head. 'Stock and Bingle.'

'Oh?' said Lareina. 'What do you do out there?'

'I'm a rabbit trapper.'

'Really. I like to eat rabbits.'

'You'd eat anything,' said Les.

'What was that?'

'I said, you can eat them with anything.'

'Yes. Especially curried.' Lareina swallowed the glass of wine she brought with her and poured another one. 'So what are you doing in Katoomba, Marvin?' she asked.

'I'm here for the Songs of the Wind Festival,' answered Les.

Lareina gave a squeal of delight. 'What a coincidence. I'm a playwright.'

'You're a what?'

'I write plays.' Lareina nodded to the bottle of cheap fizz. 'That's why I'm celebrating. They're performing one of my plays this weekend. And I've won a grant to write another one.'

Les looked at her impassively. 'Fair ... dinkum?'

'Yes. It's called *The Sculptured Chrysanthemum*.'

'Go ... on.' Les had a mouthful of beer and stared at Lareina. Shit! How do I find them? I've got to get a T-shirt made with Come and Talk to Me, I Love Idiots printed on the front. And a matching cap.

Lareina started waffling on about her fabulous play and how Les shouldn't miss it. She could get him a ticket. Then the musicians returned and started flogging Cat Stevens's 'Where Will The Children Play'. While this was going on Les didn't notice a bloke wearing a disposal-store army jacket, jeans and black Timberlands walk in. He had dark hair and an earring and was walking to the hotel across the railway line when he saw the mud spattered green Berlina out the front of the Kensington. Inside there was no missing Norton's craggy red head. The bloke got a middy and quietly watched Les from the bar.

By now Les had had enough of Lareina, and the music wasn't doing anything for him either when Lareina pulled out a packet of Winfields from somewhere in her dress. She groped around for her lighter, got a cigarette going then managed to knock Les's beer over when she picked up her glass of wine.

'Oh I'm sorry,' she giggled, blowing a mouthful of smoke in Norton's face as she flicked ash over the table.

'That's quite all right,' said Les. 'You did me a favour.' He rose from the table and walked straight out the door to his car.

Fuckin fat pain in the arse, Les scowled, zipping his leather jacket up against the cold. I was enjoying that beer. Three would have been just nice, too. He licked his lips. I suppose I can have another one back at the Medlow. He was about to get in the car when he noticed the hotel across the railway line. Why don't I have one more in there. It's not that far and some fresh mountain air would be good after putting up with her. They might have some music going, too. Les shoved his hands in the pockets of his jacket and started walking.

A tunnel ran under the railway station, and the taxi drivers parked in front of the nearby shops thought Les was an approaching fare and nearly ate him. Les smiled as he walked past and took the steps on his right. An opening to the station went off to the left and beneath a grey metal girder the tunnel ran straight ahead. It was fairly well lit. There were some framed posters on the walls and at the end of the wall on the right was a long mural of an indigo night sky full of stars, viewed from over a row of pine trees. Les gave it a grudging nod of approval as he walked past then turned right coming up at a pedestrian crossing leading to the hotel.

It was a fairly big hotel featuring a small beer garden out the front beneath an art-deco style verandah and windows. A blue awning with Fosters printed on it swung round to the bars on the right. Les crossed over to the footpath and walked in the glass doors at the end. Inside, one long wooden bar curved around to the left to an alcove with a fireplace. On the right was a games room and in front of that a pool room with one unoccupied pool table. Through a corridor was a lounge with a small ticket office next to a door with a sign, BANDS WED AND FRI NIGHTS $3 ADMISSION. The decor was mainly brown and yellow, with old wooden fittings and lights hanging from the ceiling on chrome pipes. The fire in the alcove was going and about fifteen punters were spread along the bar including three very sour-faced blokes at the games room end wearing dark tracksuits and trainers. Les had a quick look around, then ordered a middy of VB and walked down to the alcove at the other end.

There was no music and absolutely nothing to perv on as Les sipped his beer and gazed at the fire over a table full of drunks. The crowd was older and more into plain drinking than at the other hotel. It might have been warm and the beer wasn't all that bad, but it was just too boring. Gazing absently at the fire Les didn't notice the bloke in the army jacket walk in the same door he did. He went straight up to the sour-faced men in the tracksuits and pointed to Les. Their sour faces suddenly turned even sourer. Well, there's not much doing here, thought Les. I think I might call it a night. I'd have been better off staying home. No. If it hadn't been for that wobbegong putting her fat head in at that other place it would have been all right. The music wasn't that bad, and the beer was good. Les finished his middy, put the glass on the bar and left through the nearest door.

Walking back through the tunnel, Les stopped momentarily to have another look at the mural and noticed the artist had included a few UFOs in the background. I suppose on those clear nights up this way they'd see a few strange lights in the sky now and again, Les chuckled to himself. Woody should move up here. She'd cough in her rompers if she saw that mural. He'd started walking again when an angry voice shouted out from the end of the tunnel, echoing round the walls.

'Hey, you in the fuckin leather jacket.'

Les stopped and turned around. 'Are you talking to me?' he asked politely.

'You're the only fuckin one here, cunt.'

The three men from the bar, plus the one in the army jacket, marched up to Les. The one doing the shouting had dark hair and a flattened nose, pushed into a mean, sallow face. He was the biggest. The man in the army jacket was about medium build and another one on Norton's right was tall with short brown hair and looked like he might be able to handle himself. The fourth bloke was skinny with a bony face full of acne, and although he was doing his best to look tough, Les felt he was there only to make up the numbers. The four men formed a half circle around Les, who was standing a couple of metres out from the wall.

'What seems to be the trouble fellahs?' smiled Les, taking his hands from his pockets.

The biggest bloke glared at him. 'You were out Medlow Bath today. Weren't you?'

Les shook his head. 'I only just got here a couple of hours ago.'

'Fuckin bullshit!' The big bloke nodded to the one in the army jacket. 'Jimmy was working out there and saw you parked in Red Gum Road. You were cruising around all day.'

Les looked at the bloke in the army jacket. 'I think Colin Combat needs to get his eyes tested.'

'I don't need my eyes tested,' said the bloke in the army jacket. 'That's your Berlina outside the Kensington. And that was you out Medlow Bath today.'

'You got me mixed up with someone else,' said Les.

'We ain't got you mixed up with no one,' said the big hood. 'And I got one dog dead, and another in the vet's with a fractured skull.'

'Well,' suggested Les, 'maybe you shouldn't let your dogs roam the streets. Keep them on a lead and they won't get hurt in the traffic.'

The big hood's face reddened with anger. 'They didn't get hurt in no traffic you cunt. Somebody hit them with something. Something hard. Like this.'

The big hood reached under his tracksuit with his right hand and whipped out a length of pipe. He raised it above his head then swung it at Norton's face. Les had been expecting something like this. He moved in closer, caught the hood's wrist with his left hand, gripped him at the elbow with his right, then twisted left, turning the big hood with him. When the hood's back was facing the tunnel wall, Les swept his right leg away and banged the back of his head into the wall. He followed this with a smashing right knee into the hood's groin. The big hood gave a yelp of pain that echoed round the tunnel and dropped the length of pipe. Les let go of him and snatched up the pipe. In almost the same movement, Les backhanded it against the side of Army Jacket's right knee. Army Jacket gasped in a breath then howled and grabbed at his shattered knee. Before he could howl again, Les gave him an uppercut with the pipe, splitting his chin open and dumping him on his back. Les kept going round in a half circle with the length of pipe and collected the brown-haired bloke across one side of the face, then swung it back across the other. The first blow broke Brown Hair's jaw, the second one smashed several teeth. Brown Hair clutched at his face as blood started oozing through his fingers, then turned his back on Les and sank to his knees. Les split the back of his head open with a quick rap of the pipe and he pitched forward, unconscious. The big hood was sitting on his backside holding his groin: stunned and in a lot of pain, but still conscious. He looked up at Les and the last thing he saw was the length of pipe coming towards his face before it crunched into his forehead, splitting it to the bone. Blood poured into his eyes, he let go of his groin and fell back amongst the others, out cold. This left the last bloke looking down at his mates horrified. His poor, skinny, acned face was contorted with fear and a trickle of urine had started running down the inside of his jeans. Les poked the length of pipe at his groin.

'Hello me old,' said Les. 'How are they hanging? Long and loose and full of juice?'

'Ohh look mate,' begged the skinny hood. 'I had nothing to do with this. Fair dinkum. I was just sitting in the pub. I don't even come from round here. I'm from Muswellbrook. I drive a bread cart. I swear mate. I hardly know these blokes.'

Les gave the skinny hood a cursory once up and down. 'You know something? I believe you. You're just an innocent bystander.'

'That's right mate. I'm telling you the truth. Honest I am. You got to believe me.' The trickle in the bloke's jeans turned into a torrent. 'I've never lied in my life.'

'Yeah. You're an honest man,' said Les. 'So I'll tell you what I'm gonna do.' The skinny hood yelped with terror as Les jammed the length of pipe up under his chin and pinned him against the wall. 'Now listen to me, you pimply faced streak of cat shit,' hissed Norton, his eyes about an inch away from the hood's. 'I'm a secret agent with the taxation department. I'm up here looking for an Israeli banker, stole fifty million dollars from the government. So I'm not in the slightest bit interested in you. Or your shitty mates. You listening?'

'Yeah mate. Yeah,' gasped the bloke. 'Every word mate.'

'So tell your friends when they're back on their feet: keep their mouths shut about what just happened, and I won't tell the drug squad about their little hydro operation in Red Gum Avenue. You got that?'

'Yeah mate. Every word. No one'll say nothing.'

'Good. Because I don't need the paperwork. But if you don't, you know what I'll do?'

The bloke shook his head. 'No mate. What?'

Les shoved the pipe between the bloke's legs. 'I'll come back and audit you.'

Les could see the poor bloke was seconds away from crapping his pants as well as pissing himself. He wiped the hair and blood off the pipe on the bloke's tracksuit top and left him.

The taxi drivers were watching Les as he came up the stairs. Les tucked the piece of pipe under his arm, but he thought one driver saw it. When Les got to his car, the piano man and his mate were pounding the life out of Fleetwood Mac's 'Don't Stop'. Les opened the door and threw the piece of pipe on the passenger seat. Whether any of the cab drivers took any notice as he drove past, Les wasn't sure. A couple of kilometres down the highway, Les opened the window and flung the piece of pipe into the bush. He wound the window back up and drove to the hotel.

Back in his room, Les packed his jeans away and changed into his blue tracksuit. He got a little bottle of Jim Beam from the mini-bar, poured it into a glass, topped it with water and swallowed some. It went down well, so Les swallowed some more. He sat on the edge of the bed and looked at the silent TV. What just happened should have had a funny side to it; especially when the skinny bloke piddled himself. But Les wasn't laughing. He was worried. And he felt like kicking himself in the arse. I knew I should have stayed home. There's cops looking for me all over the state. But no. I have to go to a fuckin pub and get into a fight. I need rooting. Les took another mouthful of bourbon. When those heroes drag their sorry arses off to hospital, the doctor or the nurses are going to call the police. Then there's those taxi drivers. They couldn't miss me. And I'm sure one of them saw me with that iron bar. Shit! My only chance is if they don't go to hospital before I get out of here tomorrow. Yeah, right. If they don't get their heads stitched up they'll bleed like stuck pigs all night. Les looked at his bags packed and ready to go. I should piss off now. But where am I gonna go? I can't hang around Sydney or my place. I can't win. I'm fucked if I stay here. And I'm fucked if I go home. Les caught his reflection in the mirror next to the bathroom. You're a nice goose, Norton.

He finished the first bourbon and had another. The second one settled him down a little. Yeah, but surely those hillbillies wouldn't say anything after I drummed it into that dill's head about their hydro system? They couldn't be that stupid. No. I think I'm pretty sweet. And by the time the cops sort all the shit out, how are they going to find me? They could if they wanted to. But I reckon they'd have better things on their minds than a bunch of wallys getting a belting. They're probably local hoods anyway. Les took another sip of bourbon. Yeah. I think I'm drama queening here just a bit. That's me, Les Norton aka Bette Davis. He caught his reflection in the mirror again. You dill. Les was about to switch the TV on when there was an urgent knock on the door.

Norton's blood went cold, and this time he did start to panic. Ohh shit! They're here already. Fuck! How did they find me so quick? God! What am I going to do? He looked at the window. It was a ten-metre drop. Don't answer the door? The cops'd smash the fuckin thing in. Les was trapped. There was only one thing he could do. Answer the door and face the music. Bugger it. Two days he'd lasted. Two lousy, bloody days. And just when it looked like there might have been a tiny light at the end of the tunnel. With a heart full of lead, Les opened the door.

'Mr Forrest McNamara?' It was a woman.

Les gave a double blink. 'Yeah. That's me.'

'My name is Odessa Hatfield. I'm a friend of Blythe Selby's.'

'You are? Well ... come on in, Odessa. Tell me what I can do for you.'

Totally flabbergasted, Norton stepped aside to let the young woman in. She was almost as tall as Les, with straggly auburn hair combed up at the back. Her face was strong, with a firm mouth and wild green eyes and totally devoid of make-up. A thick black cardigan hung loosely over a maroon dress clinging to her whippy body and across one shoulder was a small leather sling bag. Clutched in her hands was a manuscript. It wasn't far from stepping inside to the mini-bar near the end of Norton's bed, but by the time she got there, Les noticed Odessa had a shapely arse with a swing like a new back door.

Odessa turned around, her chin up, a look of defiance on her face. When she spoke her voice was firm yet eloquent. 'If I've barged in on you like this Mr McNamara,' she said, 'I'm sorry. But Blythe told me you're looking for poets.'

'Yeah. We sure are,' replied Les. 'Are you a poet?'

'Yes,' asserted Odessa.

'Unreal,' said Les. 'So ... what have you got for me, Odessa?'

'This.' Odessa thrust her manuscript at Norton.

Les took the manuscript and looked at the title, *Silicone Thoughts and Plastic Dreams*. 'Are these all your original works, Odessa?'

'Yes.'

'I thought so. All right. Well why don't you relax and make yourself a drink while I read one.'

'Thank you, Mr McNamara.'

Odessa flustered nervously round the mini-bar and made herself a scotch and water while Les fumbled around opening her manuscript, still not quite sure what he was doing. Odessa watched intently as Les sat on the bed and chose a poem at random. It was called 'Muriel's Milk Box'.

Talk to me in lecherous detail,

my heart demands it.

Is there cream,

yoghurt,

Lite-White,

Ricotta.

I swim in a sea of masochistic love,

with chocolate sharks,

and raspberry stingrays.

Les closed the manuscript and looked at Odessa. Odessa stared back challengingly.

'Well. What do you think?' she said. It was a demand as much as a question.

'What do I think?' answered Les. 'I'm not sure how to put this, Odessa. But you're definitely in the same league as Blythe Selby.'

'I am?' Odessa gave Les a double blink.

'Reckon. Of course I've only read one poem. But hey ...' Les made an open handed gesture.

'So you like them?'

'Of course. They're great.'

Odessa fell back against the mini-bar. 'Oh, I'm so thrilled,' she said.

Les smiled serenely at Odessa. 'But I do have to ask you something, Odessa, before we continue.'

'And what's that, Mr McNamara?'

'Are there any poems in here about sex?'

Odessa shook her head almost imperceptibly. 'I'm trying to keep sex out if it. At this stage.'

'Fair enough, Odessa,' nodded Les. 'What about blow jobs?' Les tapped the manuscript with an index finger. 'Is there any chance of finding a polish in here?'

Odessa's green eyes flashed. 'Mr McNamara,' she smiled. 'There's a sheila in there could suck a medicine ball through a didgeridoo.'

Les nodded cognizantly. 'Did Blythe mention my company's contractual arrangements? Half the advance initially. The rest on publication.'

'Blythe told me everything,' said Odessa. 'Everything.'

'Excellent,' beamed Les. 'Now, why don't I join you in a drink and I'll read another poem.'

'Do that, Mr McNamara.'

Les made another bourbon and found his hands were shaking slightly. What just happened was an astonishing, almost unbelievable turnaround. He had a mouthful of bourbon and settled down at one end of the bed. Odessa cradled her scotch and sat at the other. Les chose another poem at random. It was called 'Prismatic Impulsiveness'.

Moonbeams and rainbows,

nailed her to a wall of proclamation.

But despair and scandal

would never be the sword of righteousness,

in the hands of the separatists.

Nor reticence,

the slings and arrows

of the nebulous ungodly.

Les closed the manuscript and looked at Odessa. 'I don't think I need to read any more, Odessa. Just give me your phone number. And I'll tell you how you can contact me.'

'Marvellous,' said Odessa. 'Oh, I'm so glad I was brazen enough to call around.'

'Me too,' said Les.

She wrote down her phone number and address and her phone number at work. Odessa lived in Blackheath and worked for the council. Les gave her the same phone number he gave Blythe and told her to contact him through Mr Edwards.

'So there you go, Odessa,' said Les, placing her phone number in his wallet.

'You're on your way. I can envisage dual readings. You and Blythe.'

'This is amazing,' said Odessa. 'Absolutely amazing.'

'It sure is,' winked Les. 'Now, Odessa,' he said, undoing his tracksuit pants, 'there's some other contractual arrangements need to be taken care of. I've got a silent partner who'd like to get involved in this deal.' Les whipped out Mr Wobbly and gave him a couple of shakes. Mr Wobbly raised his head up to see what was going on and liked what he saw. 'He's in public relations. You know anything about public relations Odessa?'

'I certainly do.' Odessa moved along the bed. 'And you know something Mr McNamara? You're even better looking than Blythe said you were.'

'Call me Forrest, Odessa.'

Odessa was cool. She kissed Les and let him slip his hand under her dress and give her boobs a squeeze. They were round and firm with hard pointy nipples and her kisses were warm and sweet. It wasn't long before Norton had a rock hard boner and Mr Wobbly was frothing at the mouth. Odessa gave it a few strokes then slipped her mouth over the knob. Les felt a shiver run up and down his spine as Mr Wobbly started to get very red and angry. Odessa got right into it, adding some discreet moaning and groaning to show she was getting off a bit herself. It wasn't long before Les was spreadeagled on the bed, his eyes closed, sighing with sweet agony. Odessa hit the vinegar strokes and Les felt like he was levitating above the bed as he let go. Odessa took the lot. Licked her lips and looked around for more. Les collapsed against the pillows; eyes rolled back in his head and his toes twitching.

Odessa went to the bathroom and came back adjusting her dress. Les pulled his tracksuit pants up and tucked Mr Wobbly back into his little bed.

'I might leave now, Forrest,' said Odessa.

'Okay,' replied Les. 'I'll walk you to your car.'

'You don't have to. Stay where you are.'

'All right.'

'You won't lose my manuscript, will you?'

Les shook his head. 'I'll copy it as soon as I get back to the office. You've got other copies just to be on the safe side?'

'Oh yes.'

'Good.'

Odessa gave Norton a kiss. 'Goodnight, Forrest,' she smiled. 'I look forward to seeing you again.'

Les smiled back. 'Me too, Odessa. It's been a delight.'

Odessa stepped out the door, closed it behind her, and was gone.

Les looked at the door for a moment then placed Odessa's

manuscript on the table and stared out the window. Suddenly he felt beat. It wasn't just driving around and being stuck in the car half the day. Or the beers, the fight and the romp with Odessa. When he heard that knock on the door, Les thought he was gone. When he opened it and it wasn't the police, the feeling was almost indescribable. Shock, followed by sheer elation. Like diving into a pool full of chilled champagne. Les knew the cops wouldn't be around now. He could relax. He cleaned his teeth, left his tracksuit on then crawled under the doona and switched off the bed lamp. Norton's last thoughts before drifting off were that he couldn't really blame that big bloke and his mates for wanting to sort him out after he'd killed one dog and fractured the other one's skull. But he honestly didn't think he'd hit the dogs that hard. And maybe he shouldn't have smashed the blokes as much as he did. But on the other hand, what would those blokes have done to him if he hadn't got hold of the iron bar? He probably wouldn't be walking. And Odessa wouldn't be getting a contract with Roulette Publishing. Les yawned and jammed his head into the pillows. Anyway, it was all behind him. Tomorrow was another day. And with a bit of luck he'd be in Adelaide and something might turn up. Les yawned again. It wasn't long and he was out like a light.

Les was out of bed, washed and in the breakfast room by eight wearing the same tracksuit; not being out to impress and knowing he was only going to be sitting in his car all morning he didn't bother getting changed. He filled a bowl with cereal and fruit and a plate with bacon and eggs, got some toast and coffee and found a table overlooking the Megalong Valley. Outside it was cold and raining again. He didn't bother turning on the radio or reading the paper. David would only be screaming his name to the rafters and some journalist would be doing the same. Les felt what he didn't know wouldn't hurt him. After one last cup of coffee he checked out, and by nine o'clock Les was in his car and heading for Sydney. He'd worked it so he had plenty of time to get home, grab a change of clothes, pick up his tickets and get to the airport, yet not be hanging around long enough for the police to arrest him. If he could make it to the airport Les felt he'd be able to hide in Golden Wing and he'd be all right.

Because of the weather, the drive down was slow and Les didn't like being a fugitive one bit. Five kilometres the other side of Linden a highway patrol car pulled in behind him and he began to sweat. He kept to the left and drove like Grandma Duck, when the cop suddenly switched on his siren making the butterflies in Norton's stomach start line dancing. But the cop went round him and pulled over a driver towing a trailer with no brake lights. Les exhaled audibly. That's it. Time for some music. He found a tape and Jools Holland and his Rhythm and Blues Orchestra started tickling the ivories with 'Travelling Blues'. After that the trip went noticeably smoother. The other side of Penrith Bob Margolin was cranking out 'Up and In' like there was no tomorrow and B. B. King had just belted out 'Pauly's Birthday Boogie' when Les switched off the stereo and came down O'Brien Street Bondi. He pulled up on the corner of Cox

Avenue and Lamrock and peered through the windscreen. He couldn't see any police cars out the front of his house or the State Protection Unit hiding somewhere. Oh well, thought Les. Here goes nothing. He screeched to a halt outside Chez Norton, grabbed his bags then quickly locked the car and sprinted inside.

There were two messages on the answering machine. Les didn't bother to listen to them. It would only be Price or Eddie telling him what an idiot he was and he could do without that. Instead Les rang for a taxi. While he was waiting, he dumped his dirty clothes out of his bag, filled it with fresh ones and whatever else he thought he'd need in Adelaide then changed into a clean pair of jeans and a black Lee Kernaghan T-shirt. A horn bipping out the front told him the taxi had arrived. Les threw his leather jacket on, picked up his bags and Wednesday's paper from where he'd left it in the kitchen, then made sure the house was locked and ran outside.

'Clovelly Road. Then out to the airport,' said Les, jumping in the back seat of the taxi.

'No worries,' replied the driver.

Les buried his head in the paper, kept quiet and avoided any eye contact with the driver. Gary wasn't in his office when the taxi pulled up out the front of Travelabout Clovelly. One of the girls working there handed Les his tickets and wished him a good trip. The traffic wasn't too bad and he was outside Ansett Departures before he had a chance to re-read the sports pages. At the desk it was automatic drive. Mr Ullrich had his bags tagged Priority and was politely told his plane was leaving from gate sixteen. Les couldn't help the butterflies fluttering a little as he passed through the uniforms at security, but nothing happened. Safely through there, Les stopped at a newsagency and bought a map. Suburban and Regional Adelaide. He took the escalator to Golden Wing, got a smile from the girl at reception when he showed his card, and stepped inside.

There were a few casually dressed people in Golden Wing, but it was mostly suits waffling into mobiles or using the phones provided. Les found a table in the corner, made a cup of tea, got a plate of cheese and crackers and a *Bulletin* and spread his map out. The drive to Victor Harbor looked like a piece of piss. Les saw Mount Compass on the map and from there, Victor Harbor was almost straight down a highway, sitting in a long, wide bay. You can't tell which way the train went by looking at the tracks, thought Les, and you can't tell much about a town by looking at a map. At least I know where it is. Les folded his map up, put it in his backpack and read the *Bulletin* while he kept an eye on the other punters. By the time he had another cup of tea and a few more crackers it was time to board the plane. Les had the very front seat to himself and plenty of leg room and one of the flight attendants had dark hair and a pretty good pair of legs in her black stockings. She gave Les a nice smile and a glass of orange juice. She came back to make sure Mr Ullrich's bag was stowed in front of him and they were on their way. Les had decided to brush *The Portable Beat Reader* for the time being. He'd read and heard enough nutty poetry to last him a lifetime. Instead he got a book from Warren's room. *Once A Jolly Swagperson* by Lawrence Held. *Politically Correct Tales For Our Times.* Les had just finished 'The Differently Statured Adult Male of Notre Dame' when it was time for lunch. Salad with sesame soya vinaigrette and mixed grill with honey carrots and sautéed wild mushrooms. This went down easily with another glass of orange juice and Les picked up his book again. He'd just finished 'Beauty and the Superficially Non-Humyn Animal' when the pilot announced they were making their descent into Adelaide. The plane bumped down on the tarmac and a few minutes later Mr Ullrich got another smile as he disembarked.

Adelaide airport was nowhere near as big as Kingsford Smith. It was only a short walk to the arrivals lounge and standing on the right, wearing a grey uniform, cap and sunglasses, was a driver holding a sign: ULLRICH. Les walked up to him a little cautiously.

'I'm Conrad Ullrich.'

The driver was about thirty, dark complexioned and looked fit. 'Thank you, Mr Ullrich,' he replied pensively. 'I'm Vincent. I'll get your luggage.'

Les followed Vincent over to the carousel without saying anything. Vincent seemed to expect this. Norton's bag arrived, Vincent picked it up and Les followed him out to a white Ford LTD and got in the back. The weather was cloudy and cold and it looked like there had been some light rain. Vincent didn't say anything as they left the airport. Les thought it might be best if he did the same and peered out the window.

After the smog, traffic gridlocks and high rise of Sydney, Adelaide was like a big country town. Long flat roads, roomy wooden houses and plenty of parks and trees. A sign ahead said BURBIDGE ROAD A–6 CITY. Further on Les noticed a nice old hotel with a verandah round it called the New Market. Before long they were in the city. Vince turned this way and that then came out on a wide, straight road divided in the middle. There were office blocks on the right and railway lines on the left. Behind the railway lines was a park with a river running through it. Vincent turned left into a curved driveway and pulled up in front of the Adelaide Grande.

The hotel looked quite swish. Thirty storeys high, plenty of chrome and glass, neat gardens and a split-level restaurant out the front. On the right was a casino. Vincent got Norton's bag from the boot and gave it to a porter with a brass luggage trolley then opened Norton's door.

'I'll see you at five-thirty on Sunday, Mr Ullrich,' he said.

'Okay. See you then, Vincent. Thanks,' replied Les.

'Enjoy your stay in Adelaide, sir.' Vincent got back in the LTD and drove off.

'Just the one bag, sir?' asked a porter in a black vest.

'Yes.'

'This way, sir.'

Les followed the porter into the lobby. Inside was even more swish than out. A ring of marble and gold columns rose out of a shiny parquet floor and circled a set of marble stairs with brass railings, leading down to a ballroom and function centre. The lifts were on the left next to a spacious bar called the Torrens Room. Just round from this were the doors to a sundeck overlooking the river, then an open doorway to a large dining room. To the right from the main entrance was the concierge, then behind a barricade of shiny black marble was the reception desk. Les followed the porter to reception. Checking in was automatic drive again. An extremely pleasant woman in a blue suit soon fixed everything with a minimum of fuss. Les signed in as

C. Ullrich, Clovelly Road, Sydney and was given his key and charge card. He then checked with the concierge about the car. No problems. Avis was straight across the road, the car was available at nine, bring it back to the hotel and it would be valet parked for him. Les followed the porter across to the lifts and even though Les would have made two of him, he let the porter carry his bag and they swooshed up to the twenty-third floor.

As he stepped out of the lift, Les walked to the windows at the end of the lift lobby to check out the view. On the right was the park and the river, ahead in the distance was the ocean and to the left a ring of hills surrounding the city. Walking to his room Les looked down two floors onto the Regency Club, a tastefully furnished, lovely green area with a bubbling fountain, servery and a bar where Gary had said the continental breakfast was on the house. Les couldn't wait for breakfast.

After the Medlow, Norton's room was like a home unit with a fabulous view over the city, the casino, and all the way to the distant hills on the left. There was a queen-size bed, a TV, ample furniture and wardrobe space and a marble bathroom with a shower and spa. The mini-bar was well stocked with assorted booze, chocolates and nibblies. And to think I would have settled for a room at the Y, Les chuckled to himself. He gave the porter two dollars and got a bottle of Heineken from the mini-bar. While he sipped that, Les unpacked then checked out the hotel directory and the room service menu. He had another look at the city as he finished his beer and noticed the clock radio: Adelaide was half an hour behind Sydney. It just gets better. Now I've got thirty minutes up my sleeve. Les lay back on the bed, closed his eyes and wondered what to do. The bed was very comfortable and Les lay on it longer than he intended. Another minute and he would have dozed off. He got up, splashed some water on his face and took in the view over the city again. Why don't I go for a walk? Check out beautiful downtown Adelaide. I won't get much chance tomorrow. Or Sunday. Les threw his leather jacket on and got the lift to the lobby.

He walked past the entrance to the casino and turned left at the old railway station. Les hadn't gone five metres before he tensed up. Three uniform cops were standing just inside the station. Les watched them out the corner of his eye, but they didn't appear to notice him. Shit! This is ridiculous, he told himself, I'll finish up in the rathouse. Les went right at King William then strolled past an office block and a group of girls huddled on the footpath, puffing desperately at their cigarettes. They were all dressed in black or purple with long dark hair and chalk-white skin. Very different to the girls at Bondi. After unexpectedly seeing the wallopers, Les felt like something soothing. A Jack Daniels or a coffee would be nice. He sprung a health bar that was all bright colours and vinyl stools called the Boost Juice Bistro. Les ordered a shot of wheatgrass and a Brain Boost. Carrot, beetroot and apple with ginseng and ginkgo. The wheatgrass tasted exactly like licking the blades on a lawn mower, but you got a slice of lemon for a chaser. The brain booster was delicious and went down splendidly. It might have been Norton's imagination, but as he strode off, his head did feel clearer and there seemed to be an extra kick in his step as he crossed King William Street to check out Rundle Mall.

Les found himself walking down a long flat mall crammed with shops on either side and entrances to arcades and malls with more shops. There were crowds of shoppers and groups of unfamiliar mall hangers amongst the shoppers. Skinheads wearing black T-shirts with Korn, Fear Factory, Witchery and Crypt on the front and pale-skinned Gothic chicks wearing dark dresses and layers of weird dark make-up who looked like they'd just flown in on broomsticks. Fruit barrows and paper stalls were scattered along the middle and near one fruit barrow were several bronze pigs, one on its haunches eating out of a garbage tin. Les wished he'd brought his camera. There were plenty of music shops catering mainly for thrash and grungeheads. Les had a look in one. It was all dark and mysterious with dark and mysterious-looking staff. On a bookshelf was a whole section on Wicca, Paganism, Ritual Magic, Goddess Studies. I wonder if I could get *The Beach Boys Greatest Hits* in here and a few Barbara Cartlands. I don't think so. Les crossed an intersection and now it was hotels, restaurants and sidewalk cafes. The mall ended near a gift shop selling cute little portable fountains. Les crossed over and came down the other side. It was much the same, except for the ubiquitous McDonalds and the usual kids, with faces full of pimples, that like to hang out the front. Les walked back to where he started, crossed over from the mall and found himself in Hindley Street.

Traffic drove back and forth and now there was a noticeable sleaze. Head shops, disposal stores, adult book shops, triple-X-videos, video games arcades, Wild Night Review, takeaway food shops, tourist trap hotels. Bigger and better Gothic shops. Strip joints. Hello, thought Les, I'm home. I'm back at the Cross. All that's missing is a few hundred assorted hookers and junkies. Although he knew he shouldn't go near it, something about the local police station fascinated Les and he had to have a discreet look. There was only one young cop in there with his head down and his window was shaded by a venetian blind, so his view was restricted. What fascinated Les was the other window. It was covered in posters for missing persons. MISSING. MISSING. CAN YOU UNRAVEL THE MYSTERY? DO YOU HAVE A CLUE IN MICHAEL'S MURDER. REWARD. DISAPPEARANCE. SUSPECTED MURDER. There were photos of at least forty missing people, most of them young girls. Not counting all the Murder–Reward posters. Christ, thought Les, that's a lot of missing people for a small city. Then he remembered he'd heard a few stories about South Australia. They had some good murders and things in Crow Eater Territory. It wasn't long ago they found eight bodies stuffed in barrels in an old bank vault. They still hadn't found out what happened to the three Beaumont children. I'll bet there's a few Jeffrey Dahmers and Charles Mansons running around out there, mused Les. What about all those Witchcraft shops? And those spooky looking Gothics? There was one bright light in Hindley Street, a music shop called The Blue Note. It had the best selection of blues and rock 'n' roll music Les had ever seen, plus Latino and Cuban and all that. There were blues bands Les had never heard of. The proprietor was a friendly young bloke wearing a stars and stripes vest with his hair combed across his forehead in two thick bangs. He offered Les assistance. But how was Les going to tell him that if he wasn't going to gaol on Monday he'd have bought half his shop out? Les browsed round for a while, drooling over the CDs and told the bloke he'd be back.

Outside, Les noticed it was getting dark and took a glance at his watch. Across the road was a lane leading down to the Grande. There was a hotel on one corner with an enclosed verandah around the top and an unused picture theatre on the other. Les crossed Hindley Street and walked down, passing a dirty little alley on the left with a skip bin out the front. Further down on the right was the foyer of another glitzy hotel that ran down to a bar on the corner. Les had a quick peek in the window as he went past. It looked all right; black furnishings and shiny chrome fittings. But not many customers. Les waited for the traffic then jogged over to the Grande.

Back in his room Les sucked on another Heineken and stared out the window as the lights came on across the city. Now what will I do? he asked himself. I know, there's a heated pool downstairs and it doesn't close till nine. Why don't I have a mullet and bream. I tossed my Speedos in before I left. Les changed into his black swimmers and got a white bathrobe out of the wardrobe. He took a nice fluffy towel from the bathroom and barefooted it for the lift down to the pool.

The pool was on the third floor, down a corridor and in the open. When Les stepped outside, the wind felt like it was coming straight from Antarctica. Shit! I don't know if this is such a good idea, he shivered. No wonder I've got it to myself. When he dropped his robe the wind flayed him like an icy whip. Oh well, here goes nothing. Les bolted across the sundeck and plunged straight in. It might have been cold out, but the water was beautiful. At least ten degrees warmer. Even though the pool was only fifteen metres long, Les started doing laps like he was Ian Thorpe. Freestyle, breaststroke, backstroke any stroke or style you like. It was great and the water seemed to wash away his cares. It was almost like he was in Adelaide on holidays. Les flopped around, duck dived, lay on his back and spurted water in the air. Soon he noticed people looking down at him from the rooms above. Evening everybody, grinned Les, then pulled his Speedos off, rolled over and mooned the surrounding windows. Would you like another look? Sure you do. Les rolled over again and spread his freckly, white cheeks. There you go. What do you reckon that is? A cut or a burn? Les flopped around a while longer then got out and climbed back into his robe. He tossed his towel over his shoulders and dripped water in the lift all the way to the twenty-third floor.

Back in his room, Les showered and shaved and changed into his back-up tracksuit, a dark blue Brooks. He got a bottle of Hahn premium from the mini-bar and studied the room service menu. Les picked up the phone and ordered hoummos, taramasalata and toasted pita bread plus a Caesar salad with Cajun chicken for starters. Lamb rack with mashed potato and vegetables for mains. And coffee and bread rolls. The person at room service told Mr Ullrich it should be there in thirty minutes. Les flopped back on the bed, swivelled the TV round and watched *Seinfeld*. It wasn't a bad one: Kramer is a theatre guide, Elaine shows a bit of cleavage and George gets dressed up as Henry the Eighth. Les was still laughing over a bottle of Hahn when his meal arrived. He gave the waiter two bucks and got stuck into it over Adelaide's version of the *7.30 Report*.

Les couldn't knock the food. It was delicious. The vegetables were steamed to perfection and the lamb was tender. The Caesar salad was exceptional. Les bored in then put the trolley out on the landing, saving the hoummos for a late night snack. He started flicking through the TV guide. There wasn't much on the commercial channels and SBS were having another racist witch hunt. A doco about the Vietnam War on the ABC looked interesting. Les got his map out and went over it again while he waited, when the phone rang. It was Gary Blair from Travelabout.

'Gary,' said Les. 'What's up?'

'Nothing,' replied Gary. 'I just thought I'd ring up and see if everything was okay. All part of our after-sales service.'

'Thanks, Gary. No, everything's as a bean, Gary. The driver picked me up okay. The hotel's the grouse. In fact I've just been for a swim in the pool.'

'You've been swimming? What's the weather like down there?'

'Cold and cloudy. But the pool was heated.'

'It's pouring bloody rain up here.'

'Fair dinkum?'

'Hey, I just thought I'd tell you, Les. The reason that bloke never picked up his ticket. The poor bastard got run over.'

'He what?'

'A motorbike collected him near Rose Bay golf links. He died on the way to hospital.'

'Shit!'

'So you won't have to worry about Mr Ullrich wanting his room back.'

'Jesus, Gary. I hope this isn't some kind of omen. Like the *Twilight Zone* and he turns up delivering my room service or something.'

'Hey, you never know, Les. Adelaide's a spooky place.'

'Thanks, Gary.'

'Anyway, I'm glad everything's all sweet. Anything goes wrong, give me a ring.'

'No worries. Thanks, Gary.'

Les hung up the phone. Bloody hell! One minute I'm going through a dead bloke's house. Now I'm staying in a dead bloke's room and using his name. Not a very nice coincidence. Les gazed absently out the window for a moment. Not much I can do about it though, I suppose. Les got the last Heineken from the mini-bar and settled back in front of the TV.

The doco wasn't bad and showed how easily the Vietnam War could have been avoided if the Yanks had used their heads. Instead they blew JFK's off then managed to kill three million Vietnamese along with fifty thousand Americans. After that there was nothing. Les switched off the TV and stared out the window at the city lights. It was too early to go to bed, and that cooped up feeling started kicking in again. You know what I should do, he told himself, instead of flopping around after all that food. Go for a walk. Even if it's just up to that music shop and have another look through those CDs. Yeah. Why not. Les put his Nauticas on and walked out to the lift.

The bar on the corner had picked up and so had Hindley Street when Les got there. Les stopped outside the empty theatre at the end of the lane and had a look around. Gangs of youths were roaming around in baggy clothes and baseball caps on back the front, swearing and trying to act tough, while packs of hoons cruised up and down the street like sharks in old Kingswoods and Commodores, yelling out at any passing girls. Across the road in front of a Time Zone, gangs of black kids, aged from ten up, swarmed around the

148

footpath managing to swear louder than anybody. Young girls hobbled past in long black boots with high heels, each one wearing a black mini, a black top and five layers of make-up. Mecca appeared to be the hotel and strip joint on the opposite corner. Several lumpy girls in minis and high heeled boots were bumping and grinding out the front to a blaring disco version of Rod Stewart's 'Do Ya Think I'm Sexy', trying to entice any passing blokes to come in. Behind the enclosed verandah upstairs, you could be a star for the evening and dance on a little stage placed in full view of the street below. Rod Stewart finished and 'Bus Stop' started thumping out from the hotel at a thousand decibels plus. Les walked across to the music store.

Latino music was playing and the owner was busy behind the counter talking to a South American bloke when Les walked in. Although the shop was crowded, Les managed to earwig the conversation. The customer had just bought some tickets to an Afro-Latino Fiesta and he and the owner were discussing Latino bands. Les stepped over to the blues section and started flicking through the CDs. There were bands Les had never heard of. Sax Gordon, Red Rivers and the Rocketones, CJ's Blues Band. Eddie The Chief Clearwater. Blue Katz. It was torture. All that music to be bought and he was going in the nick. Les would have loved to have heard a few tracks. But all the headphones were being used and the owner was playing Latino for the benefit of the people buying tickets for the concert. Les could only take so much. He flicked through the CDs again and left.

There was a Lebanese takeaway two doors up from the music store with a few chairs and tables out the front. Les walked in and got a bottle of OJ from the fridge. As he paid for his drink, Les inadvertently flashed several one-hundred dollar bills. A young black homeboy standing out the front in a Sweat Hog jacket noticed and hurried back to the Time Zone to tell four of his mates. Les stopped next to one of the tables and downed his OJ, not noticing the severe eyeballing he was getting from five young hoods wearing baggies and floppy beanies. Three were blacks, another was white and the fifth could have been anything from a Yemeni to an Eskimo. The oldest was around fifteen. Les dumped his empty bottle in the nearest bin then sidestepped through the passing cars across Hindley Street and proceeded down the lane. He was level with the skip bin at the alley when he heard a young voice behind him.

'Hey mister. You got a cigarette?'

Les stopped and slowly turned around. The tallest of the gang, wearing a red beanie, was doing all the talking. The others were grouped behind him, rocking up and down on their toes.

Les didn't need a degree in atomic physics to know what their intentions were. 'Sorry,' he said slowly. 'But I don't smoke.'

'Then give us all your fuckin money. You cunt,' snarled Red Beanie.

Norton's face turned to stone. 'Get fucked. I'll give you nothing.'

'Yeah? Then I'll fuckin stick you.' Red Beanie pulled out a knife and waved it in front of Les, close enough to put a tiny nick in Norton's jacket. 'I'm tellin' you, I'll fuckin stick you, man. Give us your fuckin money.'

Les looked at his jacket. 'My fuckin good tracksuit,' he howled. 'You little cunt.'

Norton wasn't in the mood to play games. If the kids wanted to be men, then they'd better learn to take it like men. He pivoted slightly on his left foot and with his right instep kicked the knife straight out of Red Beanie's hand, breaking the kid's wrist. The young hood screamed with pain and grabbed his shattered wrist as the knife landed in the skip bin. Les followed up with a full-blooded right into the young hood's face, almost taking his skinny head off. Before the kid hit the ground, Les turned and left hooked his nearest mate, dumping him on his skinny backside with blood pouring down his chin and no front teeth. Realising things weren't quite going as they'd planned it, the other three turned and went for their lives. One wasn't quite quick enough and Les was able to kick him fair up the arse. He yelped with pain and lost his balance for a moment then tottered forward before catching up with his mates.

'We'll fuckin remember you, mate,' one called out.

'Good,' Les called back. 'Make sure you do.'

'Fuckin white cunt.'

'At least I know what I am,' said Les. 'Do you?'

Les looked at the two young hoods moaning on the ground and felt like doing a bit of Balmain folk dancing on their heads. Instead he gave them a kick in the thigh each and walked briskly to the end of the lane. He ignored the people in the bar on the corner, jogged straight across the road and up the driveway into the Grande.

Les stopped near a column in the lobby to gather his thoughts. Can you believe that? he asked himself. I go up to have a lousy look at some CDs and I nearly get rolled. Bloody hell! Does trouble follow me around or what? Shaking his head, Les felt like a drink. But not in his room. Why don't I have one in the Torrens Bar? he thought. Maybe with a bit of luck somebody'll pick a fight with me in there, too. Or pull a gun on me. Or a knife or something. They'd be mad not to. I mean, that's what I'm here for.

A bar built low to the floor with low seating ran around as you walked in on the left with a sunken lounge on the right and plenty of chairs and tables in between. A mirrored ceiling looked down on the punters and at the rear a three-piece jazz combo was backing a girl in a silver-blue lamé dress wailing 'My Baby Don't Care For Me'. The air was thick with smoke, most of it coming from a plentiful selection of cigars available in a cabinet near the entrance. Along with the cocktails and beers going down, every second man in the place was smoking a cigar and every woman was smoking a cigarette. Everyone was dressed up, mainly in black, and the average age was thirty plus. There was a casually dressed group of people at one end of the bar that looked like flight attendants on a stopover. Looking around, Les surmised the Torrens Bar was one of the places to be seen in Adelaide. He walked over to the bar, ordered a bottle of Hahn and a JD and ice and charged it to his room. Some bloke in a dark jacket got up from a table near the cigar cabinet leaving a butt smouldering in an ashtray. Les took the table, dumped the cigar butt into a pot plant and sat facing the bar. He took a belt of JD and washed it down with almost half the bottle of beer.

Well that's it, Les told himself. No more going out while I'm away. I'm a walking fuckin disaster area. Kids with knives, blokes with iron bars. Coppers. Stop the fight! He took another hit of JD with his beer chaser and looked at the nick in his tracksuit. No. Tomorrow night

I'll be in my room watching TV or reading a book. In fact I shouldn't even be in this rotten bloody smoke box. Knowing my luck, the cops'll come in here looking for whoever belted those little pricks, and I'll get charged with assault. Along with every bloody thing else I've been charged with. Fuck it. I'm out of here. Les downed the rest of his drinks and caught a lift to his room.

The room temperature was perfect. Les took his tracksuit off, cleaned his teeth and turned the TV on. There was still nothing worth watching, but Les lay on the bed and watched it for a while anyway before turning everything off and getting under the doona. As he squashed his head into the pillows, Les couldn't help but think about Conrad Ullrich being dead. It *was* a little eerie. And Gary saying Adelaide was a spooky place. I wonder why he said that? Buggered if I know. Buggered if I know anything to be honest. Les yawned and stretched out a little more. This bloody bed's comfortable. I know that. Before long Norton was snoring peacefully.

Les was out of bed, cleaned up and staring out the window at eight o'clock the next morning, picking over the remains of last night's hoummos. Outside it was windy with patchy rain and it looked cold. So. What should I wear today in my search for the good ship Lollipop or whatever it is? thought Les. I'll probably be doing a fair bit of running around. I reckon my tracksuit and gym boots. And my Bugs Bunny cap. Les got changed, put what he thought he'd need in his backpack and left it on the bed then got the lift down to the Regency Club to sample the continental breakfast.

A smiling girl in a black uniform checked Norton's room charge card when he walked in. There were plenty of comfortable chairs and glass tables and about a dozen guests seated round the fountain. Les placed his room key on a table near the entrance and walked across to the servery. He didn't go far. Next to the fresh fruit and stewed peaches was a tub of fresh Bircher Muesli thick with blueberries. Les got the biggest bowl he could find and ate enough to fill a pothole in a road. He followed that with toast, smoked salmon and coffee and more toast, and finished with two sparkling glasses of fresh OJ. Nothing wrong with the continental breakfast, thought Les, rubbing his stomach as he took the lift back to his room. I can't wait for tomorrow. He checked his map again, made sure he had everything, and headed for Avis.

There were two girls in red uniforms looking after two customers at the far end of the office when Les walked in, and a man at this end using the phone. The man was wearing a button-down collar shirt with the collar buttons undone and a crumpled red tie. He put the phone down and moved his eyes wearily to Les, looking like he'd sell his soul if he could get out of having to work that morning.

'Yes, sir,' said the bloke, expressionlessly. 'How can I help you?'

'Have you got a car here for Ullrich?' said Les. 'Through Travelabout in Sydney?'

'Just one moment, sir.' The bloke punched the keys on a computer like he was shifting furniture. 'That's right, sir. A Hyundai Grandeur. For Mr C. Ullrich.'

Norton couldn't help himself. He had to try an impersonation of Jelly in *Analyze This*. 'Mr Ullrich's been detained,' said Les. 'Not only that. He ain't going to be here. So I'll be taking it instead. My name's Norton.'

The bloke looked at the computer screen again. 'No problem, Mr Norton. Do you have your driver's licence and credit card?'

'I sure do.'

Les soon filled out the forms and was handed a receipt, the keys, a small map of Adelaide, a pamphlet for the Avis Navigator and told where to collect the car.

'You know how to work the Avis Navigator, sir?' asked the bloke.

Les looked at the pamphlet like it was a Chinese newspaper. 'I wouldn't have a clue.'

'Just read the pamphlet, sir. It's quite simple.'

Les looked at the pamphlet again. 'Simple, eh?'

'Yes, sir. Just read the instructions, sir,' repeated the bloke, tireder than ever. 'It's quite simple.'

'Yeah righto,' replied Les, staring blankly at the pamphlet. He walked out of the office into a small arcade with a few Saturday shoppers and through a doorway into the car park. The Hyundai was up on the next level in bay 37.

The car had a silver duco with a neat grille and looked a little like a small Mercedes. Les clicked the locks up with the remote, opened the door and got behind the wheel. Inside it was all soft leather seats that adjusted every which way and a wooden dash that looked like it belonged in a MiG 21. Les had a look around and tried to familiarise himself with everything. The handbrake was a footbrake with the release in the dash, you couldn't take the keys out of the ignition unless the gear shift was in park and the electric windows were especially designed so you'd push the wrong buttons all the time. There was a small screen below the dash and sitting near the gear shift was the control module, something like a TV remote. Les had another look at the pamphlet.

Avis Navigator is easy ... Control Module. Cursor direction control. Repeat direction. Confirmation key. Main menu. Plan an alternative route. Volume down. Volume up. 1. Turn on ignition. Les turned on the ignition and the screen lit up. Main Control. Destination input. Stand-by. Settings. Les pressed a minus button and a woman's voice said,

'Softer.'

Les pressed a plus button and the voice said.

'Louder.'

Well, I'll be buggered, thought Les. How about that. Les pressed more buttons and the screen changed to: Destination Input. Country. Junction. Guidance. Les pressed buttons and more buttons and got nothing except the woman's voice saying softer and louder. After a while he threw in the towel. Fuck this! You'd have to be Bill Gates to work one of these. Les locked the car, went back to the office and got the bloke to come and have a look at it. The bloke followed Les like he was being led to a firing squad.

'Fair dinkum mate,' said Les, as they both got in the front seat, 'I can't work this thing out to save my life. It took me all my time to find the handbrake.'

The bloke looked at the pamphlet. 'They can be a little tricky,' he conceded.

'A little tricky?' echoed Les.

'Where are you going, sir?'

'Victor Harbor.'

Even the man from Avis had a little trouble. But eventually he pushed the right buttons and the screen lit up like the keys on a typewriter. He ran Les through it; Les nodded, understanding less than a third of what he was saying. Finally the bloke punched in Victor Harbor. And told Les how to punch in his way back to Adelaide.

'There you go, sir,' he said. 'You'll be all right now.'

Les had another look at the pamphlet. Approximately ten to twenty-five per cent of the traffic network is changing each year. Because of this one hundred per cent accuracy is not possible.

'Hey mate,' asked Les. 'Do these things play up much?'

'No more than anything else, sir,' replied the man.

'Yeah. But do they play up?'

A polite half-smile appeared on the man's face before vanishing. 'No more than anything else, sir,' he repeated.

'Thanks,' Les watched as the man got out of the car and dragged himself back to the office.

Terrific, thought Les. That means they can play up. Knowing my luck I'll probably finish up in Perth. Les got his backpack from the back seat and put it next to him with the map on top. Oh well, here goes nothing, he thought, and started the car. The engine was that quiet and smooth you hardly knew it was running and after fiddling around with the seat the car seemed to mould itself around you. Les drove to the boom gate, gave the parking attendant his ticket, then turned right into a lane and came out facing the Grande. There was a break in the traffic and Les turned left looking for West Terrace then Anzac Highway and South Road. He took a quick glance at the map when an arrow and a number appeared on the radar screen and the woman's voice said.

'In two hundred and fifty metres, turn left.'

'Huh? Oh, thanks sweetheart.'

Sure enough, there was West Terrace. Les waited for the lights and took off. He was about to check the map again, when the voice said, 'In five hundred metres, turn right.'

'If you say so, sexy,' smiled Les.

A little further on a sign said ANZAC HIGHWAY. And another, A.13 NOARLUNGA. CAPE JERVIS. VICTOR HARBOR. Yes, smiled Norton. We're on our way.

The traffic was constant, but compared to Sydney it was a drive in the country.

There were plenty of parks and trees and the road was wide and flat like the old houses going by on either side. Les passed a hotel on the left called The Avoca and smiled as he briefly remembered walking along the beach with Jimmy Rosewater. The traffic thinned out a little and he came to a slight rise so Les put his foot down to see what the Hyundai could do. Instantly it kicked silently down into second and took off. Les found himself congratulating the late Conrad Ullrich on his choice of cars. The Grandeur was a real pocket rocket. Les zipped effortlessly past the other cars then eased up. The last thing he needed was to get pulled over and a check done on his licence.

'Right turn — ahead.'

'What?'

Les looked at the radar screen and an arrow saying 2700 metres. Minutes later, Les found himself cruising up a winding hill and noticed in the distance a low range of mountains that ringed Adelaide. He crossed the Onkaparinga River and the voice said,

'Left turn ahead.'

After that it was plain sailing. A shower would fall now and again, but mostly it was light drizzle. The countryside was green rolling hills with patches of forest here and there, but it still looked a little barren; probably because it was such a miserable bleak day. Les didn't notice many birds. The only signs of life were cows standing around waterholes with ibises picking at the grass near their hooves. He went through Mount Compass. It was more a big hill than a mountain, with a set of lights, then a few shops and a hotel on the left. Les was tempted to put on a tape but he thought it might be best to concentrate on the road rather than start bopping. The road curved up and down. The weather had probably turned away the weekend drivers so there wasn't a great deal of traffic. A sign on the right said. MINIATURE VILLAGE. It's certainly bloody miniature, thought Les, cause I'm buggered if I can see anything. The farms thinned out and houses began to appear. Then a Lutheran church with a sign out the front. YOUR CHILD'S TOMORROW DEPENDS ON YOUR LOVE TODAY. I'll go along with that, thought Les. Unless it's got a skateboard that should be wrapped round its pointy little head. A garage loomed up on the left and Les got a glimpse of ocean. A sign on the left pointed to Goolwa and another on the right said, VICTOR HARBOR.

'Right turn ahead.'

'Thanks, baby,' smiled Les. 'I couldn't have got here without you.'

The road curved down a hill with houses on either side, the ocean on the left, and surrounding hills off to the right. Ahead was just a huge bay edged by a strip of sand. There were a few rocky islands and waves breaking over reefs near the shore, a long row of pine trees faced the ocean and in the distance a long jetty ran out to another rocky island, and that was it. It looked nice enough. But Les was expecting wharves, jetties, piers, marinas, boats, fishing fleets. Not just a big, blue bay. The smile vanished from Norton's face. This is Victor *Harbor*, he asked himself? Railway lines appeared on the left, and coming up was the shopping centre. Suddenly a sign on a small blue wooden building on the right in front of a brown wooden fence caught Norton's eye and he pulled over. I. V.H. Sea Scouts. Hello, thought Les, I'll bet that's where Knox and his mates got their T-shirts. I'm definitely on the right track. The building was locked and the wind blew a sudden patch of rain against the car so he didn't bother getting out. He doubted if he'd find what he was looking for in there anyway. But he'd keep it in mind. Heartened by what he'd found, Les drove on.

He bypassed the shopping centre and followed the road as close to the coastline as he could with no idea where it would lead. Around him were mostly houses or holiday lettings, a few small blocks of flats and the odd motel. Parks and reserves overlooked the bay and he crossed a couple of creeks. A smile flickered in Norton's eyes for a moment. Next door to a bowling club was The Ezy Rest Motel. The sealed road finished at a blue building called The Whalers Inn Resort and Conference Centre, then a narrow dirt road curved round the water's edge towards a low bluff. There were still no boats or jetties, not so much as a canoe or a paddle pop stick floating in the water. Just a few clumps of granite rocks smeared with bird shit sticking up through the seaweed with the odd pelican sitting on top. Les followed the dirt road till it ended at a turning circle next to a small wharf and a low granite wall facing the ocean. Parked near a granite cliff was an old white station wagon and sitting on the wall were two surfboard riders. Les pulled up near the wharf, got out of the car and stretched his legs. The rain had eased, but a gusty offshore wind was blowing and it was quite cold. Les shoved his hands in his pockets and had a look around.

The wharf was a fish measuring station, with a noticeboard at one end showing the different kinds of fish. Across the bay, houses built on the low hills overlooked the ocean and there was another island in the distance, but still not a boat in sight. Les was shaking his head, completely baffled, when he heard the two board riders clapping their hands and calling out to something in the water. He sauntered over for a look. Swimming next to the rocks were half a dozen seals. Les watched fascinated as the seals rolled on their sides, dived under the water then came up again, snorting and blowing as they floated on their backs, wiggling their flippers and looking up at you with big soft eyes. Les had never seen a seal before. He got his camera from his backpack and, despite his disappointment at not finding any boats, took a few photos. The two surfies gave him a smile, then got in their car and drove off. Les was about to take another photo of the seals when a movement on the right caught his eye.

A woman wearing just a pair of check shorts and a black T-shirt rattled up on a battered old push bike. A white helmet sat loosely on her head and a pair of well-worn thongs clung to her feet. She had black hair and a plain face and Les would have put her age at around forty. The cold didn't seem to worry her at all. Les caught her eye as she rested her bike against the granite wall and smiled. She smiled back then turned to watch the seals. Les walked over to her.

'Excuse me,' he said. 'Would you mind doing me a favour?'

'Ohh yeah,' answered the woman. 'What is it?'

'Would you mind taking a photo of me standing next to the car?'

'Okay.' The woman looked at the camera as Les handed it to her. 'How do you work this?'

'It's easy.'

Les showed her how, then sat against the bonnet of the Hyundai with the ocean in the background. The woman clicked off a photo. Les got her to take another one of him standing on the wharf.

'Thanks very much,' he said, taking his camera back.

'That's okay.'

The woman seemed quite friendly, so Les thought he'd try a few questions. 'You from round here?' he asked.

The woman pointed to the houses facing the bay. 'Over there.'

'You lived here long?'

'All my life,' she replied, sounding rather proud of the fact.

'Hey, how come there's no boats around? It's supposed to be a Harbor.'

'The marina's at Goolwa. They keep them there.'

'Oh? Where's that?' asked Les.

The woman pointed across the bay. 'About twenty kilometres that way. It's nicer than Victor Harbor, too. Not so touristy.'

'Right,' nodded Les. Yes, she's a local all right, he smiled to himself.

'There's another marina on Hindmarsh Island, too.'

'How do I get there?'

'You get the ferry at Goolwa.'

'Fair enough,' nodded Les. 'Hey, have you ever heard of a boat called the *Trough Queen*? I'm looking for the owner.'

The woman looked at Les and shook her head. 'No. Can't say I have.'

'Okay. I'll ask around Goolwa.'

'If you don't do any good there, ask the fishermen in the pub.'

'Fishermen?'

'Yeah. They'll all be in the pub Saturday night. They'd know.'

'Which pub?'

'The Harbor Hotel. There's two pubs near the jetty. The Harbor and the Royal. They'll be in the Harbor.'

'Thanks,' said Les. 'You've been a big help.'

'No worries.'

The woman went back to watching the seals and Les got in the car. Well, there you go, thought Norton as he drove back along the dirt road. All you have to do is ask the locals. I'll take a run over to Goolwa. If I don't do any good I'll come back and ask the fishermen in the local boozer. Be funny if I bumped those blokes in the photo. Les stopped at the end of the dirt road and had a quick look at his map. On the way to Goolwa was a place called Port Elliott. I suppose I'd better have a look in there while I'm at it, he thought. It says port.

Yeah. Like this place says Harbor. Les bypassed the shopping centre again, figuring he'd check it out later and get a coffee. Just past the sea scout building on the left, Les noticed a sign. VICTOR HARBOR, WHERE YOU'RE ALWAYS WELCOME. Yeah. That's me all right, Les smiled to himself. Everybody's mate.

The road to Goolwa was straight and flat through wide green fields and barren hills. Sitting amongst the farms and houses on the side of the road was an abandoned drive-in and an old sign, TEN DOLLARS A CAR LOAD. At a row of shops Les turned right into Port Elliott. The street leading to the ocean was narrow and flanked by old heritage buildings preserved in the original red-brick and sandstone. It was all very colonial and beautiful, but not what Les had come to see. He drove to the end and came out at a bluff overlooking a wide deep bay with a rocky island in the middle. The wind had picked up, pushing a light drizzle before it and the ocean looked grey and uninviting. On a fine day it probably would have looked a picture. But not today. And again there was not a boat to be seen. Les turned around and got back on the main road.

Entering Goolwa, Les drove past more old red-brick and sandstone buildings with verandahs built out over the footpath, and a sign said WELCOME TO GOOLWA. SOUTH AUSTRALIA'S TIDIEST TOWN. At the start of the main street another sign near the local war memorial said HINDMARSH ISLAND FERRY. Les hung a right then followed the signs, almost going round in a circle, before coming out at a railway line opposite a row of pine trees in front of a floating motel. Towering over a strip of water was a bridge under construction and just past that two rows of cars were waiting for the ferry. One lane

said. PRIORITY. Les pulled into the other and turned off the motor
There were other buildings back amongst the trees and a restaurant
on the wharf. Norton's timing was good. Just as he pulled up the ferry
pulled in. The cars in front started moving and a bloke in overalls
guided them on to the ferry.

The ferry took about a dozen vehicles and two minutes to reach
Hindmarsh Island. Les followed the other cars off the ferry and
started looking for the marina. The road was sealed, but all Les could
see was reclaimed swamp covered in flat tundra with patches of scrub
and no trees. The only touch of colour was an Aboriginal flag painted
on a sheet of corrugated iron at the end of a paddock. Secret women's
business, thought Les. Christ! Why waste millions of dollars arguing
over the joint? It's a swamp. The roads seemed to circle every which
way till eventually Les came across some new homes, bulldozers
clearing the swamp and a blue-grey tavern with an olive green roof.
Near a ring of townhouses down from the tavern was the marina.

Les drove down to a parking area in front of a long, flat green
building with a radio antenna on the roof that overlooked the
marina. He parked the car and got out. Several grey wooden jetties
pushed out from the grass in front of the parking area and along the
jetties, rows of boats moved gently at their moorings. There was no
one about; the only sound was the wind and a solitary crow
squawking in the scrub. With a light drizzle softly swirling around
him, Les pulled his collar up and started combing the jetties looking
for the *Trough Queen*.

The boats were all cruisers and yachts named *Wind Move*, *Lazy
Life* or *Lady Celene* with numbers on the bow: MR 6034, IF 1731, TQ

555. Definitely no old wooden clinkers. Les went over the last jetty then got back in the car. Well, it's definitely not there. I'll try the one in Goolwa. He started the car and drove back to the ferry. This time there were more cars and he had to wait a little longer. While he was sitting in the car Les noticed the other marina off to the right on the mainland. After cooling his heels for fifteen minutes they were herded aboard for the two-minute journey then he bumped off the ferry behind a small white truck.

Les circled round once more then came down the main street of Goolwa. Like Port Elliott it was all old red-brick and sandstone buildings with galvanised iron roofs and verandahs built out over the footpath. There was a hotel amongst a row of shops, a garage that looked like it had been shut since nineteen fifty, craft shops and cafes and a small horse-drawn tram displayed in a shelter. Very interesting, thought Les. He did a U-turn at a motel, stopping for a woman with a pram, then drove back and took a left at an op shop on a corner. There were more heritage buildings and houses, then Les bumped over a railway line and the marina was on the right, running alongside a park and a long patch of bullrushes. There was a small parking area in front of a brown building with BOAT SUPPLIES on the side. Les stopped the car and got out.

The Goolwa marina was much the same as the one on Hindmarsh Island only more spread out and the boats looked a little less expensive. They had names like *Big Bird*, *Onawa* and numbers on the bow. LP 2545, MJ 663. At the end of one pier Les thought for a moment he'd found the *Trough Queen*. But it was only an old grey wooden clinker called *White Coffee* TF 3192. Les went over it just to be sure it wasn't the *Trough Queen* renamed and done up. It wasn't. Feeling a little disgruntled, Les walked back to the car.

Well, that's that, thought Les. My only chance now is to ask those fishermen tonight. He looked at his watch. But I don't fancy hanging round till dark. I may as well drive back to Adelaide and come back tonight. This little car's fun to drive and I'm doing nothing else. I wouldn't mind a quick bite to eat right now, though. What about some fish and chips in Victor Harbor? I still haven't had a look at the place yet. Les started the car and headed for Victor's shopping centre.

When Les got there, he went past the main street and turned left further on, doubling back down a wide road running alongside the bay. He had a quick look around then parked near a row of pine trees next to the tourist centre, where you caught a horse-drawn tram across the jetty to Granite Island. Over the road were two hotels with a park and a fountain in between and a building to the right with ENCOUNTER COAST DISCOVERY CENTRE on the side. Behind the building was a much larger park where a longer row of pine trees faced the ocean. Two small streets and a number of shops ran up from the hotel on the left and the main street started behind the hotel on the right. There weren't many cars and people around. The main activity was a group of bike riders in coloured lycra and safety helmets. Les locked the car and crossed the road.

The hotel the woman had mentioned, the Harbor, was the one on the left and looked quite modern with long, wide windows facing the ocean. The other hotel on the right, the Royal, had a green verandah above the footpath with signs on it saying DANCE CLUB SATURDAY, BAND

FRIDAY. Set in in pavers around both pubs were lovely old gas lights and small trees. Les walked past the Royal and up the main street.

There were the usual coffee shops, a newsagent, clothes and sporting stores, fish shops and banks. Les heard music playing — The Eagles, 'Hotel California'. A little further on was a radio station, 99.9 FM, Great Southern Radio and a DJ in his forties sitting in a window facing the street. Les turned back and found a fish and chip shop opposite the bank with a wooden table and bench seat out the front. This'll do, he thought, and went inside to see what was on offer.

There was a dark-haired woman in a white tunic standing behind the counter and a blackboard menu on the wall. Les ordered three King George whiting fillets and chips and an OJ. This didn't take long to cook. Les paid the woman then went outside and sat down at the wooden table. He spread his fish and chips out to cool and started eating. The whiting fillets were delicious and the chips weren't bad either. A car parked in front of where Les was sitting pulled out and seconds later a flock of seagulls arrived, squawking and arguing with each other around Norton's feet, waiting for a handout. Les threw them a few pieces of batter and some burnt chips to shut them up. But the more he gave them the more they wanted and the more they fought amongst each other. Les was tossing the seagulls another couple of chips when a bloke driving an old, white Jaguar with Victorian number plates pulled into the vacant parking spot, scattering the seagulls. The bloke got out of the car and locked the doors. He was wearing a blue cheek shirt tucked into a pair of blue King Gee trousers and he was bigger than Les with a beefy, florid face and long black sidelevers. For some reason he gave Les a dirty look before crossing over to use the ATM outside the bank. As soon as he left, the seagulls returned for another handout. A couple landed on top of the bloke's restored Jaguar and shat on it. Les tossed the seagulls some more chips as the bloke came back from the ATM. As soon as he saw the seagulls sitting on his car his florid face turned purple.

'Ahh get off the car you mongrels,' he cursed, scattering the two seagulls. 'I just washed the fuckin thing.' The bloke looked at Les finishing his fish and chips and muttered something under his breath.

Les smiled up at the bloke good naturedly. 'They reckon that's a sign of good luck,' said Les, nodding to the two piles of white shit on the roof of the car.

Sidelevers glared at Les. 'You're lucky I don't shove those fuckin fish 'n' chips down your throat, you prick,' he growled.

Norton's eyes narrowed. It hadn't been a good day, even without the weather.

'Yeah?' replied Les. 'Well how about you shove your old bomb Valiant up your fat arse instead, you big goose.'

'What did you fuckin say?' snarled Sidelevers.

'You heard,' said Les. 'What? Are you deaf as well as ugly?'

'Why you smartarse fuckin cunt.'

The big bloke came charging round on the left to grab Les by the front of his tracksuit and pull him out from behind the table. Les edged back a little, then quickly stood up and slammed the top of his head into Sidelever's nose stopping him dead in his tracks. The big bloke howled with pain as blood started pouring out of his mangled nose, and down his chin. Les pushed Sidelevers back, then bent slightly at the knees and belted him under the ear with a short, devastating left hook. The big bloke's legs went from under him and he fell down in the gutter next to his car, out cold. Les looked at him for a moment, then picked up the wrapping paper from the table and scattered what was left of his fish and chips all over Sidelever's chest. In a squawking, screeching frenzy, the seagulls immediately swarmed onto the big bloke's check shirt and started gobbling up the scraps. One dropped a shit on his forehead. Les scrunched up the wrapping paper, tossed it in the nearest bin along with his empty OJ container and walked back to the car. On the way out of town he saw the sign again: VICTOR HARBOR, WHERE YOU'RE ALWAYS WELCOME. Yeah. That's me, nodded Les. Making friends wherever I go.

Les stopped at the garage near the Goolwa turn-off and bought a packet of jaffas and some mineral water. He had a fiddle with the navigator while he was sitting there, getting Route Selection, Optimise Distance. And the woman's voice saying softer — louder. Les had a pretty good idea how to get back to Adelaide anyway, so he just left the navigator turned on and kept his map next to him. Well. So much for beautiful downtown Victor Harbor in the daytime, thought Les, popping a jaffa in his mouth. I wonder what it'll be like when I come back tonight? Cold, I'd reckon. He hit the blinker and headed for Adelaide.

The farms and turn-offs to local hamlets went by. Les wasn't thinking about much. There wasn't much to think about. Things hadn't quite turned out the way he expected. But it wasn't over yet.

He still had one shot left. And trying not to be over optimistic, Les had a feeling something would turn up in the hotel when he met the local fishermen. He took a tape from his backpack and popped it in the stereo. Next thing Lee Kernaghan was twanging 'Aussie Dog House Blues'. Mount Compass went by and further on a turn-off to some place called Yundi. It didn't seem long and Professor Ratbaggy was singing 'Love Letter' and Les was in downtown Adelaide.

'Right turn. Five hundred metres.'

'Okay, baby,' said Les.

'In two hundred and fifty metres, take the next turn on your right.'

The navigator hadn't been saying all that much and whether it was working properly or Les had somehow fluked it, he didn't know. But the Bar Kings' 'Treat Me Right' faded out just as Les pulled safely into the driveway of the Adelaide Grande. He opened the door to get out and pushed the minus button on the navigator. As the concierge approached, the voice said,

'Softer. Softer.'

Les gave him a smile. 'Be nice to my girlfriend, won't you.'

The concierge smiled back and gave Les his receipt. 'No problems, Mr Ullrich. We'll look after her.'

Les caught the lift to his room and got out of his damp tracksuit. After spending most of the day sitting in the car, he felt like another swim in the heated pool to stretch out a bit. He put his Speedos on, climbed into the bathrobe and with a towel over his shoulder, caught the lift down to the pool to give the guests another glimpse of his freckly backside. Except when he got there, two other guests were in the pool — a couple of young Japanese honeymooners who went awfully coy when Les dived in alongside them. Les gave them a smile then spent an enjoyable time flopping around and breaststroking up and down the pool. The only chilling thought, apart from the weather, was knowing it all had to end and he wouldn't be doing any swimming in the remand yard at Long Bay. Les finally got out and went back to his room. He rang room service and ordered another Caesar salad, plus a club sandwich and coffee. Then he got under the shower. His food arrived, Les switched on the TV and ate it watching a wildlife documentary. After putting the empty tray outside the door, he changed into a pair of jeans, a clean grey T-shirt and his leather jacket. He checked everything he needed was in his backpack, then went down and collected the Hyundai. Minutes later Les was taking a night drive through the suburbs of Adelaide. Somewhere along the way the voice said,

'Right turn, five hundred metres.'

'Righto, sweetheart,' replied Les. 'You don't have to nag. I think I know where I'm going by now.'

A bit further on the voice said, 'In two hundred and fifty metres, take the next turn on your right.'

'Hey, I won't tell you again,' said Les. 'Knock up on the nagging. You don't know who you're dealing with, woman.'

Bloody sheilas, smiled Les. You can't tell them anything. He slipped on a tape and Steely Dan started bopping out 'Cousin Dupree'. The Hippos were 'Three Steps From The Blues' when Les drove into Victor Harbor.

Les pulled up facing the park opposite the Harbor Hotel and switched off the motor. He got out of the car and there was a bitter wind blowing straight in off the ocean; as he'd surmised earlier, it was cold all right. There weren't many cars around and the surrounding cafes were almost empty. From the hotel further down Les could hear music coming from upstairs and see the punters drinking in one of the bars below. Across the road at the Harbor Hotel two bars faced the street; a lounge on the left and a smaller one on the right. Oh well, here goes nothing, thought Les. He shouldered his backpack and walked over to check out the lounge first.

A long bar faced the door as you entered and inside it was split into two sections, a raised lounge on the left with a gaming room behind, and a betting room on the right. The barmaids wore white shirts and rugged up in jackets and scarves was an average crowd of all ages and sexes, seated or standing around enjoying a drink and a smoke. The betting room was full of TV sets showing the prices and a TAB doing brisk business on the trots. Above the bar were photos and paintings of racehorses and a wooden cabinet full of cups and trophies. Set up in the lounge was a duo called Joe and Danny who were currently on a break. Les had a quick look around then walked into the lounge first. Nothing much was happening in there so he walked back to the betting room. After checking out the punters, Les got a feeling he was in the wrong part of the hotel. He stepped across to the bar and caught one of the barmaid's eye.

'Excuse me,' asked Les. 'Where do the fishermen drink?'

'Fishermen?' said the barmaid.

'Yeah.'

She pointed to the left. 'Try next door.'

'Thanks.' Les walked back out into the street and went into the other bar.

It was smaller, just a room with two pool tables, more betting facilities, a juke box against the far wall and blue curtained windows looking out on the street. There was a solitary barman in a shirt and tie and behind the bar were sporting photos and one of two blokes standing next to a monster crocodile they'd just shot and hung from a rope. About a dozen men were standing or seated on stools round the bar with one bloke in a floppy captain's hat sitting at a table pencilling a betting card. All Les knew about drinking in South Australia was, certain beers were pretty ordinary and instead of pots and middies, they drank butcher's. He walked over to the bar and ordered a butcher's out of a red tap, then stepped over to one of the windows and took a mouthful. It tasted like dog's piss. Bloody hell, thought Les. No wonder they call them butcher's. A couple of these and you'd be butcher's hook all right. You'd be dead. He took another sip to make sure he wasn't imagining things, shook his head and placed the beer on a small table beneath a glass noticeboard. Something inside the noticeboard caught Norton's eye. J.D. won Friday night's meat raffle. Under that another short notice said, *Victor Harbor Angling Club will close if we don't get members' support.* Les read it again then stared out the window. Angling club? Les was expecting professional fishermen. Not anglers. And the angling club was folding up. No wonder that woman on the bike didn't feel the cold. She wouldn't know what day it was. There wouldn't be two fishermen in the whole bloody joint. Les stared out the window and shook his head. I don't believe it. After a few moments, Les shifted his gaze from the window back to the bloke in the captain's cap. He had a trimmed beard and a weathered face. Fuck it, thought Les, I'm here now I suppose. He took the photo from his backpack and approached the man in the captain's cap.

'Excuse me, mate,' said Les.

The bloke looked at Les indifferently. 'Yeah, what's up?'

'I'm looking for the crew of a boat. You wouldn't know these blokes, would you?' Les showed the man in the cap the photo.

The bloke looked at the photo for a second, laughed and called out to the bar. 'Hey Merv, Harry. Come over here.' Two rugged looking men in their late twenties, wearing check shirts and beanies, left the bar and came over. One of them had a brown moustache, the other had two tear drops tattooed next to his left eye. 'Have a look at this. This bloke's looking for the crew of this boat. What do you reckon?'

The two men looked at the photo then all three of them started laughing amongst themselves. Les couldn't see what the big joke was. The bloke with the tattoos stopped laughing, took a drag on his cigarette and turned to Les.

'So you're looking for the crew of that boat, are you mate?' he said, breathing smoke all over Les.

'That's right,' replied Les.

'You're not a poofter, are you?'

'What?' said Les.

'Are you a poofter, mate?' asked the bloke with the moustache.

'No. I'm not a bloody poofter,' said Les indignantly.

'You sure?' said the bloke in the captain's cap.

'Yeah — I'm sure,' said Les.

Tattoos shook his head. 'I reckon you're a poofter.'

'So do I mate,' added Moustache.

The bloke in the captain's hat gave Les a very indifferent once up and down. 'I reckon you are, too.'

Les could feel his fuse starting to burn out rapidly. Another half a minute and they'd soon know whether he was a poofter or not. Les took a deep breath, slid the photo into his backpack and closed it.

'Sorry,' said Norton quietly. 'I was just trying to find those blokes in the photo. It appears I've made a mistake. Thank you for your trouble.'

'That's all right — sweetheart,' said Tattoos.

Moustache gave Les a wink. 'Are you sure you wouldn't like a pink lemonade before you go?'

'They got straws,' said the man in the captain's cap. 'And little umbrellas.'

Les smiled thinly. 'No thank you. I'm not thirsty. And I think it's best I leave.'

Les swallowed his anger and headed for the door. Fuckin wallys. I should have known better. He was just about to open the door when who should walk in but the big bloke with the sidelevers he'd flattened earlier. He was wearing a black leather jacket and white sticking plaster all over his nose. Two enormous black eyes blinked painfully from behind the plaster and his jaw was wired up. Close behind him were two blokes almost as big. One was wearing a grey gaberdine trenchcoat, the other had on a bulky white jumper. As soon as Sidelevers recognised who it was, his face darkened and he turned to his two mates.

'Grrhhnngggmmgh. Grmrngh brrghh,' he grunted, pointing angrily at Les.

176

'Ohh go fuck yourself,' replied Les, and stormed past them out the door. He was across the footpath, heading for his car when he heard a voice behind him.

'Hey. You with the fuckin backpack.'

Les stopped and turned around. It was the bloke in the woollen jumper. Sidelevers and his two mates had followed him straight out of the hotel with Sidelevers bringing up the rear.

'Yeah, fuckin what?' replied Les.

'We want to see you,' said the one wearing the trenchcoat.

Norton's fuse suddenly burnt out. 'You're going to wish you hadn't,' he hissed, and dropped his backpack on the footpath.

Les walked up to the bloke in the woollen jumper, feinted a left to his chin then belted a short right under his floating rib. The bloke's eyes bulged and his mouth gaped open as Les doubled up with another short right over the top. The bloke's legs wobbled as it slammed into his jaw and he fell down on his backside, eyes glazed, wondering what hit him. The bloke in the trenchcoat on Norton's right swung a left at Norton's head. Les stepped outside it and grabbed the bloke by the arm with his left hand then pulled him forward and back-fisted him in the mouth, ripping his lips open. Les gave him another one then straightened his right arm under the bloke's chin and thumped his right knee into the bloke's kidneys. The bloke fell back over Norton's leg and banged the back of his head on the footpath as he landed at Norton's feet. Les left him and walked across to Sidelevers who was looking for a hole he could crawl into and something he could drag over the top with him.

'You big weak prick,' said Les. 'Look what you've done.' Les jerked a thumb at Sidelevers' mates lying bleeding on the footpath. 'I hope you're happy.'

Sidelevers looked like he was ready to crap his pants. 'Nnghhh. Nghhh.'

'Shut up,' ordered Les. 'This is all your fault. And now you're going to have to pay the penalty.'

'Nnnnhh. Nnnhh. Gmmh nnh unh mghh.'

Les was going to belt Sidelevers in the jaw again and smash it up some more. But he just couldn't be that cruel. Instead, he stepped back and kicked him hard in the balls. Sidelevers grunted with pain and sank to the ground clutching his groin. The worst part was he couldn't scream and everything bottled up inside him. Eventually the strain and the pressure were too much and the capillaries in his eyeballs burst, sending blood seeping onto the white sticking plaster across his nose. Les watched him for a moment then looked up. The three blokes he'd shown the photo to had come out to see what was going on.

Les smiled at them. 'Now. Which one of you hillbillies reckons I'm a poofter?'

The one with the tattoos shook his head vehemently. 'Not me mate,' he said, and scurried back inside.

'Me either,' added Moustache, turning to join his mate. 'Never said a word.'

'What about you, Captain Ahab?' asked Les. 'What have you got to say?'

'I was just thinking,' said the bloke in the captain's cap, 'that was a really clear photo. What sort of camera did you use?'

Les picked up his backpack and got in the car. A few people had gathered in front of the hotel and he knew the best move now would be to put as much distance between himself and Victor Harbor as possible, before the wallopers arrived.

Rather than take the main street after reversing out, Les turned left, past a video arcade and a second-hand bookshop, and came round a back way near a garage. On the way out of town Les saw the sign again: VICTOR HARBOR, WHERE YOU'RE ALWAYS WELCOME. Yeah terrific. Unless you feed the seagulls or you're a poofter looking for a boat.

The turn-off to Goolwa went by, then the farms and countryside. Les stared into the twin beams of light splitting the darkness ahead of him and shook his head. The trip to Adelaide had turned out to be a complete waste of time and money. And deep inside Les had had a feeling it would. He just didn't think it would end in so much violence and people laughing at him and calling him a poof. On the other hand, it would have been no use staying in Sydney. He had to take a punt. Maybe if he hadn't breached his bail conditions it would have worked out differently. Who knows? Anyway, it was too late now and he was looking at a very dismal future when he got home. Very dismal indeed. He started thinking about some of the things that had happened on the trip and flashed on to the romp he had with Blythe at the Medlow. That was fun all right, mused Les. But you still can't beat a good root. Les laughed mirthlessly. That's something I can forget about, starting Monday. My sex life. Unless I want to chase drag queens around Long Bay. Yes, it had certainly turned out a bummer all right. Les blanked his mind and just stared through the windscreen, totally zoned out. He didn't bother listening to a tape; he didn't even notice any of the hamlets or turn-offs going past. Les just stared ahead, thinking about absolutely nothing.

'Right turn. Five hundred metres.'

Les slowed down and swung the Hyundai right. He didn't notice the name of the road, but glimpsed a sign saying WATCH OUT FOR LOW LEVEL BRANCHES. Les drove on down a narrow sealed road covered with a thin layer of mist, the headlights picking up dense forest on the right side of the road and a plantation of tall pine trees on the other. Beyond that the car was enveloped in total darkness.

'In two hundred metres, take the next turn on your right.'

Les slowed down again and turned right into the forest. A narrow, dirt road full of potholes and gutters rose up through the trees. Next thing a bumping, banging sound came from under the car. The noise seemed to snap Les out of his trance.

'Hey! What the fuck am I doing?' he exclaimed. 'This isn't the way to Adelaide.'

Les stopped the car and looked around him. Christ. Am I a nice goose or what? I was bloody miles away. I deserve to have that navigator shoved up my arse. What was that noise though? Shit! Knowing my luck, something's probably gone through the fuckin petrol tank. Les quickly turned everything off, found the torch in his backpack, then got out and shone it beneath the car. A branch had jammed itself under a firewall. He wrenched it away, tossed it to one side of the road then switched the torch off and stood next to the car. It was quite eerie standing out in the middle of nowhere, surrounded by a black, leaden silence that seemed to close in on everything. It was also very exhilarating. Suddenly the sky lit up and great shafts of light beamed down through the trees. At first Les thought it was a UFO. It turned out to be the biggest, brightest full moon Les had ever seen, drifting momentarily between a bank of clouds like a huge ball of beautifully polished silver. Les stared at it in awe before it disappeared back behind the clouds again and darkness returned. Shit! What about that? thought Les. That was unreal. Les was about to get back in the car when somewhere in the distance he heard the most awful scream he'd ever heard in his life. It split the darkness like a bolt of imaginary lightning and clamped an icy hand around Norton's heart. It was a woman's scream. Not of pain. A scream of sheer, hysterical terror. There was another scream, followed by a horrific wail.

'No. No. Help me. Somebody. Please HELP me.'

It seemed to be coming from somewhere near the top of the hill. Another scream sent a chill up Norton's spine, then it abruptly stopped. Les found his heart starting to quicken. Shit! I don't like the sound of that. Some poor sheila's in bad trouble. Les stared into the darkness towards where the screams had come from. Fuckin hell! As if I can't get into enough trouble as it is, he cursed, without playing Dudley fuckin Do Right. Why me all the time? Shit! Leaving the car where it was, Les picked up the branch, broke off the skinny end to make a club, and followed the dirt road up the hill.

As he approached the top Les could hear people chanting, ringing bells and beating drums. When he got there, he could see a driveway leading back to an old abandoned farmhouse with cars parked around the front and lights glowing out the back. Les stopped near some trees for a closer look. The farmhouse was red-brick and sandstone, just like the old buildings in Goolwa, but not very big. The front door and windows were boarded up and two chimneys along the side squatted on a rusty galvanised-iron roof. A stone wall with several gaps in it formed a perimeter around the farmhouse and the remains of a high wooden gate stood out the front. At the end of the driveway, a man wearing a Driz-A-Bone and a woollen beanie was leaning against a tree with a gun over his shoulder. He had his back to the road and seemed more interested in what was going on at the back of the farmhouse than anything else. Quieter than a silkworm tiptoeing on a silk hanky, Les snuck up on the man and belted him across the side of his head with the branch, knocking him unconscious. As the man fell silently to the ground, Les grabbed the gun; it was a fully loaded pump-action shotgun. Les cradled it for a moment, then left it against the tree, knowing it was there if he needed it. There was a piece of cord hanging from the man's coat; Les ripped it off, tied the man's thumbs together then stuffed his beanie in his mouth. Gripping the piece of branch, Les kept low and snuck across to a gap in the stone wall to see what the man in the Driz-A-Bone had been looking at.

The stone wall formed a backyard at the rear of the farmhouse. Outdoor heaters were placed round the yard and candles and hurricane lamps flickered on the walls. A wooden table sat against one wall, draped with a sheet of black satin. Placed on the sheet was a solid bronze candelabra, a chalice, several animal figurines and black velvet cushions embroidered with gold stars and pentangles. Standing in the yard were about twenty naked old people in varying degrees of ugliness and obesity. The men wore chains and medallions round their necks and carried small drums. The women had weird masks made from bird feathers over their eyes and held tiny bells. One particularly grotesque old man was wearing a fur hat made from a ram's head complete with horns; in his hands was a long silver knife with a black handle. Next to him was another old man wearing a silver mask shaped like a hawk; he was carrying a ram's horn painted with gold to look like a penis. They were all grouped around a wooden altar covered with a sheet of white satin. Tied to the altar by her hands and feet with a gag over her mouth was a struggling, terrified young woman, her blonde hair tied at the back and adorned with flowers. She was dressed in a long white gown, cut low across her shoulders with wide billowing sleeves and laced round her waist was a maroon bodice. Standing behind her was an old woman holding a hypodermic syringe. She removed the gag from the young woman who immediately started screaming again. The man wearing the ram's head started waving the knife about, reciting some ritual, while the others beat their drums and tinkled their bells.

'Oh mighty Azalzak, lord of earth, water, wind and fire, wand and sword. Prince of Darkness, Ruler of Spirits, come ye unto life as the sacrifice is made.'

'Azalzak. Azalzak. Azalzak,' chorused the others.

'Hear the offering's screams, oh mighty Azalzak. As they waken ye from the night. And beckon ye unto our desire.'

'Azalzak. Azalzak. Azalzak.'

'Oh ye mighty Azalzak, hear her screams. Soon you shall taste her body. Then you will drink her blood from the witches' blade.'

At the word blood the woman on the altar almost screamed her lungs out and started thrashing around that much it looked as if she'd break her bonds. The man wearing the silver bird's mask then lifted the young woman's dress up and began working the ram's horn towards her vagina. The man in the ram's head gave the woman with the syringe a nod and with the help of another woman she was able to prepare a vein in the young woman's arm and stick the syringe in. A steady push with her thumb and the woman went completely comatose.

Watching grimfaced through the gap in the stone wall, Les was almost sick as he realised what he had stumbled across out in the Adelaide Hills. It was a coven of Devil worshippers, Satanists, AntiChrists, or whatever their ungodly trip was. Not a bunch of flower-smelling, spell-casting, flute-blowing Wiccas. These were full-on, black magic, murdering nutters, complete with a high priest ready to perform a human sacrifice. You could bet this was where half those people in the photos outside the police station had finished up — as offerings to Azalzak or whoever. The chanting, drum-banging and bell-ringing got louder. The man in the ram's head raised the knife above his head.

'Now mighty Azalzak. Now. Taste her blood.'

'Taste the blood. Taste the blood. Azalzak. Azalzak. Taste the blood.'

That was enough for Dudley Do Right. Les stood up and flung the branch at the high priest. It turned end over end and the thick part whacked the high priest in the mouth. He gave a surprised shout and fell back, dropping the knife over the altar. A hush went through the coven and they all stopped chanting and banging their drums and ringing their bells. The man with the bird mask turned to see what had happened to the high priest as Les leapt through the gap in the wall, shouting and yelling at the top of his voice to get the coven off guard.

'Go on. Get back. Get back,' Les clamoured. 'Keep away from her. Leave her alone. Piss off, the fuckin lot of you. You horrible-looking bags of shit.'

Les ran across to the altar and picked up the knife from where the high priest had dropped it. He brandished it at the coven and kept yelling at them.

'Go on. Get back you rotten, evil fuckin things,' he shouted. 'Get back. Or I'll cut your fuckin heads off. I'll kill the lot of you. I'll rip your guts out.'

The coven drew back with shock as Les slashed the cords tying the woman's arms and legs, and took her round the waist. She was a completely dead weight and it was like trying to pick up a wobbling sack of jelly. Still shouting his head off, Les managed to get the girl over his shoulder in a fireman's carry while he waved the knife at the coven.

'Go on. Keep away, you motherless bastards,' he howled. 'Fuck off.'

The coven withdrew from Les. A couple started to taunt him and hiss obscenities. Les didn't see one old woman sneak up behind him with the heavy brass candelabra. She raised it and swung it at his head just as Les bent a little to shrug the girl from round his neck. The candelabra missed his head but thumped down hard on Norton's shoulder, making him drop the knife.

'Ow shit,' yelped Les, the pain almost paralysing his arm.

He spun around just as the old woman brought the candelabra up to hit him again. She was fat and ugly with grey hair and great, droopy breasts and looked eighty-five if she was a day and was probably somebody's dear old grandmother. Les smashed her with a straight left that split the old woman's mouth open, cracked her top plate and dumped her on her flabby, wrinkled backside. Les reshuffled the young woman on his shoulder as the man in the bird mask picked up the knife.

'Come on. Get the unbeliever,' he called to the others.

The coven advanced on Les. Some started picking up rocks, another had hold of the brass candelabra as they grouped behind the one holding the knife. On his own Les would have left them for dead, but juggling a dead weight on his shoulders slowed him almost to a walk. Under a hail of rocks, Les got through the gap in the wall and made it to the tree where he'd left the shotgun. He dropped the woman on the ground, took the shotgun and aimed it at the parked cars.

'Blam! Blam! Blam!'

Les shot out the three nearest windscreens, sending wiper blades and pieces of glass flying everywhere.

'Look out,' shouted the old man with the knife. 'He's got Martin's gun.'

Blam! Les sent another blast into one of the outdoor heaters, spewing gas and sparks across the backyard.

'My bloody oath I have', shouted Les. 'Now piss off, before I blow the lot of you to hell. Where you fuckin well all belong.'

The coven stopped in their tracks. Les fired another shot into the galvanised-iron roof, then picked up the girl and jogged back to the car. He opened the door and dumped the girl in the front seat, quickly doing up her seat belt. Before he got in alongside her, Les emptied the shotgun into the trees near the farmhouse, then threw the gun into the scrub. As soon as he was behind the wheel, Les shoved the Hyundai into drive and spun it around in a tight circle, sending rocks and clods of mud everywhere. He straightened up, belted back down the dirt road, did a screeching left turn at the end, then further on fishtailed a smoking right onto the main road back to Adelaide. A few kilometres along the road Les slowed down a little, took a deep breath and tried to stop his heart from pounding its way out of his chest and through the seat belt.

Bloody hell! What about that. Those ratbags were just about to cut that poor girl's throat. Thank Christ I came along. Or thank Christ that navigator's on the blink, or whatever. I don't know about those other directions it was giving me. Half the time I was looking at the map. But that was just sheer coincidence. Les looked at the night sky and shook his head. Or an act of God. The girl had slid around inside the seat belt. Les adjusted it and straightened her up so she didn't bang her head on the door. I don't know who you are, sweetheart, but you've got a guardian angel, that's for bloody sure. Les started checking her out.

She looked to be in her early twenties with a pretty face, nice lips and corn blonde hair, which looked quite beautiful with the flowers in it. She had big breasts and could have been a little overweight, but a bit of exercise and she'd be a stunner. I wonder who she is? thought Les. And I wonder where she comes from? Then another thought struck Les. What am I going to do with her? Shit! I can't take her to the police, or I'll go with her. And I can't just dump her somewhere. She's out like a light and anything could happen to her the way she is.

Les caught his reflection in the rear-view mirror. Good old Dudley Do Right. I'm going to have to take her back to the hotel. Let her sleep there and if she doesn't wake up by the morning call a doctor before I split for Sydney. I wonder what they hit her with? That old tart looked like she might have been a nurse at one time the way she prepared her arm before she shoved the pick in. Probably valium or something like that. Christ! I wonder what she'll think when she wakes up? I hope she doesn't start screaming blue murder. Les looked at the girl, her head down, moving with the motion of the car behind the seat belt. Poor bastard. After what she's just been through, you wouldn't blame her if she did.

Les cruised on into the night and started to relax. Even though his trip to Adelaide had turned out a complete disaster, it did have one redeeming feature: he'd saved some poor girl from a terrible fate. Les laughed mirthlessly. I wonder if the beak'll take that into account when he throws me in the slammer? Whether or not, Norton's good deed did make him feel better. A bit further along he switched on the radio and got some FM station playing mouldy oldies. Sam the Sham and the Pharaohs were singing 'Little Red Riding Hood'. Les looked at the unconscious girl and started singing a bodgie version of the lyrics.

'*Hey there little Miss May Queen baby, watcha doin' out in that South Australian bush alone.*'

He topped a hill and suddenly beneath the night sky the lights of Adelaide burst across the horizon like a ribbon of beautiful flowers. Les turned to his unknown passenger again and smiled at the uncanny resemblance in her hair. How about I nickname you the May Queen, sweetheart. It suits you in that outfit. The next song on the radio was 'Lucy in the Sky With Diamonds'. Les was singing away as he swung onto the Southern Expressway. He'd reached the traffic lights at the end when he heard a familiar voice.

'Right turn, five hundred metres.'

'Yeah, that'd be right you dope,' said Les, turning left to follow the traffic into Adelaide. 'I'll finish up in Port Lincoln.'

'In two hundred metres, take the next turn on your right.'

'Sure. Straight into the oncoming traffic you moron. Right. That's it for you, you low-life slut,' said Les. 'You're sacked. You'd think Muhammad Ali was a street in Cairo.' Les jabbed at whatever buttons on the navigator he could find. 'Piss off. I never want to see you again.'

'Softer. Softer.'

'Ohh shut up. You're nothing but a slaggy moll.'

Some more old pop songs played, Les saw a familiar street sign, then another and another. He hung a right and finally pulled up in front of the Adelaide Grande. The concierge came over and opened the passenger door first. He gave a double blink when he saw the girl lolling behind the seat belt wearing a long puffy gown, a maroon bodice, flowers in her hair, no shoes and no knickers. Les picked up his backpack, came round and got the girl out of the car and put her left arm around his neck.

'Can you manage all right, Mr Ullrich?' asked the concierge.

'Yes. My fiancée's just had a few too many magic mushrooms, that's all,' replied Les, and dragged the girl into the foyer.

As luck would have it, there was a ball downstairs in the hotel, so plenty of half plastered girls wearing long gowns were getting shouldered all round the foyer by plenty of half plastered men in tuxedos. None, however, were completely out on their feet with their boobs flopping everywhere like the girl with Les, and they were wearing a lot more under their evening gowns as well. The more sober patrons gave Les a double blink as he dragged the May Queen over to the lifts, as did the three young Japanese tourists waiting for a lift and two young girls with their shoes off behind them. A lift pinged and Les bundled the May Queen inside. From there it was an embarrassing silence all the way to the twenty-third floor.

Les dragged the May Queen back to his room, pulled the sheets back and lowered her onto the right side of the bed, lying her on her left side. He got a towel from the bathroom and placed it under her head, then put a small rubbish bin by the side of the bed in case she woke up sick. He checked the girl's pulse again then watched her for a moment and wondered what else he could do. Nothing. But at least she was safe. What Les felt like now was a drink and a debriefing. He splashed some water over his face, then got a lift down to the foyer.

The Torrens Bar was packed with revellers from the ball along with the normal Saturday night punters. A duo in black, comprising a skinny brunette and a skinny dark-haired bloke, were warbling 'My Guy' in front of a half full dancefloor. Like the night before, the place was full of cigarette smoke and the cigar cabinet was doing a roaring trade. Les blinked at the smoke and had half a mind to give it a miss. He got a JD and ice with a bottle of VB and fluked a stool next to a pillar facing the dancefloor. The duo cut into 'Blame It On The Boogie' and the dancefloor filled up with shuffling couples. Les took a belt of JD and washed it down with beer. Yeah, he thought grimly, don't blame it on the sunshine, don't blame it on the moonlight, don't blame it on the good times, blame it on the devil. Bloody hell! What a fuckin freak-out. Imagine if that old sheila had clobbered me with the candelabra. I'd have finished tied up on the altar with the May Queen as an offering to Zamzak or whoever it was those lunatics were praying to. He swallowed some more booze. Gary sure was right. This is a spooky fuckin joint. I haven't got much to look forward to when I get home, but I'll be glad when I'm back in Sydney. Les sipped his drinks and let his eyes drift around the bar at the punters in basic black with sequined bolero jackets, silver belt buckles or whatever as the duo struck up 'Celebration Time'. Les finished his drinks. Celebrate without me, folks. It's all yours. He left the revellers to it and got the lift back to his room.

The beer settled Les down and on the way back to his room he began to feel weary. Plus he was aching where the old woman had hit him with the candelabra. When he opened the door, the May Queen still hadn't moved. Les checked to see if she was all right, then stripped off and got under the shower.

He had a nice bruise coming up on his left shoulder and another near his kidneys where someone had got him with a rock. Les stayed under the shower for a while letting the hot water soothe his aches and pains then dried off and got into a clean white T-shirt and jox. He took a bottle of mineral water from the mini-bar, stared out the window while he drank it, yawned a couple of times, then switched off the lights and got into bed with his back to the girl.

It was odd being in bed with someone after sleeping on his own and Norton's share of the pillows weren't comfortable the way he was.

He was forced to roll over. He tried to close his eyes, but he kept staring at the May Queen. The rise and fall of her shapely body looked truly delicious bathed in the soft light coming through the hotel window. Christ, this is going to be nice, thought Les. Trying to sleep with that lying in front of me. The girl still hadn't moved and it didn't even look like she was breathing. Les thought he'd better check her pulse again to make sure she hadn't expired. No. Her skin was warm and there was a steady pulse in her neck. Les slipped his hand under the May Queen's arm. She also had a good heartbeat. She also had a great pair of tits. Les knew he shouldn't do it and there was guilt written all over his face, but he started giving them a little squeeze. They felt sensational. Mr Wobbly started to thinking the same thing too. As Les squeezed the May Queen's boobs, Mr Wobbly forced Les to rub his evil little head against her shapely backside. Within minutes Les had a horn that hard you could have shattered roof tiles on it, and he was in a pitched battle between himself, his conscience and Mr Wobbly.

By rights the girl shouldn't even be there. She should be dead. Another half a minute and she would have been. Les had risked his neck to save her from the devil. So, literally, she owed him her life. Okay, it was wrong. Very wrong. It was statutory rape. But on Monday he was going to gaol anyway. What did he have to lose? And what could they do if they found out? Give him another ten years on the life sentence he was already going to get? Besides, the May Queen was that out of it she wouldn't know anyway. Les squeezed her lovely big boobs. Christ! I'd kill for a root right now. And she definitely owes me one. What the fuck, I'm going to give her one. Better the devil you don't know, my child, thought Les, slipping off his jox, than the devil you almost did. Mr Wobbly wholeheartedly agreed. Les lifted up the May Queen's gown, placed his hands on her hips and slipped Mr Wobbly in from behind.

Right wrong or indifferent, the May Queen's ted felt fabulous; warm and tight and juicy. Plus it was the taste of forbidden fruit. Les also didn't have to worry whether he was going too hard, too fast or too slow. Just do your own thing in your own time. It still wasn't as good as going off with someone. But hey, it was on the house. And who's complaining? The May Queen certainly wasn't. She didn't bat an eyelid. Didn't say a word. Les felt the vinegar strokes coming on so he started going for it. A minute or two later he squeezed his eyes shut, groaned with ecstasy and emptied out.

'Whoah ho! Shit! Bloody hell! Oh yeah, ohhhhh yeah.'

Les finally shuddered to a halt and pulled out a very happy Mr Wobbly. After he got his breath back, Les smiled to himself, put his jox back on and got a towel from the bathroom. He gave the May Queen a wipe, wiped around the bed then dropped the towel on the floor and rolled over. That, Les chuckled to himself, I say that, should solve any problems I've got about sleeping. Les reached behind him and gave the May Queen a pat on the behind. Goodnight, sweetie, he smiled in the darkness. Les closed his eyes and crashed out.

Les was in a field somewhere. He was naked. Covered in flowers. He started running. All these strange people in weird masks were chasing him. They had shotguns. A flock of seagulls flew over his head. They started shooting the seagulls. Dead seagulls started to fall around him. The field turned into a tunnel. At the end of the tunnel was a pack of snarling dogs. Rottweilers. Albert Knox had them on a lead. He dropped the lead. Les woke up and blinked at the clock radio. It was four in the morning. The girl was still lying just as he'd left her. Les checked to see if she was all right. She was. Next thing, Mr Wobbly wanted to know if the girl was all right too. Still half asleep, Les started giving the May Queen another one. It felt just as good as the first. Maybe better and it took a little longer. Les emptied out and wiped up again. Well, he thought as he closed his eyes, that should keep me going for the next thirty years or so. Les crashed out. He didn't have any more bad dreams.

Les woke up about nine. The girl had rolled over onto her back during the night and now she was gently snoring. Although the flowers in her hair had wilted, she still looked beautiful in the morning light. Les got out of bed and had a shower. He dried off, got back into his tracksuit and a clean T-shirt and stared out the window. There were patches of blue in the sky, but the trees below were moving steadily with the wind and it still looked cold. Les was starving hungry and would have loved to have gone down and eaten another bucket of Bircher Muesli. Only he didn't fancy leaving the May Queen on her own in case she woke up totally freaked out and started running round the hotel screaming her head off. He made a cup of tea and chewed a hotel biscuit. Les was staring out the window and thinking of ringing room service for some food when he heard movement behind him. He turned around and saw the girl was starting to sit up. Les put his tea down, got a bottle of soda water from the mini-bar, opened it and sat on the end of the bed like a family doctor on a house call. The girl rolled her head around as if it weighed a tonne, then blinked her eyes open. They were a soft hazel. She looked up and saw Les at the end of the bed and a puzzled look came over her face. Then she noticed what she was wearing and saw the flower petals on the bed and her face went white. She shrank back, wide-eyed with terror and looked as if she was going to scream. Les placed his hand gently over her mouth.

'It's all right. It's all right,' he said softly. 'You're okay. You're safe. No one's going to hurt you. Don't scream. Don't scream.' He took his hand away and offered the girl the bottle of soda water. 'Here. Drink this. It's only soda water and it'll make you feel better. Come on. Take a sip. It'll do you good,' Les assured her.

The girl's hands were shaking as she took the bottle. She had a few mouthfuls but never took her eyes off Les. Les eased back to the end of the bed as the girl drank some more soda water, then belched lightly into her hand. She took a quick, nervous look around the room and stared at Les again.

'Where am I? Please tell me where I am,' she pleaded. 'I'm all confused. Who are you? What's ... ?'

'Take it easy. Everything's all right,' said Les. 'You're in a hotel in Adelaide.' Les opened his wallet and showed the girl his driver's licence. 'That's me. My name's Les Norton.'

The girl looked at the driver's licence. 'You're from Sydney?'

'That's right,' nodded Les. 'This is my hotel room.'

'How ... ? How did I get here?'

'I'm going to tell you. But would you like a cup of tea first? Or a coffee?' The girl shook her head. 'All right. Well, I'd better warn you, it's not a very pretty story. What's your name, anyway?'

'Roxy. Roxy Boswell.'

'Okay Roxy. This is what happened.'

Les picked up on driving back from Victor Harbor and taking the wrong turn because of his Avis Navigator. How he heard her screams. Knocking out the guard. What he saw. Everything. Roxy stared at Les wide-eyed as she gulped down the rest of the soda water. Les told her how he got her in the car then wasn't sure what to do. He was a bit shook up himself. So he brought her back to the hotel and put her to bed. If she hadn't woken up before long, he added, he was going to call the hotel doctor.

'And that's about it Roxy,' said Les. 'Like I told you. It wasn't pretty.'

'Oh my God,' she gasped. 'It's all coming back to me now. Those horrible old men and women. And that man with the ... Oh God!' Roxy started to hyperventilate.

Les read her mind, took her by the arm and steered her towards the bathroom. 'Why don't you have a shower and that while you're in there,' he said. 'There's plenty of towels. And there's a hair dryer next to the mirror.'

'Thanks,' mumbled Roxy.

Les closed the door behind her and settled back on the bed. Everything had turned out fine. Apart from being very shaken up, Roxy wasn't too bad. She didn't start screaming and she didn't faint. Considering what she'd been through, she showed a lot of heart. Les switched on the TV and got *Sunday* with Jim Waley. He watched it till Roxy eventually came out of the shower. She'd taken off the bodice and let her hair down and the colour had returned to her face.

'How do you feel now?' asked Les, switching off the TV.

'A lot better thanks,' answered Roxy. She gave Les a coy smile. 'I hope you don't mind, but I borrowed your swimmers.'

'That's okay,' said Les. 'Would you like a coffee or something?'

'I wouldn't mind another bottle of soda water, if that's all right. I'm so dry.'

'Sure,' said Les. He got a bottle of mineral water from the mini-bar and handed it to her. 'Are you hungry?'

Roxy took a healthy swig on the bottle of mineral water and belched quietly into her hand. 'I'm absolutely starving.'

'Good. So am I. And they do a continental breakfast here, make you jump fences.'

'All right.' Roxy finished the bottle of mineral water, closed her eyes for a moment and shook her head. 'God I'm still ...'

'Don't worry about it,' said Les easily. 'Come on. Let's go and eat, and we'll have a talk over breakfast.'

They caught the lift and Les escorted Roxy into the Regency Club. The May Queen got a few second looks from the other guests before Les settled her down at a nice table by the fountain. He told her to stay there and be his guest then got a tray and loaded it up with Bircher Muesli, fruit, coffee, toast and OJ and they both ripped in. They followed up with smoked salmon on toast and ham and finished nibbling croissants and sipping more coffee.

'Well, how was that?' asked Les.

'It was delicious,' replied Roxy, patting her stomach. 'Thank you very much, Les.'

'I'm glad you enjoyed it.' Les sipped his coffee and smiled at the May Queen. She definitely looked more relaxed after a good meal, but Les sensed she was still nervous. He decided to try a little light conversation. 'So tell us a bit about yourself, Roxy. Are you from round here? Or ... ?'

Roxy flicked some long blonde hair across one eye. 'Tell you a bit about myself. There's not really that much to tell, Les.'

Roxy was twenty-nine. She grew up in Adelaide but she'd lived in Victor Harbor with her mother for the last ten years since her parents were divorced. She had an older brother in Adelaide who owned a computer shop. He was married with two children. She worked in an office in Victor Harbor for her uncle who had a car dealership there. Roxy wasn't seeing anyone in particular at the moment. She had a boyfriend, a musician. But he moved to Melbourne and he was too into drugs for her liking anyway. She liked Victor Harbor. It was quiet and it suited her because she was trying to write a book. She'd done a writing course and had a couple of short stories published in women's magazines. She didn't go out that much. If she did, she'd go to Adelaide and stay at her brother's house in West Beach.

'And that's about it, Les,' said Roxy. 'I'm just a battling little Crow Eater doing her best.'

'You're writing a book,' said Les. 'Unreal. What's it about?'

Roxy shrugged a little self consciously. 'It's about a girl who joins a rock band and gets involved in murder and drugs and ... has to sort it out.'

'Yeah? What are you going to call it?'

'I was thinking, *While My Guitar Gently Screams.*'

'Hey. I like it,' smiled Les. 'I reckon you could be on a winner.'

'I hope so. I'd love to be a writer.'

'Well, I hope you get there, Roxy.'

'Thanks, Les.'

Les got two fresh coffees and another croissant between them. Roxy had opened up, but Les sensed she still had something bottled up inside her. He decided it was time to uncork the bottle.

'So how come you finished up with those ratbags in the old farmhouse?' he asked.

'How come?' Roxy took a deep breath and stared into her coffee for a moment. 'I was out having a walk. I walk for an hour nearly every day. I was near some bush not far from home when this old couple in a campervan pulled up and asked me how to get to Hindmarsh Island. When I told them, they asked me to come closer to the car because they were a bit deaf. I went over and the next thing I knew, someone had come from behind and put a cloth over my mouth with something on it. I went all giddy and they bundled me into the back of the campervan. I didn't have time to yell out or anything.'

'What time was this?' asked Les.

'About six. It had just turned dark and I was on my way home.' Roxy sipped some more coffee. 'They tied me up. Gagged me and blindfolded me. I came to a couple of times, but they put that cloth back over my nose. I remember coming to and I was in these clothes. Then I woke up in that farmhouse tied to an altar or whatever it was out in the open. There was a huge full moon for a few moments.

Then I saw all those horrible old people standing around me beating drums. And that man with the knife and that other man with the ... ram's horn. Then they took the gag out and I started screaming.'

'That's about when I arrived,' said Les. 'I heard you half a kilometre away.'

'Thank God you did.'

'Yeah,' conceded Les.

'After that it was a nightmare. That man waving the knife around. The other man with that ... that thing. Then I heard one say something about drink my blood. And the other said ... something else. And I just flipped out. I went crazy. Then that woman stuck a needle in my arm and that was it. Next thing I remember waking up in bed and you're offering me soda water. I didn't know where I was.'

'I'm sorry I had to put my hand over your mouth. But I thought you were going to start screaming again,' said Les. 'You've sure got a good set of lungs on you Roxy. I mean ... noisewise,' added Les. 'But you didn't, you were cool. You're a brave girl.'

Roxy shook her head. 'I don't know about that. I was absolutely terrified.'

'Who wouldn't be?'

Roxy gave Les the same coy look she gave him when she borrowed his Speedos. 'Les,' she said, a touch of colour in her cheeks, 'there's something I have to ask you.'

'Sure,' replied Les. 'What is it?'

'That man in the bird mask holding the ram's horn. Did he ... ?'

Les nodded slowly. 'Yes, I'm afraid he did, Roxy. I just didn't quite get there in time to stop that. I'm sorry.'

'That's okay,' said Roxy quietly.

'But it was only for a few seconds or so. It wasn't long. What makes you ask, anyway?'

'Oh. It's just that I'm a little sore down there. That's all.'

Les sipped some coffee. 'Yeah, well. At least I got there before that other nutter got in the act with the knife. Or ... well, we won't go into that.'

Roxy reached over the table and took Norton's hand and squeezed it. 'You're very reassuring, Les. You know that. And you're very understanding too.'

'Whatever,' shrugged Les. 'But I know how you feel, Roxy. You've been through hell. And now you've got to try and put it behind you.'

Roxy let go of Norton's hand sat back against her chair, taking him in. She seemed a lot brighter now that she'd faced up to what happened and got certain things off her chest.

'Anyway, what about you? Mr Les Norton from Sydney,' she smiled. 'What brings you to Adelaide? I suppose you're on some sort of business trip?'

Les threw back his head and laughed. 'A business trip? Yeah. That'd be right.' He smiled at Roxy for a second or two. 'All right, Roxy. I'll give you the whole deal. Shit! I got nothing to lose.' Les took another sip of coffee. 'Was there anything on the news down here about a film set getting blown up in Bondi?'

'Yes,' answered Roxy. 'I saw something on TV. And there was a photo in the paper.' She gave Les a double blink. 'Wait a minute. Norton. That wasn't you, was it?'

Les nodded. 'It sure was.'

Les gave her pretty much the whole story. Where he lived. Where he worked and what he did. What happened on Tuesday. How he was trying to clear his name. And how he finished up in Victor Harbor looking for a boat called the *Trough Queen* and the crew. He didn't say he killed the bloke's dog. But he did tell her how he broke into the house at Medlow Bath.

'So that's it, Roxy,' shrugged Les. 'It was a waste of time coming down here. But I was desperate. Now I'll get bundled off to the nick on Monday. Probably when I get home tonight. It's not much to look forward to.'

Roxy was both surprised and sympathetic. 'Golly. That's tough,' she said. 'And it wasn't even your fault. That's awful.'

'Try telling that to the two cops who nicked me,' said Les.

Roxy shook her head. 'So what do you intend to do now?'

'What do I intend to do now?' Les looked at his watch. 'Well, I intend driving you back to Victor Harbor, for starters.'

'Oh. Thanks very much.'

'Then you're going to have to go to the police. You've got to report those nutters before they do the same thing to somebody else. And you can bet you're not the only one they've abducted.'

'Yes. They've probably been watching me walking for a while,' agreed Roxy.

'But we'll discuss that on the way to Victor Harbor. Anyway, I have to go back to my room and get a couple of things. We've got plenty of time. But I have to fill the tank and all that.'

'Okay,' said Roxy. 'Let's go. And thanks again for the lovely breakfast.'

'My pleasure, Roxy,' replied Les. 'And I'd like to rephrase something too.'

'Oh? What's that?'

'Well, when I said it was a waste of time me coming down here, it wasn't. It was one of the best things I ever did.'

'Thank you, Les,' replied Roxy. 'In fact I don't even know how to thank you.'

They walked round and caught the lift. On the way up Roxy started giving Les some odd looks. Les couldn't quite pick up on the vibe. But he had a feeling Roxy suspected he'd been doing a bit of heavy tampering through the night. Les smiled at her and said nothing. Back in his room, Les started sorting a few things out. Roxy had to use the bathroom and Les offered her a T-shirt to put on under her dress if she wanted it. Les was staring out the window when he felt Roxy come up behind him and slip her arms around his waist.

'You know what, Les,' she said.

Les turned around. 'No, Roxy. What?'

'How did you sleep with me last night without ... you know?'

Les looked at Roxy as if he had no idea what she was talking about. 'I was tired. I crashed out. Besides, what sort of a cad do you take me for Roxy?'

'You're a decent sort of man, aren't you, Les,' said Roxy.

'Ohh, I don't know,' said Les. 'Maybe if I'd taken my Viagra things might have been different.'

'Are you tired now?'

'No. I had a terrific night's sleep,' replied Les. 'Why?'

Roxy went a little coy again. 'Well, I was thinking. You going to gaol. And me living down here and all that. We might not get the chance to see each other again.'

'Yeah,' agreed Les. 'It's a bit of a bummer.'

'Well. And don't get me wrong about this, Les, because I don't do it very often. But seeing as I owe you my life, why don't we make love before you drive me home? I owe you one.'

'You don't owe me anything, Roxy,' smiled Les. 'I just did what any half decent, red-blooded Australian man would have done. That's all.'

'All right,' conceded Roxy. 'I don't owe you anything. But shit! I don't know. For some reason I'm as horny as buggery this morning.'

'You sure it wasn't the Bircher Muesli, Roxy? It's full of vitamins, you know.'

Roxy shook her head. 'No, Les. It wasn't the Bircher Muesli.'

'Well, in that case.'

Les put his arms around Roxy's waist, bent his head a little and kissed her. That's what was missing last night. The kissing. And Roxy's lips were soft, warm and horribly inviting. And when she slipped her delicate little tongue in, Les felt like putting his foot straight through the hotel window. He ran his hands up Roxy's ribs and lifted her dress up over her head. Roxy stood at the end of the bed with Norton's speedos tied round her waist and her huge boobs sticking out.

'Jesus Christ, Roxy,' said Les. 'You've sure got one hell of a good body.'

'Don't say things like that, Mr Norton,' replied Roxy. 'You'll only make me hold it against you.'

Les got out of his tracksuit, slid the Speedos off Roxy and eased her back onto the bed. He spread her legs then pushed his face in and gave Roxy's blonde ted a monster eat. Roxy oohed and ahhed and wriggled on the bed while she jammed Norton's head into her. Les came up for air and Roxy reached under and gave his knob a polish that sent Norton somewhere into the fifth dimension. Just when Les thought he was going to stay permanently cross-eyed she stopped and he got between her legs. Roxy gave a howl of joy as Les slipped Mr Wobbly in and started going for his life. They made love on the bed from all angles. Les got Roxy's ankles behind her head, sat a pillow under her behind. She got on top. They had a doggy. A sixty-niner. It seemed to last forever till Les finally pulled the plug and emptied out, with much moaning and groaning from him, and plenty of wailing and flailing from Roxy. On a scale of one to ten, Les gave it a nine point nine. He reluctantly deducted a percentage of a point because she had been wearing his old Speedos. In a pair of knickers, Roxy would have romped in a ten.

They got cleaned up a little, pulled the sheets back over them and lay on the bed getting their breath back. Les had one arm around Roxy. Roxy had her head on Norton's chest.

'Well, I have to say one thing Mr Norton,' said Roxy, running a finger around Norton's chest.

'Yes. What's that, Ms Boswell,' answered Les.

'You certainly don't need Viagra.'

'Oh? What makes you say that?'

'You're there for the long haul, aren't you? You don't just squeeze the trigger and empty the magazine in one burst.'

'Yes, Roxy,' admitted Les modestly. 'I am a bad mamma jamma, a couple of metres out from the fence and the track's good.'

'Between that and the Bircher Muesli,' replied Roxy.

Yeah. And having a couple earlier in the piece slows things down a bit. 'Bad luck I've got to get you home, Roxy,' kidded Les. 'Or I'd be very tempted to pounce on you again.'

'Sounds good to me,' smiled Roxy. 'But how about when we get back to my place?'

'Whatever you say,' Les gave Roxy a cuddle and a big sloppy kiss on the forehead and they got dressed.

Les gave Roxy his address and phone number. He probably wouldn't be there, but she'd get his friend Warren and he'd tell her what was going on. Roxy gave Les her home details and said she'd be in touch and for Les to at least write to her. Les promised he would. They finished dressing. Roxy put Norton's Lee Kernaghan T-shirt on. Bad luck his shoes didn't fit. But it would be warm once they got in the car. He tossed a couple of bottles of mineral water in his backpack and they caught the lift downstairs. It was a different concierge from the night before, but he knew who Les was.

'Good morning, Mr Ullrich,' he said brightly.

'G'day mate. How's things,' replied Les.

'Good morning, ma'am.'

The concierge opened the door for Roxy, getting a good look through the gown at her boobs and black Speedos, as he closed the door.

'I got to get some petrol,' said Les, as they turned right at the front of the hotel. 'Do you want anything while I'm there?'

'No. I'm all right thanks, Mr Ullrich,' replied Roxy.

'Roxy. Please,' said Les. 'After what went on upstairs. Call me Conrad.'

Roxy gave Les a clip under the ear. 'Keep that sort of talk up and they'll be calling you an ambulance.'

'Hey Roxy. What do you call a woman with no clitoris?'

'I don't know. What?'

'Call her what you like. But she won't come.'

'Right. That's it.'

Les stopped at the first garage he came to, filled up and they proceeded on their way to Victor Harbor. He didn't put the Avis Navigator on. But he pointed it out to Roxy and told her again that was what saved her life. Roxy went a little quiet so Les thought this was the time to get serious.

'Okay Roxy,' he said. 'I've told you all about me. And this is what I'd like you to do.'

'Sure Les. What?' answered Roxy.

Les suggested she didn't go to the police till around six. Say she was still in shock. This would give him time to be on the plane back to Sydney. But tell the police the truth and give them all his details, then they'd extradite him back to Adelaide to give evidence. In the meantime, tell the cops to check round the local panel beaters and find out who was getting new windscreens put in their cars and if there were any signs of shotgun pellets. Also check the hospitals for an old lady with a busted mouth, an old man with a lacerated face and some tall bloke with dark hair who could have a broken jaw. Les wasn't sure where the farm was. It was pitch black. But it was a turn-off to the right coming back from Victor Harbor. There wouldn't be too many abandoned farmhouses out there. A helicopter would find it in five minutes. And tell the cops to make copies of any tyre prints in the mud and match them up with the cars getting new windscreens. The coven had to be stopped before they killed someone else. They might even come back looking for her. This sent a chill up Roxy's spine. But on the plus side, if they got rounded up and the police found out who they'd murdered in the past, there would probably be a reward. Which she could claim. Roxy agreed this all made sense and she'd do what Les asked.

The trip back to Victor Harbor seemed to take no time at all with Roxy in the car and Les found himself getting quite attached to the May Queen. He was going to be very sorry when it was time to say goodbye. He sensed Roxy was feeling much the same way, too. She started to go quiet just before they reached the turn-off to Goolwa.

'You okay, Roxy?' asked Les. 'You're very quiet there.'

'Yes. I was just thinking of something,' deliberated Roxy. She turned to Les. 'You know how you were saying you came to Victor Harbor looking for a boat, but it turned out there was no Harbor?'

'Do I what,' replied Les.

'Well there used to be a boat in Victor Harbor. But it wasn't in the water.'

'Wasn't in the water?' Les stared at Roxy. 'What do you mean?'

'It used to be in a park. I'll show you.'

Wondering what Roxy was on about, Les followed the road into Victor Harbor. The long wide bay curved round in front of the car and in the distance Les could see the island with the jetty running out to it.

They went past the houses and shops then, before they reached the shopping centre, Roxy told Les to turn left. They crossed a railway line and she told him to pull up next to a big green park with a long row of tall pine trees alongside the footpath. Les turned off the engine and had a quick look around. A row of two-storey holiday homes stood across from the park and on the corner was a red-brick and sandstone restaurant with a lattice work balcony around the top floor. An old cannon sat in the park, facing out to sea, and near where the park met the ocean was a row of young pine trees protected with hessian.

'It used to be over there,' said Roxy, pointing out her window. 'Come on. I'll show you what I mean.'

Les got out of the car and followed Roxy across the park to the rocks at the water's edge. The wind had eased and the sea was calm and grey under a leaden sky. The thin strip of beach was covered with seaweed up to the rocks. Roxy looked at the rocks for a moment then walked back into the park a little and turned to Les.

'It used to be here,' she said, pointing to her feet.

'What used to be here?' said Les. 'I'm not sure I follow you.'

'An old wooden boat,' said Roxy. 'It had something to do with the bad old days of whaling. People were always getting their photos taken next to it.'

'Photos,' said Les.

'Yes. The tourists. And there used to be a wooden sign saying Victor Harbor.'

'A sign?'

'Yes. Next to the old boat. But some vandals set fire to the boat one night. They burnt the sign too. The council never replaced it.'

209

Les stared at Roxy for a moment. 'Roxy. Just wait here for a second, will you?'

Les jogged back to the car and got his backpack with everything still in it from the night before. He jogged back, pulled out the photo he stole in Medlow Bath and showed it to Roxy.

'Is this the boat?' Les asked her.

'Yes. That's it,' replied Roxy. 'It wasn't called the *Trough Queen*, though. It never had a name.' She looked up at Les. 'Are the men in the photo friends of yours?'

Les shook his head dumbly. 'No, Roxy. They're not friends of mine. The one on the left is the bloke that got blown up on the movie set. Albert Knox.'

'Oh.'

Les stared at the photo then lined it up with the ocean. From the way it was taken and if you didn't know better, you'd think the old boat was sitting in the water. The name *Trough Queen* on the bow also started to take on a different perspective, and you could bet if you examined the photo under a magnifying glass or a loupe, you'd see it was held on with tacks or something.

'How long ago did they set the boat on fire?' he asked.

Roxy shrugged. 'About five years. Something like that.'

'Five years. Thanks, Roxy.' Les stared at the photo, had a look round the park and felt like his arse had just caved in.

'Are you all right, Les?' asked Roxy.

Les looked at her for a moment and an ironic half smile crept over his face. 'Am I all right? Yeah, Roxy, I'm all right. For a complete Dubbo I'm real good.' He put the photo back in his bag and took out his camera. 'Anyway, let me get a photo of you with the ocean in the background.'

'Okay,' smiled Roxy. 'And I'll take one of you.'

They clicked off the photos then Les placed the camera back in his bag. 'Come on, Roxy,' he said, putting his arm around her. 'I'll get you home. It's too cold to be standing round here in your bare feet.'

Roxy lived back towards where they drove in. She told Les to take a left next to a park and a garage, then he followed a hill up past a wedding reception building that looked like an old medieval castle. Roxy's street was on the right a bit further along. The house was a single-storey brick house with a garage underneath and a verandah with a skinny iron railing round the front. There were trees on either side and a well-kept garden out the front. Parked in the driveway were two Ford Lasers, a blue one and a white one. Les surmised these would both be from her uncle's dealership. Les pulled up in the driveway behind the white one.

'So this is your place, Roxy,' he said, switching off the engine.

'Yes. It looks like Mum's home,' she replied. 'Would you like to come inside and meet her? I don't like your chances of getting my Speedos off again, though.'

'No. I think I'd better make a move,' replied Les. 'By the time I get back and all that.'

'Okay,' replied Roxy softly.

There was a silence between them for a few moments as they looked at each other. Les tried to smile, but all it did was make Roxy's eyes well up and a tear rolled down her cheek.

'Hey, Roxy,' soothed Les. 'What's all this, mate?'

'I don't know,' answered Roxy.

'Well, don't start. Because I feel pretty ordinary as it is.'

'Oh Les.' Roxy buried her head in Norton's chest and put her arms around his neck. 'It's not fair.'

Les held Roxy and stroked her hair. 'What's not fair?'

'Everything. You going to gaol. Me down here. And I'll never see you again.'

'Hey. You'll see me again. Even if I have to tunnel my way out. I'll smuggle a spoon in with me. Or a hacksaw blade.' Les was putting on a brave face, but inside he felt as empty as an old mailbag. In a very short space of time the May Queen had managed to bore her way right into the big Queenslander's heart.

'Yeah. You'll see me,' said Roxy. 'How?'

Les got his hanky out and wiped away her tears. 'You never know what might happen, Roxy. Your guardian angel could fly up to Sydney and keep an eye on me for a while.'

'Les, promise me you'll keep in touch,' said Roxy. 'You saved my life. Besides, I like you. A lot.'

'I know. And I like you too, Roxy. A lot. And I will keep in touch.'

'You promise?'

'I give you my word. Hey, I got to come down and give evidence when the police round up those ratbags. I'll probably see you then.'

'Yeah. From across a courtroom.'

Les put a finger under Roxy's chin, lifted her face up and kissed her. The kiss was long and hard and he could taste the salty warmth of Roxy's tears as they trickled down her face onto his lips. After a while Les had to finish.

'Roxy, I have to go,' he told her.

'All right,' sniffed Roxy. She placed her hand softly on Norton's cheek. 'I'll never forget you, Les.'

'And I won't forget you either, Roxy.' Les kissed her again. 'Goodbye Roxy.'

'Goodbye, Les.' Roxy got out of the car and looked at Les for the last time. 'It's still not fair.' She closed the door and ran up the driveway. Les watched her disappear into the house, then started the car and drove off.

Norton's jaw ached and his mind was full of sadness as he went past the Goolwa turn-off. He got a bottle of mineral water from his backpack and swallowed almost half of it. Yeah, you're not wrong, Roxy, mused Les. It's more than not fair. It's completely fuckin shithouse, if you ask me. Les swallowed some more mineral water and stared at the road ahead. Just when I meet a girl I truly like and I might be able to share some good times with, I get the rug pulled straight out from under me. She wasn't only a good sort, she had something going for her. She's trying to be a writer. Well, I hope she cracks it and makes a bundle. She deserves it after what she's just been through. Les swallowed some more mineral water. Christ! I'd have loved to have shouted her a trip to Sydney. Then taken her away somewhere, like a top resort and just given us both a spoil. But, I guess it just ain't to be. The only holiday I'll be getting is a long one care of the government. Les drained the bottle and dropped it on the floor of the car. Still, I've had a bloody good run. I guess my karma had to catch up with me sooner or later.

Les put his foot down, put Roxy out of his mind and brooded on something else. Shit! All that fuckin trouble for nothing. There was no dope smuggling. The boat was just an old relic sitting in a park for people to take photos of. And that's all the photo was. Knox and his three mates having some sort of a joke when he lived in Adelaide. And me and my Sherlock Holmes, super-deduction brain went spare. I need rooting. The witchcraft thing in the house? That'd be just part of Knox's weird and wonderful lifestyle. Like putting dog shit in lamingtons. Me stumbling across those other ratbags down here was just a coincidence. Then despite himself, Les started to laugh. No wonder those three blokes in the pub called me a poof and started poking shit at me. Why wouldn't they? Some big goose comes in with a photo of a boat that used to be in the park down the road. There's four grown men standing in front of it wearing sea scout uniforms or whatever. And the big goose says, I'm looking for the crew of this boat, have you seen them? And I got the shits because they took the piss out of me. They were entitled to boot me fair up the arse. But I'll learn not to make an idiot of myself one of these days. I don't know which day it'll be. But I will learn. Even if it takes Tjalkalieri and the boys to come down from Binjiwunywunya with the first lesson written on a message stick and jam it fair up my silly big arse. Still, if I hadn't come down here Roxy would be lying in a shallow grave somewhere with her throat cut. Yeah. Bottom line, I saved a lovely girl's life. My oath I did. And they can never take it away from me. Feeling a little better, Les switched the radio on and listened to some pop music till he pulled up in the driveway of the Adelaide Grande.

'Will you be needing the car again today, Mr Ullrich?' asked the concierge.

'No. I'm finished with it,' replied Les. 'In fact you can tell Avis to come and pick it up if you like.'

'No problem, Mr Ullrich.'

Les picked up his backpack and got the lift to his room. He didn't have much to pack and there was plenty of time, so he ordered a club sandwich and coffee. When it arrived, he ate it watching TV while he waited for the driver. It was strange. Instead of waiting for a driver, Les felt like he was waiting for the hangman. It had that feel about it. Somehow the afternoon seemed to fly and soon it was time to check out. Les caught the lift down to the lobby, handed in his key and signed for the extras on the bill. He paid cash, put his wallet away and turned around to find Vincent walking towards him carrying a small attaché case in one hand and a manila envelope in the other.

'Good afternoon, Mr Ullrich,' said Vincent. 'Ready to leave, sir?'

'Yes, thank you, Vincent. I am.'

Vincent handed Les the attaché case and the envelope and picked up Norton's overnight bag. 'There's the briefcase you've been expecting, Mr Ullrich. The key is in the envelope.'

'Thank you, Vincent,' replied Les.

They walked out to the LTD. Vincent opened the back door, Les got inside and they proceeded to the airport.

Vincent caught Norton's eye in the rear-vision mirror. 'Did you enjoy your stay in Adelaide, Mr Ullrich?' he asked politely.

'Yes thank you, Vincent,' replied Les. 'It was good.'

'Everything went smoothly?'

'Absolutely. Couldn't have been better.'

'Excellent, Mr Ullrich.'

'The Hyundai Grandeur went well too.'

'They're a very nice car, sir.'

They drove to the airport in silence. Les played it cool and aloof. Softly, he drummed his fingers on the attaché case. I wonder what the fuck this is all about? Probably Ullrich's strategy for a corporate takeover. Some insider trading? I'll make sure Gerry gets it. Could be something to her advantage. Maybe mine too. Yeah. Fat lot of good it'll do me. The houses and shops went by and in what seemed like no time Vincent pulled up outside the Ansett terminal. He opened Norton's door then carried his bag into the terminal.

'Goodbye, Mr Ullrich,' said Vincent. 'Have a pleasant trip back to Sydney.'

'Yes. Thank you, Vincent,' replied Les. 'I'm sure I will.'

Vincent drove off. Les walked over to a row of seats across from the check-in counter and sat down. He placed his overnight bag and backpack at his feet and rested the shiny black leather attaché case on his knee. It had gold-plated locks and looked expensive. Stamped in gold near the handle it said CONDOTTI. Les slit the envelope with his finger, took the key out then opened the letter.

Dear C.

As you can understand I must be brief. Sorry for the way things turned out. As feared I have had to leave two days earlier than planned. Best we don't make contact for at least a year. Longer would be even better. As agreed, I have looked after J. Be cautious of N. I believe he is untrustworthy.

Take care.

K.

Well there you go, thought Les. J's cool. N's a dropkick. Now let's see what we've got here. Les clicked the key in the two locks and opened the attaché case. On top was a layer of white paper. Les peeled it back and underneath were rows and rows of hundred-dollar bills, all tied with rubber bands in neat stacks of ten. Les counted one hundred and fifty. He took out one bundle of notes and tucked it in his jacket pocket, then put the letter in the case, locked it and packed the case in the bottom of his overnight bag. There were a number of people waiting to check in. Mr Ullrich went through as smooth as butter and was told he was leaving from gate ten. Les thanked the girl, skirted round the other punters and took the escalator to Golden Wing. He flashed his card, got a smile and joined the other people inside. Five minutes later Les had a nice table facing the tarmac and was sitting down sipping tea and munching cheese and crackers while he waited for the fruit bats flapping around in his stomach to settle down before they kicked his ribs out.

Holy mother of God, whooped Les. A hundred and fifty fuckin grand. And it's all bloody mine. Ullrich's dead. And the other bloke — K — has hit the toe somewhere. Don't contact him for a couple of years. I'm bloody sure I won't. I haven't got a clue what it's all about. But thank you very much K and C and the Sunshine fuckin Band. Or whoever. Les stared out at the darkened tarmac in amazement. I can't believe my luck. Then a thought hit him and he silently laughed that ironic laugh again. Yeah. Luck. What am I going to do with it? Les turned his eyes to the night sky. You sure giveth, but you sure taketh away, don't you, boss. But thanks anyway. One thing it will get me is a truckload of good lawyers and barristers. I might even be able to get to the judge. Les tapped the thousand in his pocket. So I've got back the fifty I lost on the movie. Plus another hundred for good luck. Not bad for a quick trip to South Aussie. Christ! If only I didn't have that other shit hanging over my head, life'd be gravy. Les was sipping his tea when he felt some one sit down on the lounge next to him.

'Hello Les me old. What's happening?'

Les turned slowly to his left. It was a dark-haired man with a trimmed beard and a dark complexion, losing his hair. He was wearing jeans, a denim shirt, a black leather jacket and black Wallabees. 'Pieman,' said Les. 'What are you doing in Adelaide? Or need I ask?'

'I suppose I could ask you the same thing, Les,' replied Pieman.

'Yes, I suppose you could, Pie.'

Pieman, or Pie, was Spiro Pythagoras. A Bondi boy from a Greek family. Pie rode a surfboard and lived up the north coast with his wife and kids where he had a fishing boat and used to supplement his fishing income with a little bit of pot dealing here and there. He was a good mate of the Gull's and all the team that hung out the front of the Toriyoshi, and despite his occasional dabbling in prohibited substances, Pie was a good bloke with a good sense of humour. However, he was also keen on a dollar, and all you had to remember when dealing with the Pieman was *caveat emptor*.

'That wasn't a bad photo of you in the paper the other day, Les,' said Pie.

'Thanks. I hope you cut it out and hung it up in your boat,' replied Les.

'I did, to tell you the truth.'

'Good. Anyway,' gestured Les, 'feel free to join me Pie. I'm on the run from the law. All I need is to be seen hanging around with a notorious drug dealer.'

'Fair enough,' chuckled Pie. 'So what are you doing in Adelaide? You're a long way from Bondi.'

'To be honest, Pie, I came down here looking for some blokes I thought might be able to help me with all that Elliott I'm in back home. But I fell on my arse. Now I'm on my way back to stick my head in the noose.'

'Bad luck mate.'

'Yeah,' Les sipped the last of his tea. 'So what about you, Pie? What's your John Dory? Surely you're not moving dacca down here. It's semi legal. They give the stuff away with green stamps.'

'I know. The bastards,' answered Pie. 'No. I need some cash in a hurry. So I came down to do a little business. Now I'm on my way back to a Sleaze Ball in Zetland with a thousand caps of Ebeneezer.'

'A Sleaze Ball and a head full of eccy,' said Les. 'You'll excuse me if I don't come along and join in the festivities.'

'Oh, I don't know, Les,' said Pie. 'Someone told me you were very partial to a Sleaze Ball. I even heard you were the Trough Queen.'

Les turned slowly to the Pieman. 'You heard I was the — what?'

'The Trough Queen. The Trough Monster. The word's out it's you, Les.'

Les stared at the Pieman. 'Tell me more about this — Trough Queen, Pie. Who is he?'

'No one knows, Les. It could be a she. I reckon it's you. But whoever it is, it's been a legend in the urinals at Sleaze Balls the last few years.'

'Why? What's this Trough Queen do?'

'The only way to find out, Les,' smiled Pie, 'is to go to a Sleaze Ball and hang out in the brasco. And take a torch with you.'

Norton's demeanour was calm, but his mind had kicked into overdrive. 'Say I wished to purchase a ticket to this Sleaze Ball in Zetland Pieman. How would I obtain one?'

'You wouldn't,' replied Pie. 'It's a Sunday night special, it's been sold out for months. I happen to have one because of my ... business activities.'

'You want to sell it to me?' asked Les. 'You won't need it if you're just dropping off a bundle of disco biscuits.'

'True,' answered Pie. 'But tickets are as rare as rocking horse shit. Any donut puncher worth his sequins would kill to get one. If I was to sell you mine,' Pieman patted the inside pocket of his leather jacket, 'I'd have to charge you the full black market price.'

'How much is that?'

'Five hundred dollars.'

'You got me.' Les pulled out the thousand, whipped off five hundred dollars and handed it to the Pieman. 'Come on. Give me the ticket.'

'Jesus! You are keen, Les.'

Pie pocketed the money and handed Les his ticket. It was black in a black envelope. Embossed in silver on the front was a likeness of Oscar Wilde and the words *Take A Walk On The Wilde Side*.

Les turned it over in his hand. 'How do I know this isn't a forgery, Pieman?'

Pieman pointed to the likeness of Oscar Wilde. 'There's a magnetic strip at one end. They'll run it through a scanner to make sure. Believe me, Les, that's one hundred per cent kosher.'

'For five hundred fuckin bucks it'd want to come straight from Tel Aviv.'

Pie rested his hand on Norton's knee. 'And don't worry, Les. Your secret is safe with me.'

'Thanks, Pie,' said Les. 'Now fuck off while you're still in front.'

Pie gave Norton a wink. 'It's been a business doing pleasure with you Les.'

The Pieman got up and vanished amongst the other passengers as quietly as he arrived. Les put the ticket in his backpack, took out the photo he stole from Knox's house at Medlow Bath and started thinking. He put the photo away, got another cup of tea and was still thinking when it was time to board the aircraft.

Mr Ullrich got another nice smile as he was shown to his seat. Les buckled in and stared straight ahead. He was still staring straight ahead when the plane took off. A few minutes into the flight Les ordered a can of VB. Another two cans of VB later and Les was still staring straight ahead and thinking. He was thinking that much he even knocked back the evening meal. By the end of VB number three, Les was starting to think maybe he hadn't been barking up the wrong tree after all. Just barking at the wrong boat. And the nucleus of a plan had formed in Norton's mind.

It wasn't much of a plan and it was pretty risky. The risky part involved sneaking back to Chez Norton and getting his car. Followed by some very risky skulduggery at this Sleaze Ball. And even if he did pull the plan off, the end result would be no more than a bone to throw the two cops who pinched him. Then he was going to have to spend Sunday night in gaol. But this was his last roll of the dice. He'd pretty much stuffed things up in the Blue Mountains and South Australia. What else could go wrong? And once again, what was the alternative? Thirty long years in the puzzle. Les stared out the window at the stars etched into the inky blackness of the night sky and the clouds below tinged with silver in the moonlight. He was going to give it a go. That money falling in and bumping into the Pieman in Adelaide had to be an omen. Maybe Roxy's guardian angel had flown in? Before Les knew it the lights of Sydney were spread out below the plane and they began making their descent. The pilot circled the plane then they bumped down at Kingsford Smith Airport.

'Goodbye, Mr Ullrich,' smiled the young lady flight attendant, as they filed off.

'Thank you,' replied Les, and strode down the corridor.

He took a left straight onto the moving walkway as a uniform cop went by. His adrenalin now on the rise, Les looked straight ahead and kept moving till he got to the baggage carousel. There was the usual wait then his overnight bag came round with the other luggage; Les picked it up, feeling for the edges of the briefcase on the bottom. With his overnight bag in one hand and his backpack in the other, Les walked out to the taxi rank. There were about ten taxis and twenty punters. Les ducked and dived and pushed and shoved a little rudely before jumping in the back seat of the first cab he found empty.

'Bondi Beach, driver. Cox Avenue.'

The taxi took off and the driver smiled in the rear-vision mirror. 'Hello big Les. What's doing, mate?'

Les stared back at the rear-vision mirror. 'Bananas. I didn't know you drove a cab.'

'I don't normally. But I'm doing a bloke a favour. And I need the cashhhhh.'

'Christ! I think the last time I saw you was at the game,' said Les.

Nobody knew Bananas' last name. His first name was Louie. And everybody knew him as Lou Bananas. He was a dumpy faced, dumpy built, balding bloke with Italian parents who came from Coogee and ran bars. He once worked at the Kelly Club for a while. Lou was a likeable bloke with a dry sense of humour and an abbreviated way of talking. His main claim to fame was four daughters he called Bananarama and his love for a punt and a dollar.

'So where have you been hiding, 'Nanas?' said Les.

'I've been managing a pub in Taree,' replied Lou.

'What was that like?'

'They all got two heads and question marks on their foreheads. I stuck it out till I got back to civilizaish. Evench.'

'Fair enough, 'nanas,' said Les.

'So how have you been, Les?' asked Bananas, as they stopped in the traffic coming out of the airport. 'Nice photo of you in the paper early in the week. If your melon hadn't been covered up, I would have thought it was Brad Pitt.'

'Thanks, Bananas,' said Les. 'You know I didn't do it, don't you?'

'Oh, of course, Les. Bombs aren't your go. You just pulverise people with those big fists of yours.'

223

'Exactly, Lou. I hate violence.'

They headed for Mascot and Les started thinking again. It had to be an omen. First the money. Then the Pieman. Now Bananas. This could be just what he was looking for. It meant not having to go back to Bondi and get his car.

'So you're chasing a dollar, Lou?' said Les.

'Get four daughters, Les, and see if you don't chase a dollar.'

'How would you like to earn five hundred bucks for about an hour's work, Bananas? Cash.'

The sudden glow in Bananas' eyes shone back at Les from the rear-vision mirror like twin laser beams. 'Did you say? Cashhhhh?'

'Of course.'

'What do I have to do, big Les? Nothing too ridic?'

'No. Instead of going to Bondi, Take me to a Sleaze Ball in Zetland. Do you know where it is?'

'Yeah,' replied Bananas. 'Lachlan Street. I've been dropping freaks there all night. It's roaring.'

'That'll be the one,' said Les.

'I didn't know Sleaze Balls were your go Les. How long … ?'

'Get stuffed, Bananas. All you got to do is wait out the front. I'll be thirty minutes at the most. Here,' Les gave Bananas the other five hundred dollars he had in his jacket.

The sparkle in Bananas' eyes was like a pair of headlights on high beam. 'Sensaish. Thanks, Les.'

'That's all right,' Les picked at his chin for a second. 'On the way, stop at one of those dollar bargain joints. I want to buy something.'

'There's one in Kingsford, should still be open,' said Bananas.

'Okay. And have you got a mobile phone?'

'In the glove box.'

'Good. I might want to use it later,' said Les.

'No worries.'

'After I'm finished at the Sleaze Ball, Bananas, we'll probably be going to Waverley Police Station.'

'The wallopers, Les?'

'Yeah. I won't be coming back out. So I want you to take my overnight bag up to the Kelly Club and give it to Billy Dunne. Make sure he gets it. And tell him where I am. Billy'll know what to do.'

'Righto,' said Bananas. 'Shit! This is all very Mission Imposs, Les. Any chance of an explanaish?'

'Evench, Bananas,' said Les. 'Evench. Now take me shopping.'

Les stared out the window, still not quite sure what he was doing. Whatever it was, he couldn't finish up in much more hot water than he was already in. From now on, thought Les, I'm just burning my bridges as I come to them. Les was still thinking along those lines when Bananas pulled up on a bus stop in Kingsford outside an el-cheapo store between a Chinese restaurant and a newsagent. Lou waited in the taxi while Les ran inside. Five minutes later he was back with a plastic raincoat, a scarf, a cheap pair of women's sunglasses, rubber gloves and a Bic lighter. Plus a toy sword made of grey plastic, about the same size as a carving knife. He put the raincoat and sunglasses on then tied the scarf over his head and got back in the taxi.

Bananas couldn't believe his eyes. 'What in the fuck are you doing, Les?'

'Nothing,' replied Norton. 'Why?'

'You know who you look like holding that knife. Don't you?

'No, Bananas,' said Les. 'Who?'

'That old sheila in *Psycho*. The one who did all the murders.'

'Norman Bates's mother.'

'Yeah,' nodded Bananas. 'That's her. You're a dead ringer with the raincoat and the scarf over your head.'

Les checked himself out in the rear-vision mirror. 'Well, it is a drag scene I'm going to, Bananas.'

Bananas shook his head. 'You're kiddin,' aren't you? Fair dinkum.'

Bananas cut through Kensington, swung into Dacey Avenue and got a green light near the hotel at Lachlan and South Dowling. He followed Lachlan about half way along then pulled up on the footpath.

'There it is, Les,' said Bananas.

'I know this joint,' said Les. 'It's the old Jaeger Smallgoods Factory. I used to deliver meat here when I worked for Fields'

'Yeah? Well the only meat you'll get in there now, Les, is straight up the blurter.'

The old factory was a long two-storey brick building with a small metal door at this end and a shuttered loading dock at the other. A wall of glass bricks dotted with air conditioners faced the street and along the footpath out the front was a row of black metal posts embedded into the footpath. At the far end of the street was a park and at this end was a spare parts wholesaler. Opposite was a massive block of land that had been levelled to build a housing commission complex. There were no signs on the old building to say what was going on. The only sign of life was half-a-dozen security staff standing out the front in dark blue trousers and matching windcheaters.

'Okay, Bananas,' said Les. 'Wait here for me. I shouldn't be long.'

'Hey, Les,' replied Bananas. 'Take your time. Enjoy. You might meet the man of your dreams inside.'

'Keep smiling, Bananas,' said Les. 'You're going to look pretty funny kissing your daughters goodnight with your mouth full of stitches.'

Les got out of the car and walked across to the front door. Although he looked like a nutter, the security staff scarcely gave Les a second look. To them he was just another freak. There was a table near the door with an electronic scanner on it. A burly security man swiped Norton's ticket then another opened the metal door. Les stepped into a small corridor where a third security man opened another door. Les stepped through and it closed behind him.

Inside was complete pandemonium. At least two thousand people were either milling around or dancing at the speed of light beneath several rotating mirror balls and a bank of Bose speakers pumping out techno house music loud enough to shake the fillings out of your teeth. Lights flickered everywhere and coloured laser beams arrowed through the smoky atmosphere, making crisscross patterns on a towering row of scaffolding hung with balloons and streamers. Les moved away from a set of speakers and got his bearings while he checked out the punters. It was big on micro leather shorts with studs and leather caps and white satin shorts with gold and silver stars on each cheek and G-strings wedged up your backside. There were outrageous drag queens big enough to play front row for the Broncos. Shirley Temples, Xenas, Barbara Cartlands, Tina Turners, Marilyn Monroes, Marj Simpsons, complete with towering blue beehives. Groups of Village People were there, along with Boy Georges, boy scouts, girl guides, nurses, nuns, archbishops, rabbis, fairies, pixies. Platoons of elegant Oscar Wildes in velvet and silk mingled with legions of bull-necked lesbians in overalls, spike collars and Brando jackets, ugly enough to scare a herd of warthogs away from a waterhole. Whatever outfit you could think up with the backside cut away and a freshly waxed bum sticking out of it was in there getting down and getting dirty. There was even an Adolph Hitler, an Idi Amin and a Joe Stalin, with their freshly waxed behinds sticking out of their uniforms. And that was only near where Les walked in. Who knew what else you'd find? But there was only one Mrs Norman Bates.

Now if I remember right, thought Les, the shithouse was in that corner down there to the right. In the distance Les could make out a green sign saying EXIT. He started weaving his way through the punters, getting a great giggle when he'd stab the plastic knife around. Les was correct. There was a short corridor to the right and a sign said TOILETS. Les got the rubber gloves from his pocket and slipped them on. The Norman Bates's mother outfit was a hoot, but it also gave Les head to toe protection from the various creepy crawlies he expected to find in a Sleaze Ball toilet. The open door was just a little further down on the left. Very gingerly, Les stepped inside.

Every light bulb had been broken and it was almost pitch black. The only light was a few faint beams snaking in through a row of dusty windows high above a wall at the far end. Les could make out a row of cubicles on the right and a line of stainless steel urinals on the left. All through the middle was a congestion of seething, jostling silhouettes, sucking, fucking, licking and groping or otherwise happily engaged in all manner of sexual acts. All the lewd activity was accompanied by a chorus of squealing and moaning that hung in the dark along with the almost overpowering smell of body oil and perspiration. Good Lord, thought Les, bumping past a pair of leather clad silhouettes with their hands in each other's shorts and their tongues down each other's throats. How off's this? Les squinted into a cubicle where a silhouette with its shorts down was spreadeagled against the cistern, with another silhouette behind, choc-o-bloc up it and putting in the big ones.

It was all too much for Norton, and besides that, it was too dark. Fuck it! He cursed to himself. Looks like I've blown it again, I don't even know what I'm looking for, and even if I did, you wouldn't find it in here. No. They can stick this up their arse. They are anyway. Unexpectedly, Les suddenly found himself busting for a leak. Shit. What a time to want to have a piss. Oh well. Les weaved past several darkened figures doing whatever they were doing and stepped up onto the urinal. In the darkness he bumped into someone at his feet.

'Sorry mate,' said Les, unzipping his fly.

'Piss on me,' said a muted voice from near Norton's feet.

Les looked down but couldn't see anything. 'What?'

'Piss on me,' the tinny voice repeated.

Les pulled out the bic lighter and flicked it on. Sitting in the urinal, with its feet out in front of it and its arms by its side was a ghastly figure, clad in a full-length black leather bodysuit, complete with rubber booties and gloves. Clamped tightly on its head was a hideous black leather face helmet with yellow stripes on the front and a zipper down the back. The mouth was a small mesh grill and the eyes were a pair of dark blue swimming goggles. It was a macabre sight and reminded Les of the repulsive creature they kept locked in the cellar in the film *Pulp Fiction* — The Gimp.

'Piss on me,' the figure in the urinal pleaded again.

'Sure mate. My pleasure,' replied Les, whipping out his old boy. 'Here. Have one on you.'

After three cans of VB on the plane, Les was only too willing to oblige. He pissed all over the figure in the urinal from head to toe, giving whoever it was a real good hosing in its face while he tried to get as much as he could in its mouth. The Gimp revelled in it. Rolling its head from side to side, rubbing its hands across its face and chest and delicately flicking warm, frothy urine from its fingertips. Les gave the figure a final burst in the eyes then shook the last few drops out in its face and tucked his old boy back inside his pants.

'There you go mate. How was that?' asked Les. 'Enjoy yourself?'

'Fantastic,' murmured the figure in the urinal. 'Please come back again.'

'I will,' promised Les. 'In the meantime, try this.'

Les stepped back and kicked the Gimp in the solar plexus. The figure gasped a tiny, shrill scream then clutched at its chest unable to move. Les grabbed the figure under one arm and lifted it up from the urinal then pushed it out of the darkened toilet and started steering it through the crowd. Under the strobe lights and darting lasers, nobody took a great deal of notice. Any freaks who did, thought it was just part of the night. Mrs Norman Bates holding the Gimp and slashing at everybody with a toy sword. Les reached the first door where two security staff were standing with their arms folded.

'What's the problem?' asked one.

'My friend's having an asthma attack,' shouted Les, camping it up. 'For heaven's sake open the door. I've got to get him into the fresh air.'

'Okay.'

One of the security guards opened the door. Les hustled the Gimp along the corridor to the next door and banged on it. The door opened and Les stepped outside still holding the paralysed figure in the black leather bodysuit.

'What's happened?' asked one of the security guards standing out the front.

'My friend's had an asthma attack,' said Les. 'I've got to take him to a hospital.'

'Stay there. We'll call an ambulance.'

'It's all right,' said Les. 'I can see a taxi.' Before the security guard had time to blink, Les hustled the figure across the footpath straight into the back of Bananas' taxi. 'Righto, Bananas. Waverley Police Station.'

Bananas looked at Les, looked at the Gimp and took off. 'God strike me. You've got some funny friends, Les. Who's that?'

'I don't know,' answered Les. 'But we'll find out soon enough. Give me your mobile.'

'Here you are.' Bananas got the phone from the glove box and handed it to Les. 'Phew! You're mate's not on the nose enough, Les. Where did you find him? In a shithouse?'

'As a matter of fact, Bananas, I did.'

Bananas shook his head and drove towards Centennial Park. 'You're kiddin', aren't you, Les. Fair dinkum.'

Les got onto Telecom. Got the phone number for Waverley Police Station and dialled.

'Hello. Waverley Police,' came a policewoman's voice.

'Yeah. My name's Les Norton. Would detectives Tait and Caccano happen to be working tonight?'

'Yes. They are. But they're busy at the moment.'

'Okay. Well tell them Les Norton will be there soon. And I'm turning myself in.'

There was a pause at the end of the line. 'What was your name again sir?'

'Norton. Les Norton. You know? The bomb on the film set.'

'I don't quite follow you, Mr Norton,' came the policewoman's voice. 'What's the problem again?'

'Just tell detectives Tait and Caccano. Les Norton rang. And I'm coming in to give myself up,' said Les.

'Yes, all right, very good, Mr Norton. I'll see that they get the message.'

Bananas looked at Les in the rear-vision mirror. 'What was all that about?'

'I'm giving myself up to the cops, Bananas,' replied Les, handing Lou back the phone. 'And I'm taking the Gimp with me for company.'

'Fair enough.' Bananas kept looking at Norton in the rear-view mirror. 'You're dead set mad Les. You know that, don't you?'

'You're probably right, Bananas,' agreed Les. 'But being mad's the only thing that stops me from going insane.'

They went past Centennial Park. Les got out of the plastic raincoat and everything else and dropped them on the floor of the taxi. Bananas came up through Charing Cross and pulled up almost out the front of Waverley Police Station. The Gimp looked like it was starting to breath normally again so Les gave it a short right under the ribs to settle it down a bit.

'Okay, Bananas, you know what to do,' said Les, picking up his backpack.

'No worries, Les.'

Les had some more cash in his pocket. 'And here's another couple of hundred to help clean your cab.'

'Shit. Thanks, Les. Do you want me to wait around for a while, then come inside and find out what's going on?'

Les thought for a moment. 'No. Don't bother. Just make sure you get my bag up to the Kelly Club and give it to Billy.'

'No worries, Les.'

Norton shouldered his backpack and bundled the Gimp out of the taxi. 'I'll see you when I see you, Bananas.'

'Good luck, Les.'

Well. Here goes nothing, thought Les. He grabbed the Gimp under one arm and steered it across the footpath straight through the door into Waverley Police Station.

For a Sunday night it was very quiet. There was a young couple talking to a policewoman behind the counter on the right. Another policewoman was on the phone behind her and a burly sergeant was going through a file at a desk behind her. At the end of the counter near the noticeboard in the corner, Les could see the two detectives in sports coats and jeans. Caccano was on the phone and Tait had a notebook out, listening to what his partner was saying. Les walked past the stairs in front of the door, and bowled straight up to them, his backpack in one hand and the Gimp in the other.

'Okay fellahs. It's all right,' exclaimed Les, dropping his backpack near the counter. 'I'm here to give myself up. I'm unarmed so you won't need your guns.'

Detective Tait turned around and looked at Les without seeming to notice the Gimp. 'Hello, Les,' he said shortly. 'What do you want?'

'What do I want?' said Les. 'I want to hand myself in. That's what I want.'

'Yeah, well, we're busy at the moment, Les. Can you wait till we're finished on the phone?' Detective Tait turned back to his partner.

Les stared at the two detectives, totally admonished. What's up with these two hillbillies? he asked himself. The last time I saw them they wanted to shoot me on sight. Every cop in Australia's been looking for me. Now no one wants to even talk to me. Les looked around the police station. No one, including the young couple at the counter, seemed to notice he was there. But they certainly noticed the Gimp standing behind him. They were all wrinkling their noses and staring at it like it had just landed from another planet. Eventually Detective Caccano got off the phone. He discussed something with his partner then turned to Norton.

'What's your problem, Les?' he asked.

'What's my problem?' echoed Norton. 'I'm here to give myself up. And to prove my innocence at the same time.'

'Prove your innocence?' said Detective Caccano.

'That's right,' said Les. 'I can prove I didn't do it.'

'We know you didn't do it,' said Detective Tait.

'You what?' said Les.

'We know you didn't do it,' repeated Detective Tait.

Norton's voice rose. 'What do you mean? I didn't do it.'

'Well, if you want to be like that,' said Detective Caccano.

'No. That's not what I mean,' said Les. 'I mean. Shit! What the fuck's going on?'

'Didn't your mate Eddie tell you?' said Detective Tait.

'Yeah. Where have you been?' asked Detective Caccano.

'I've been away. I mean . . . Look, tell me what's going on, will you?'

'Eddie Salita came in and saw us on Thursday morning,' said Detective Tait. 'And he brought in one of those crackers in a cake box, Like you were telling us about.'

'He did?' said Les.

Detective Tait nodded. 'He showed us how it worked. And I have to admit, we were very impressed.'

'And you got another mate. Ray Tracy,' said Detective Caccano. 'Runs a Japanese restaurant next to the school.'

'That's right,' said Les. 'The Gull. It was his movie I put my money into.'

'Well, his partner is out here at the moment. A Mr Kobayashi,' said Detective Caccano. 'He was in the school with his video camera when the bomb went off. Ray brought him up when Eddie was here and they showed us the video. Compared to the school security camera, there's a good two second's difference between the explosions.'

'Two second's difference,' said Les.

'That's right,' nodded Detective Caccano. 'When you watch Mr Kobayashi's video, you can clearly see the cake box blow up in Knox's face. Then you see the second explosion come from the left and blow Knox down the side of the catering van.'

'We've got other forensic evidence to back this. So your story would stand up in court,' said Detective Tait. 'And even though you weren't quite fair dinkum with us at the time because you were covering for Eddie, we can see you were telling the truth. So we've dropped the charges.'

'You've dropped the charges,' muttered Les.

'That's right, Les,' said Detective Caccano. 'You've walked.'

Norton could scarcely believe what he was hearing. All he had to do when he came back from the Blue Mountains on Thursday was pick up the phone. And that would have either been Eddie or the Gull telling him he was in the clear. Instead he'd gone to all that trouble flying to Adelaide and gone through all that anxiety for nothing. On the other hand — he was laughing. Not only was he off scot-free, he had one hundred and forty-nine thousand dollars on its way to the Kelly Club completely GST-free. And a good sort's phone number in his wallet. Norton was totally out of the shit, back stroking in gravy. It was a beautiful world after all.

'I don't know what to say,' said Les. 'I'm flabber and gasted.'

'Thanks, officer, would be nice,' said Detective Tait dryly.

'Yeah,' agreed Detective Caccano. 'We'll settle for a thank you.'

'Thanks,' said Les. 'I'll give you more than thanks.' Les turned and pointed to the Gimp. 'I'll give you the bloody murderer.'

'Yeah. What the fuck is that thing?' asked Detective Caccano.

'Christ! It doesn't half stink,' sniffed Detective Tait.

'What is this thing?' said Les. 'This *thing* gentlemen. Is the Trough Queen. Sometimes known as the Trough Monster.'

A sudden, inexplicable high hit Norton as if the heavens had just opened up and the sun shone only for him. Maybe it was hanging around with the poets in the Blue Mountains playing Agatha Christie? Or just the exhilaration of not having to go to gaol. He wasn't sure, but suddenly Les thought he was Hercule Poirot or some great courtroom barrister and he started to soar.

'This foul fiend,' orated Norton. 'This devious denizen of the night. This malodorous monster. Frequents the urinals at Sleaze Balls. And other dens of iniquity. Where. It gets its perverted, lascivious pleasures. By enducing persons using the toilet. To urinate upon it.'

'It sure bloody smells like it,' agreed Detective Tait, waving a hand in front of his nose. 'Christ!'

'And I. Les Norton, concerned citizen,' continued Les. 'Have just made a citizen's arrest of this diabolical beast. Because it is my belief. This. Is the perpetrator of the foul deed. Wherein an innocent cook. One, Albert Knox. Was blown apart by a bomb.'

'Keep talking, Les,' said Detective Tait. 'I like it.'

'And it is also my belief,' said Les, pointing indignantly at the figure in the swimming goggles and black leather. 'That if you take the same sniffer dog you brought to my house. Oscar. And search this insidious fiend's premises. You will find evidence of bomb making.'

Detective Caccano sounded interested. 'Can you prove this, Les?'

'Can I prove this?' replied Norton.

No. He couldn't. Les was completely bluffing. It was just a gamble he'd taken to try and get some of the heat off himself. All he had was a photo of four blokes standing in front of an old boat. But who gives a stuff. He'd beaten a murder charge. He'd got around statutory rape. What could they charge him with now? Abduction and assault? The way Les felt, he'd beat that standing on his head.

'Yes. I can,' said Les. 'The proof is in my bag. But first. I will unmask this wretched miscreant.' Les undid the zipper, then reached behind the Trough Queen and gripped its mask. 'Gentlemen, I give you — the Trough Queen.' An audible gasp echoed around the police station as Les tore the Trough Queen's mask off.

'I don't fuckin believe it,' said Detective Tait.

'Well, if I hadn't been here to see it,' said Detective Caccano, 'I wouldn't have believed it either.'

Les stepped back and like the others stared in astonishment at the Trough Queen. Most of all Les. Possibly in amongst all the bullshit he'd done it? Maybe this was the murderer? The motive was there. Blackmail. The connection was there. Adelaide. The timing was there. Had a nose job been done? Could the Trough Queen make a bomb? Insurance coverage? Who cared? Les was off the hook.

The Trough Queen's lips curled back, trembling with anger. Eyes blazing with hatred, the figure in black glared furiously around the police station, shaking with rage. 'You vile, rotten swine,' it screamed. 'Get me my lawyer. And my agent. This is absolutely outrageous.'

Shaking his head in amazement, Les took his camera out of his backpack then handed the Trough Queen back its mask and swimming goggles. 'And to think I used to go around telling people I wouldn't piss on you. You've certainly made a liar out of me. Haven't you, Nathan.'

THE END

A MESSAGE FROM THE AUTHOR

Firstly, thanks for all your letters. It's great to hear from you and I'm doing my best to reply. But I get bogged down and I am lazy, so please be patient. Especially my readers in various big houses across Australia. I also want to thank all those people who came to the book signings for the *The Wind and the Monkey*. Particularly Newcastle. When I walked into Charlestown Mall it was like Beatlemania. I've never seen so many people. Anyway, the book went to Number One, and I'd like to thank everyone for that. You'll notice the new book is in a different size and format. That's something between my publishers and the booksellers. But it will eventually come out as a normal paperback if you prefer. The Possum Lady also said to say hello and thanks for buying the T-shirts. Actually the Possum Lady had a bit of bad luck recently. She went to a doctor to get the hair lasered off her back and it all caught fire, and poor old Possum Lady finished up with third-degree burns. New she's in a cast up to her chin and looks like the Phantom of the Opera. But she's up and about and ready by the phone in a special chair we got made for her to take your orders for T-shirts, CDs, talking books or whatever at: Psycho Possum Productions, PO Box 3348, Tamarama NSW 2026.

Now. People keep writing to me and asking me what's going on with the Les Norton movie. Well, things have fallen in a bit of a hole there. I can't elaborate on this for legal reasons. But the movie will get made. I'm just going to have to come at it from a different direction. So what I've done is this. I've paid a bloke an arm and a leg to write a film script for *Davo's Little Something*. The script is finished, it looks sensational and I reckon *Davo's Little Something* will make a red hot movie. We'll find some investors and get it up. Then when we do, I'll use the same team and make Les Norton movies the way they should be made. And it's about time. In the meantime, I hope you enjoy *Leaving Bondi*. I'm not sure what's coming up next. I might even give Les a break next year and do something else. Who knows? No matter what, thanks for your support and I'll see you in the next book.

Robert G. Barrett